Goth-Girl to Cowgirl

Book 4 in the Rescue Series

By
Award-winning Author Heidi M. Thomas

SunCatcher Publications

Advance Praise for Goth-girl to Cowgirl

Fans of the "Rescue" series will love the story from Electra's point of view.—Brenda Whiteside, Award-winning Author

"How does a young girl, completely caught up in a Goth-girl world, transfer her affections and trust to a way of life that is completely foreign to her? Electra is a completely enthralling personality in this book dedicated to her growth and development. From a sour, bitter, confused, rebellious teenager, she moves into a relationship with horses and a cowgirl named Samantha. She's a delightful young girl with a heart of gold, covered over by the scars of life and her former need for self-destruction. Take the journey with Electra ... from *Rescuing Hope* and *Rescuing Samantha* comes the Goth-girl's transformation." –Sally Bates, Award-winning Author

"If you like the show, Heartland, you'll love this...!" — Laura Drake, award-winning women's fiction author

Other books by Heidi M. Thomas

Cowgirl Dreams series
Cowgirl Dreams
Follow the Dream
Dare to Dream

American Dream series
Seeking the American Dream
Finding True Home

Rescue series
Rescuing Samantha
Rescuing Hope
Rescue Ranch Rising
Goth-girl to Cowgirl

Nonfiction
Cowgirl Up! A History of Rodeo Women

Children's
The Secret of the Ice Castle & Other Inspirational Tales

Praise for Heidi M. Thomas Books

Cowgirl Dreams (EPIC Award and USA Best Book Awards): "…Brings heart, verve and knowledge to her depiction of the intrepid Nettie. A lively look at the ranch women of an almost forgotten West." —Deirdre McNamer, MFA English Professor, University of Montana, *Red Rover, My Russian,* and *One Sweet Quarrel*

Follow the Dream (WILLA Literary Award): "I enjoyed this bittersweet novel with its accurate depiction of the lives of cowgirls in 1930s Montana and its tender portrait of a marriage." Mary Clearman Blew, award-winning author of *All but the Waltz: A Memoir of Five Generations in the Life of a Montana Family*

Dare to Dream (Book Excellence Award Finalist): "Finding our place and following our hearts is the moving theme of *Dare to Dream*, a finely-tuned finish to Heidi Thomas's trilogy inspired by the life of her grandmother, an early rodeo-rider. With crisp dialogue and singular scenes, we're not only invited into the middle of a western experience of rough stock, riders and generations of ranch tradition, but we're deftly taken into a family drama. A very satisfying read."—Jane Kirkpatrick, an award-winning, *New York Times* Bestselling author

Cowgirl Up: A History of Rodeo Women (Global e-book Winner): "The best kind of history lesson; Informative and entertaining. Thomas does a great job of showing the lifestyles of these women in a very male dominated world, and how through hard work and determination they gained the respect of many people not only in the U.S., but throughout the world. You can't help but be impressed with the toughness of these women, who competed even with broken bones and other injuries. An eye-opening look at the world of rodeo, and the accomplishments of these women. –John J. Rust, author of *Arizona's All-Time Baseball Team* and the "Fallen Eagle" series

***Seeking the American Dream* (Author's Show, Historical Fiction Winner):** "Heidi Thomas's novel grips the reader from the first opening sentence, as her nurse-protagonist struggles to face the wretched suffering in war-torn Hamburg during the final days of WWII. From there, her sweeping saga takes her away from Europe's lurching efforts to rebuild, and into building her own new life in America. From the perspective of a hard-working, and still bright-eyed young woman, we participate in America's own next chapter." –Mara Purl, best-selling author of the Milford-Haven Novels

Finding True Home (Will Rogers Medallion, Book Excellence Awards) "This sequel to *Seeking the American Dream* continues Heidi Thomas' heart-tugging saga of the life of a World War II war bride as she struggles to adjust to life on a Montana ranch, where family is everything and neighbor helps neighbor through the toughest situations. Struggling through isolation, prejudice, and self-doubt, Anna Moser finally finds peace, acceptance, and her true home through a lifetime of love and sacrifice." – Donis Casey, author of the Alafair Tucker series

***Rescuing Samantha* (Independent Press Finalist, Book Excellence Award):** "Heidi Thomas brings us a story about a young woman facing life's trials in rugged Montana. But Sam has the gumption of her grandmother and great-grandmother, to persevere and overcome. She is also compelled to rescue horses and young people.

There is drama and true-to-life dialogue in Thomas' smooth writing and the reader will become immersed. It is a joy to watch along with the characters how God brings "mysterious" blessings to their predicaments.

This is also a story of rural America that many of us long for—neighborhood rodeo, BBQ, homemade ice cream, reverence for the Star-Spangled Banner, fiddles and dancing, and (mostly) friendly neighbors. Readers will love this story." ~ Denise F. McAllister, MAPW, Atlanta, GA. Freelance editor, Member of Western Writers of America and Women Writing the West.

Rescuing Hope (WILLA Literary Award Finalist, Will Rogers Medallion, Book Excellence Finalist)

"Samantha Moser has a heart as big as Montana and it seems everyone knows it. Injured dogs, spooked horses, damaged veterans, troubled teens—they all find their way to Sam for nurturing and healing by her compassion and generosity. She sometimes wonders in the quiet of the midnight darkness if there will ever be anyone to love and nurture her and help her achieve her dream of buying her grandparents ranch."—Leta McCurry, author of *Dancing to the Silence*

Rescue Ranch Rising (Finalist NM/AZ Book Awards, and Arizona Authors Association)

"Sam Moser rescues horses, vets and rebellious teens. But who will rescue Sam from herself? Heidi Thomas does it again as her Rescue Series continues to entertain and educate. Well-paced and satisfying, a wholesome, feel-good contemporary series that deals with real issues. Suited to horse-loving teens as well as adults." ~ Anne Schroeder, award-winning author of Walk the Promise Road

"Another extraordinary story by Heidi M. Thomas. She keeps readers spellbound from the beginning to the end of her third book in the Rescue series. Samantha continues to struggle to keep her great-grandparent's ranch prosperous, while using horses to rehabilitate troubled teens and veterans recovering from PTSD." ~ Jane Laurie Hirsch, author of Murder is Brewing and Silent Shots in the Dark.

"If you like the show, Heartland, you'll love this series!" ~ Laura Drake, award-winning women's fiction author

Goth-girl to Cowgirl

A SunCatcher Publications book

Cover Design by Jason McIntyre
www.TheFarthestReaches.com

Library of Congress Cataloguing-in-Publication data is available on file.

ISBN: ISBN: 978-0-9990663-6-2

Printed in the United States of America

10 9 8 7 6 5 4 3 2 1

So do not fear, for I am with you; do not be dismayed, for I am your God. I will strengthen you and help you, I will uphold you with my righteous right hand.—Isaiah 41:10

CHAPTER ONE

Nothing in her short life prepared her for this...this emptiness.

Electra Lucci leaned against the corral fence, picking at her black nail polish. The realization had hit her yesterday as she and her mom flew over the sparse, maize-colored prairie of eastern Montana. Even the endless sky was empty, not a wisp of a cloud. They had come to the end of the earth for their so-called vacation on a dude ranch.

She sneaked glances at the three other women and their young daughters getting ready for the ride. Her mom, Alberta, rubbed the face of a big brown horse and ran her fingers through its mane. She actually looked like she enjoyed this. *Is she pretending, for my sake?* Phht! Horses. Where did Mom get this stupid idea? Because she took a few rides in Central Park when she was a kid, she thought Electra would love it too? Not!

A soft voice broke into her loneliness. "Would you like to try getting to know Ginger? She's a nice, gentle horse. Nothing to be afraid of." The woman was Sam Moser, their instructor.

Electra snorted, turned away, and slouched to the barn. She heard her mother apologizing—of all things—"I'm sorry about Electra. Ever since her father..."

She huffed again and slipped into the dark interior where she slumped onto a bale of hay. Settling down, happy that it pricked her legs through her jeans she bit her lip until she tasted copper. Anything to keep from crying.

Her father. How could he abandon her? Hadn't she always been his favorite, Daddy's girl?

The shadowy gloom in the barn closed around her, and the night of that awful accident flooded her senses. The police bringing Dad home. Telling Mom and her that Jimmy was dead. Her mother's screams. The immediate wish that it had been her, not her brother, her bestie. Even if he *was* Mom's favorite. Then her dad leaving because he *couldn't handle the pain anymore.*

She dug her nails into her arms, hard. The sharp, stabbing pain felt good. For a moment the inside hurt subsided.

***

Early the next morning, she slipped from beneath the covers, put on her black socks emblazoned with skulls and crossbones, her black baggy pants and sweatshirt. Spiking her short, ebony hair in the bathroom and reapplying her signature white makeup and black eyeliner, she crept, carrying her black Doc Martens, out the door of their cabin—*they call it rustic. I call it corny.*

She didn't care where she was, where she was going— only that she *had* to get out of there. Horses and cowgirls, blech! Some vacation. After lacing up her shoes, she clumped down the road. Surely somebody would come along and give her a ride to the airport.

Walking for what seemed like miles, she ran her dry tongue around her teeth, trying to work up a bit of saliva. *I should've grabbed a bottle of water from our mini fridge.* Her dusty Martens pinched her feet, and her legs burned.

Dark, ghostly shadows hovered in her periphery as her mind kept returning to her bleak life without Jimmy and Dad. She saw herself walking the dark hallways of their New York apartment, counting her steps, tapping lightly three times on her brother's door as she passed his room. *Remember. Remember. Remember.* It was her own private ritual. If she did that, maybe he would come back. If she didn't…

She dug her fingernails into her flesh again.

The rumble of an engine crept into her awareness. She swiveled her head to catch a glimpse of a battered, blue pickup truck, as they called them out here in the "wild West." *Oh good. A ride to town.*

The vehicle came to a stop beside her. The driver leaned over and opened the passenger door. "Going somewhere?"

That Sam woman.

She scowled into the pickup. "You."

"Yup, it's me. Hop in."

"I'm not going back there."

"Why not? Your mother's going to be worried."

A snort was the only response she could think of. *Not too likely.*

The woman kept speaking in that low, patient *mom-tone.* "Listen. Get in. I'm in a bit of a hurry to get to Miles City. I don't have time to take you back to the dude ranch right now. I'll call and let your mom know you're with me, and you can come along. Okay?"

Reluctantly, she nodded and climbed into the cab, slamming the door.

They rode in silence for a while. Electra avoided Sam's gaze and hunched against the door.

"You ever been around horses before?"

A headshake.

"So, this wasn't your idea of a fun vacation then."

She snorted again.

"What do you like to do—for fun?"

"Fun? Phht." She shrugged.

"Well, I happen to love horses." Sam chattered away. "I adopted a racehorse that was going to be put down, and I want to breed her and raise Thoroughbreds on my ranch."

Electra curled her lip in a sneer and peered at the woman from half-closed eyelids. She appeared several years younger than her mom, early twenties, maybe. She wore her chestnut-brown hair pulled back in a ponytail, and her brown eyes sparkled as she talked. *How can she be so…so* chipper *when* my *life is in the dumpster?*

"Right now, I'm going to check on a horse outside Miles City that's been abandoned and starving. I'm really worried about him, and I want to at least get him some feed until I figure out what I can do."

While Sam called Electra's mom to tell her where she was, she stared out the side window at the empty miles of prairie. *Miles City. A* city. *Good. They probably have an airport.* She fingered her mom's credit card in her pocket.

As they crested a hill and coasted down into a river basin, the tiny town looked nothing like a city. She gulped. Did it even have an airport? Maybe not. She and Mom had flown into Billings, not that big a town either. Disappointment settled like heavy netting on her shoulders as they drove on through and out into more nothingness. A half groan, half growl reverberated in her throat. *Great. I'm stuck here now.*

"Here's the pasture and the windmill where I found him yesterday." Sam steered the pickup off the main road, over a cattle guard, and approached a wooden tower with a fan of big blades on the top. Parking beside a large plastic tub, she got out, and with a hand shading her eyes, scanned the bare ground—*the pasture.*

Electra frowned at the unfamiliar terms and equipment. Oh. The horse. Maybe that's where it drank. Only a pool of scummy water in the bottom though. She curled her lip. Didn't appear all that appetizing.

Sam gasped and strode past the windmill toward a brown lump in the near distance.

Then Electra realized what she was seeing—a horse lying on the ground. A dark claw squeezed her brain, and a creepy sense of floating came over her as she got out of the vehicle and followed the woman.

The cowgirl tiptoed toward the brown horse and knelt beside him, feeling his neck.

Electra stopped just behind the pair, her chest tight. A faint mewling sound came from her lips, and she clasped her hands over her mouth. She leaned down beside Sam. Her heart shredded. She couldn't stand to see any animal suffer. "Is he…?"

Then the horse peered at them from an eye crusted half-shut. Sam gave an audible sigh of relief. "Oh, thank goodness, he's alive." She crooned to him as she stroked his face and neck. "Oh baby, howya doing, boy? Are you all right?"

As though drawn by a magnetic force, Electra reached a tentative hand out to touch his soft nose.

He lifted his head and nuzzled her hand. A feathery sensation tiptoed along her arm. A tear tickled her cheek. *He's alive.*

With great effort, the horse gathered his legs beneath him and struggled to stand, like an old man rising from a chair. Sam stood, brushed the dust from her knees, and patted his back.

Her whole body shaking, Electra ran fingers along the big animal's neck. She swallowed, pushing dread and fear and regret past a dry mass in her throat.

"Good boy." Sam kept talking to him. "Oh, I'm so glad you're not dead. You can even get up. C'mon, baby. I brought you some food."

The horse blew and gave himself a weak shake, loosening some of the dust. On wobbly legs, he followed them back to the fence, where Sam grabbed a pail full of some kind of tan oblong pellets and unloaded a bale of hay. She extended her hand, palm flat with several of the pellets—"cake," she explained. The horse bared its teeth but softly closed large lips around the treat and crunched loudly.

Cake? It didn't resemble or sound like any cake Electra was familiar with. She grimaced, imagining those huge teeth grabbing her hand instead.

Sam went to the windmill and pulled a lever. The big fan up top began to move, and water trickled from a pipe to fill the tub.

Open-mouthed, she marveled at the process. So that's how they got water for their horses out here. She shifted her gaze to the horse. His ribs showed through his dusty brown coat, and his legs wavered a bit as he stood, eyes half closed, eating a bit of hay. She took a step closer and caressed his neck. Surprisingly soft and smooth, despite the caked-on sweat and dirt. Her heart compressed and wrung tears into her eyes.

An engine rumbled, and in the distance, she saw a cloud of dust approaching, with another not too far behind. A red sports car pulled up beside Sam's beat-up pickup, bass rhythm rattling the chassis. A kid in his late teens got out. His sandy hair stood up in spikes, several earrings glinted from his ears, and he sported low-slung baggy jeans.

Electra snorted again. One of those too-cool-for-school, wannabe skater types.

A blonde woman drove up behind in her SUV, got out and nodded to them.

Sam waved. "Hi, Teresa, thanks for coming."

"Hey, that's my uncle's horse." The kid swaggered toward her. "Whatchu doin' here?"

The cowgirl moved forward. "What's it look like? I'm feeding your starving animal, the one you've been neglecting."

"Naw, naw, lady. You got it all wrong. That old nag's always looked like he's about to die. I been out here. He already had feed and water. He's doin' fine."

"That's because I left it for him." The young woman pinched her lips and swallowed hard. Was she about to punch the dude? *Go for it, Sam.* "He's almost dead. He was on the ground when I got here, could barely get up. I don't call that being taken care of."

"I don't think it's any of your business." The kid smirked, reached into a side pocket on his voluminous pants, and pulled out a pack of cigarettes. He tapped one out, flicked a silver lighter, and took a deep drag, all the while eyeing the three women from half-closed lids.

Electra glared at him from squinted eyes. *What a punk.*

The blonde woman spoke up. "Now, see here. There's no need for attitude. We're simply concerned for this horse's welfare, that's all. I'm the one who first noticed him. I spoke to the sheriff on the phone, and he said you had promised you were taking care of him while your uncle is in Europe." She gestured at the brown horse. "But he doesn't look too good."

That's an understatement. She picked at her black nail polish.

Sam leaned against a fence post. "Say, what's your uncle's name? Do you think he'd be willing to sell the horse?"

The kid shrugged as he blew a cloud of smoke. He pulled a cell phone from his pocket and punched in some numbers as he ambled out of earshot.

The other woman made a face behind his back and shook her head at Sam. "Piece of work," she muttered and then glanced at Electra. "Who's your friend?"

Sam made the introduction.

Electra didn't reply but busied herself combing her fingers through the horse's mane, trying to untangle the dirty knots, and holding tears behind half-closed lids. *How could anybody let this happen to an innocent animal?*

The teen sauntered back to where they stood. "Just talked to my uncle. Yeah. He'll sell."

"That's great! …Ah…how much?"

"Two grand."

Electra jerked her head toward the kid. *Big Yikes. That's a lotta dosh.*

Sam's eyes flashed. "That horse is not worth two thousand dollars. You'd have to pay to have him hauled to the rendering plant."

Teresa spoke up, her eyes narrowed. "Give us your uncle's number. We want to negotiate with him directly."

The kid shuffled his feet. "Naw, no need. He says I do what I want with the horse."

"Listen, friend." Teresa had a no-nonsense expression on her face now. "I'm supposed to report back to the sheriff on the condition of this horse. As bad as it appears to me, we can easily get a lawyer to draw up papers…"

"Okay, okay." The kid wiped his palms on his baggy pants. "A grand, then."

"I'll give you five hundred," Sam said. "Take it, or we'll begin legal proceedings." Her lips flattened into a hard look.

She looks majorly chapped. Electra swallowed a hard lump.

The punk gazed down at his feet. He fumbled for another cigarette.

"What's it going to be?" Teresa prompted.

He crumpled the unlit cigarette in his hand and sneered. "Okay. I'll take it."

Sam smiled. "You made the right decision. We need to write up a bill of sale right now. Teresa, do you have some paper?" She went to the pickup and grabbed her checkbook.

Teresa supplied a notebook and pen, Sam scribbled something, and handed it to him. "All right, then. Sign this and our business is finished. Teresa will notarize this, and I'll send you a copy." She offered him the check.

He stared down at it. "How do I know it's good?"

Sam leaned closer, her face inches from his. "Because I say it is. This is my signature. Take it or leave it. Either way, we're taking the horse."

"Okay, okay. Don't get your panties in a bunch." The kid smirked again.

Electra clenched her fists, wanting so badly to take a swing at him. But she dropped her hands and took a step back. *Probably couldn't whup him anyway.*

He signed the paper, showed Teresa his ID, and she notarized the document, writing down his address in her notebook. Pocketing the check, he swaggered to his car, and spun a cloud of dust as he peeled out.

Electra's gaze followed the retreating vehicle. *What a dweeb.* If he was supposed to be caring for this horse and let him get this bad…no wonder Sam looked cheesed off.

Teresa's eyes sparkled. "We did it!"

Sam gave her a high-five and twirled in the dirt. "Woohoo. We make a good team. Thanks for your help. I gotta call Horace now, see if I can get him to bring his horse trailer." She spoke to the horse. "Mister, you're coming home with me."

Sudden relief, like a pleasant spring rain, flowed over Electra. She swung her focus up to her with a tentative half-grin. "Can I come along?"

Sam grinned back. "Of course. I'm going to need some help getting this guy healthy."

Teresa left, and while waiting for Sam's neighbor Horace to arrive with his horse trailer, Sam dug out a currycomb and brush.

Hmm. Electra took in the tools and the horse. "Can I help?"

"Of course." The cowgirl showed her what to do, and she set about detangling the mane, while Sam brushed the caked dirt from the horse's bedraggled coat. He stood without moving, occasionally swaying his head toward them, as if he couldn't believe he was being cared for.

Electra bit her lip as she ran her hand over his sharply defined ribs. The poor guy. She paused her combing. "Do you know his name?"

Sam nodded. "No, I… I've been calling him Apache, after a horse that died when I was a kid."

"Oh. That's a good name." She worked on a stubborn tangle. "Do you… Will he… Will *this* Apache die?"

"Oh gosh." Sam blinked rapidly. "No, I think he'll be all right once we get him on regular feed and water. I'm going to take him by the vet's in Miles City before we bring him home, get him checked over."

With a sudden urge to connect to this poor creature, Electra wrapped her arms around Apache's neck and buried her face in his mane. *Crap. What's happening? Why do I care about an old horse? I need to get back to my friends in New York.* Then she wiped her tears in the horsehair and hardened her face.

CHAPTER TWO

An old guy named Horace wearing a battered, stained cowboy hat over his gray hair—Sam's neighbor, she said—came with a trailer and loaded the horse. They followed him into Miles City to the veterinarian clinic. Electra glanced ahead at the trailer carrying the horse named Apache. *Will he live? Or will he be another death to deal with?* She turned her head away and stared out the window, chewing her lip and digging her nails into her arms until the pain erased the questions.

"…if the vet says he's okay and we can take him home…" The cowgirl's voice interrupted Electra's dark thoughts.

"Huh?" She swung a half-lidded gaze toward her. "Is there an airport in this *city* place?"

Sam scrunched her forehead. "What? An airport? Why?"

"I need to go home." She bit the words with clenched teeth.

The light brown ponytail swung back and forth across Sam's shoulders. "We're going to have to face your mom, talk to her first. She knows what's best for you."

Electra snorted. *Right. Like this lame vacay out here in Nowheresville. If she thinks this is going to make me forget Jimmy being dead and Dad leaving…*

"…he's going to need a lot of extra care. Do you want to come tomorrow and help?" Sam talking again.

Just be quiet. Leave me alone. I don't want… She jerked her head back to peer at the woman. *Wait. What?*

"I think Apache responded to you, even more than he did to me. If it's okay with your mom, and if you'd like to come over for a few days, you would really be a big help to me, trying to get him back to health."

Images floated behind her eyelids of the brown, nearly-dead lump lying in the dirt, ribs straining against the filthy coat, the soft nose as he nuzzled her arm. Her heart crumbled. Could she help him? Would he survive if she did?

"Um…" Her voice rasped, and she cleared her throat. "Well…um…I dunno…you think I can?"

"Sure." Sam's brown eyes sparkled. "I've seen miracles when the right person comes along for the right horse."

Miracles? Really? Still skeptical, she snorted, but then made throat-clearing sounds again to cover it. "Well, okay. Just for a couple of days." *Then I'm going home.*

***

The vet pronounced Apache "sound, although malnourished, and he's going to need a lot of care, but I think he'll come out of this with little damage."

Sam's shoulders visibly relaxed as she whispered, "Oh, thank God."

Electra was surprised to find herself holding her breath, and her hands shook. A smile lifted her mouth out of its perpetual downward pull of sadness, and she met the woman's gaze full-on.

Sam paid the vet and then helped him and Horace reload Apache, and they headed to Sam's ranch. On the way, she called Electra's mom to let her know how the day had gone. When they arrived at Sam's, Mom was waiting beside Clyde's ranch vehicle.

Electra stepped out of the truck, and her mom enveloped her in a rib-crushing hug. "Oh my goodness, am I glad to see you. I was *so* worried when I woke up and you were gone."

She let Electra loose and sent Sam a glance. "Thank you for calling and letting me know you found her."

"No problem."

"And you found a starving horse?" Mom peered into her face. Something fluttered in her chest. *Is Mom actually interested in what I have to say, for once?*

"Yeah. Come and see. The poor guy… I…we thought he was dead…but I petted his head and then he got up, and then Sam bought him from this nasty punker, and we took him to the vet, and his name is Apache, and I'm going to help Sam take care of him. Is that okay?" She paused to take a breath, her chest squeezing with hope.

Her mother cocked an eyebrow and put an arm around her. "That's wonderful, honey. I'm so glad. Show me the horse." As they headed toward the barn where Horace unloaded Apache, Mom faced Sam, blinking rapidly. "Thanks," she whispered.

Electra huffed. She really hadn't thought her mom would miss her one little bit.

Later, after they'd all shared a meal of venison stew, Horace—a pretty nice guy, even if he was probably older than God—went home. Electra excused herself to go check on Apache. She paused just outside the kitchen door when she heard her mom say, "Sam. Wow. She hasn't talked this much or smiled since…since her brother was killed."

"Oh my gosh. Killed?"

"Car accident." Mom's voice choked.

Accident. Killed. Electra leaped off the porch and ran, leaving the dark, nasty words behind. Inside the dim, musty-smelling barn, she wrinkled her nose at the stench of horse poop—manure, Sam called it. Clumping to Apache's stall, she threw her arms over the top of the gate and dropped her head heavily on them. *Why does she always have to talk about it? Why did she have to tell Sam?* Trying to slow her fretful breathing and angry, galloping heart, she gulped back sobs. *Stop! Stop this! You're tough. You're a Goth-girl. Nothing bothers a Goth-girl.* She bit her cheek and ground her teeth, as if by sheer force she could will away the ache.

Something touched her arm. She jerked her head up and pulled back. Apache had draped his head over the stall and nuzzled her shoulder. His huge brown eyes held her gaze as if he somehow understood.

She mewed a tiny whimper, slipped inside, and buried her face in his mane, her arms encircling his neck. He occasionally turned his head to nuzzle her. Funny how she felt no fear of this horse… Funny how she was able to forget…for just a few minutes…

"Time to go, dear."

Electra jumped when she heard the voice. "Aw, Mom."

Sam grinned beside her mother. "I'll see you tomorrow at the dude ranch. Be ready to ride."

Electra's lower lip trembled as she patted his neck one more time. *Will he be all right without me?*

The cowgirl added, "And you can come back tomorrow evening to help me with him. It's okay with your mom."

Pivoting slowly, her hand still reaching toward him, Electra left Apache, and the three said good night.

***

Electra lay awake, listening to the wind and a branch tapping against her window. *Remember. Remember.* She scrunched her face. As if she could forget. She fluffed her pillow and rolled to her other side. *Remember. Remember.*

"Race ya." Jimmy takes off running up the hill in the park. His laugh echoes, his lanky teenage frame silhouetted against the sky at the top. "I won again!"

"You cheated. You ran before I was ready."

"Naw. I didn't need to cheat. It's cuz you're a shrimp."

"Am not!" She sticks her lower lip out in a pout.

"Are too!" He rubs his knuckles over the top of her head. "But a cute one."

Remember. Remember.

She's on the school playground, a little girl huddled under the slide, tears and snot running down her face. The bigger boys stand just out of reach, holding her book bag, taunting her. "Can't get it. Can't get it."

Jimmy's deep, ominous voice. "What are you punks doing? Give me that bag."

The boys drop it and run.

Jimmy. Her hero.

Remember. Remember.

After they tell her he is dead… After the funeral—*What a farce. That preacher didn't even know him, but he's talking about him like his own son...* After Mom finally let her go back to school… She's numb. The girls who were supposed to be her friends hang back. *They don't know what to say.* Nothing matters. Her best friend is gone. There's a hole the size of a moon crater in her chest. Her grades plummet. She doesn't care.

She sits alone at lunch, picking at her sandwich. A girl with a ghost-pale face, black lipstick, eyeliner, and nail polish sits down across from her. A black cape hangs from her stick-thin body. "Hi. I'm Ashley."

She stares at the white face. *That fits.* She grunts.

Turns out she's part of a group of misfits—*yeah, that's what I am*—who call themselves Goth-girls.

Remember. Remember.

***

Electra awoke to piercing sunlight, the remnants of her dreams hanging like wisps of spider webs in her head. Mom's bed was empty. Already up and gone. She hung her legs over the side of the bed and yawned. *Ugh.* That Sam woman was going to be there again, and she'd promised her she'd ride today. Then Apache's eyes and his nuzzling nose popped into her head. The quicker she did what Sam and her mom wanted, the sooner she'd get to see him again.

She tugged on the same black clothes from the day before, laced up her Martens, and ran her hands through her hair. No time to spike it or do makeup. Grabbing a granola bar from the table, she headed to the corral, where the dude ranch guy, Clyde Bruckner, was getting their horses ready for the day's ride. She didn't see her mom or the other women and their girls yet.

"Mornin'." Clyde touched the brim of his cowboy hat with two fingers. "You're early. Eager to get out and ride today?"

She shrugged. *No, not really.* These horses were big. Strong. Intimidating. Not like poor Apache, with his ribs sticking out and head hung low. Her mouth dry, she tried to swallow. *No. I can't do this.*

"This here's Ginger. She's our best and gentlest horse. Here, try giving her some cake." The rancher held out a handful of those weird pellets. *Wonder if it's chocolate or vanilla.* She huffed a little laugh.

"Just hold it out in your flat palm, like this." He demonstrated, like Sam had done yesterday.

Well, okay. I'm gonna have to do this…if Mom and Sam are going to let me see Apache again. He needs my help. Rolling her eyes, she took the cake and held it out. Ginger closed soft lips around it and moved her head back to chew. Electra widened her eyes. *Oooh. Her nose is so soft. And she didn't bite me.* Involuntarily, the corners of her mouth curved up. She slowly reached out a trembling hand to touch the mare's neck. Flattening her palm, she caressed the soft hair. *Softer than poor Apache's—all matted with gunk.* Her heart flipped at the thought of brushing him to this kind of softness.

Ginger swung her head around and nuzzled her. "You want more?"

Clyde reached into the pocket of his blue checked shirt, offered another handful, and she fed the horse again, giggling a little at the tickle on her palm. "Why do you call this *cake?* It's not sweet, is it?"

The man chuckled. "Naw. It's grains and oils and minerals for extra nutrients. I dunno, really. I think it's cuz it's all formed—kinda caked or clumped together."

"Oh." *Whatever.* Still seemed like a strange name for a hard, crunchy pellet. *Why not horse Cheetos or something?*

"There you are." Her mom came up beside her.

"I see you're getting acquainted with Ginger," Sam's cheerful voice added.

She sighed. *Is that woman always this happy?*

The cowgirl took a brush from a bucket she carried and offered it to Electra. "Would you like to groom her before we go for our ride?"

"Okay." *If I have to. Just get this over with and you can go see Apache later.* She took the brush and gently swept it down Ginger's neck.

"Honey," her mom patted the mare's face, "Sam has invited you to stay with her for the summer and help her here at the dude ranch and with Apache. Is that something you'd like to try?"

Electra jerked her head, and her stomach somersaulted. "What?" She regarded her mother and then Sam, one eyebrow raised. "Really? You don't…mind?" *After all the months of barely allowing me out of her sight, she's going to leave me here and go home by herself?* Oddly, she didn't even have the desire to go back with her.

Sam grinned. "You're going to be working awful hard."

"I don't care. I'll do whatever you want." She flicked her gaze back to her mom. Her chest squeezed tight. "But you'll be all alone…"

Mom hugged her. "I know. I'll miss you like crazy. But I think this will be good for you."

For the first time since they'd arrived, a tiny light glimmered at the end of that long, dark hallway, where she remembered, and tapped, and missed her brother.

CHAPTER THREE

The day passed quickly, the group of women and their daughters getting into the spirit of the ride, laughing, and teasing each other. Despite her fear of climbing all the way up on top of that horse, Electra managed to accomplish the task, with a little boost from Sam. And she didn't even fall off.

Once her body relaxed and she fell into the rhythm of the horse's walk, she let her white-knuckled fingers loosen from around the saddle horn. Gazing over the endless prairie to low, flat-topped hills in the distance, she breathed in the fresh air—no smog out here—and allowed herself to imagine cloud shapes as teddy bears or whales or even horses. She and Jimmy used to do that—lie on their backs in the park and point out formations. "That's Snoopy," she'd say.

"Nuh-uh, it's the Red Baron," he would tease.

"Same thing," she retorted.

She smiled, remembering, the pain a tiny twinge this time.

When they finished their ride, she slid out of the saddle, her legs threatening to buckle under her.

Mom lifted a palm for a high-five. "Good job, kiddo."

"Ohmygosh, will my legs ever be straight again?"

"You'll get used to it. It's a good kind of stiff and sore." Sam chuckled beside them. "Go ahead and unsaddle your horses and brush them down. Then we can head out to my ranch and see how Apache is doing."

An arrow of anticipation zinged through her middle. *Will he be okay? Will he still be alive?* She bit the inside of her cheek and hurried to take care of Ginger, so she could go see him.

Mom asked to come along, and she drove Clyde's truck so she could take her daughter home later, while Electra rode with Sam in a more companionable atmosphere than the day before. The cowgirl glanced at her. "I like your hair today."

"Oh." She scrubbed fingers through the short mop. Yikes. It must look as flat as those hills out there. "Ran outta gel." She shrugged.

"Easier to wear with a hat," the woman said. "I have an extra one at home you can use, if you'd like."

She snorted. A cowboy hat? What would her friends say about that? She could only imagine the derisive remarks. Then she huffed a laugh. *Who cares? I'm here now. When in Rome…right?*

"Yeah. I'd like that."

Sam flashed her a grin. "We'll make a cowgirl out of you yet."

Me? A cowgirl? "Ha."

She was out of the pickup almost before it came to a complete stop and sprinted to the barn. Fear prickled like a thousand tiny needles, and she held her breath as she entered the building and tiptoed toward Apache's stall.

When he heard her footsteps, he lifted his scarred, bumpy face over the gate and let out a low, rumbling sound. Her breath escaped in a loud whoosh. "Oh, Apache, you're okay." She slipped inside the stall and threw her arms around his neck. "I missed you today."

She nuzzled her nose in his black mane and took in his musky, horsey smell, letting her fingers trail through the tangled hair.

"He doin' good?" Sam's voice startled her, and she flinched, a flush rising into her cheeks. Caught, going goo-goo over the horse.

"Yeah, I think so." She raised her brow. "He actually seemed glad to see me. He made this funny rumble in his throat."

The cowgirl smiled. "That's a sure sign he likes you. I'm glad." She stroked the brown horse's shoulder. "How're you feeling today, mister? You look better." Taking a handful of cake pellets from her pocket, she offered them to Electra. "Here, go ahead and give him a treat. I'll get the brushes, and we can try to get him prettied up."

Clyde's truck rumbled to a stop outside, and her mother joined them in the barn.

Sam checked his temperature and gave him vitamins and a shot. Mom brushed his back, while Electra painstakingly worked on the knots in his mane. "You poor guy," she murmured. "Nobody combed your hair or gave you a bath or did anything nice for you, did they? How could that creep be so mean?"

Apache closed his eyes and appeared to grin as she caressed and talked to him. The hole in her heart seemed to fill…just a little, like a dry pond after a summer rain.

***

The pattern of their days repeated like a patchwork quilt. Riding at the dude ranch with Mom and the others and then going home with Sam at the end of the day to brush and pat and nuzzle with Apache.

On one of Sam's days off from Clyde's, Mom drove her to the ranch, where they found the cowgirl unsaddling Sugar, her Thoroughbred rescue.

Electra ran toward them. "Hey, you didn't start without me, did you?"

"No, I saved Apache for you. You can walk him around the corral awhile, then brush him down." She reached inside her truck. "I have something for you." She held out a well-worn straw-colored cowboy hat.

"Oh! Thanks." With an embarrassed smirk Electra put it on over her smooth hair and posed for her mom. "Do I look like a cowgirl now?"

"You sure do." Mom appeared pleased. One of the few times lately she actually approved of something Electra did.

"We'll find you some boots too," Sam added. "You look great."

A pleasant wave of acceptance washed over her. She started toward the barn at a skip, but abruptly slowed to a more *who-cares* Goth-girl saunter.

As she walked away, she heard her mom say, "She's a whole different girl. I haven't seen her like this in months. Thank you, Sam."

Really? Electra slowed her pace, listening, hardly breathing. No way. This…this *cowgirl* experience wasn't changing her.

"Oh, I haven't done anything," the cowgirl protested. "It was the horse."

"Whatever it was, it's a miracle." She swiveled her head slightly to see her mom pat Sugar's neck. "I don't feel quite as bad about leaving next week. I know she's in good hands."

Her chest expanded, and she strode six feet tall as she headed to see *her* horse.

The afternoon passed quickly, with Sam giving her many of the grooming and feeding chores.

"What kind of a horse is Apache?"

"Good question. He's a Quarter horse—that's his breed, a buckskin—the light brown is his color, and he's a gelding." She explained what that meant. "The vet thought he's about ten years old, so that's still pretty young. He apparently was somebody's valued saddlehorse once." She sighed and ran a hand over the scarred face. "He must have had a run-in with a barbed wire fence at some time."

Electra swallowed the prickle of sorrow that welled in her throat. "Yeah. He's really a nice horse…Quarter horse…buckskin…gelding." She rolled the terms around in her mouth.

Finally, Sam hung up her feed bucket. "C'mon, let's go up to the house. I have some chicken marinating, and I'll fire up the barbecue."

Sam poured a glass of wine for her and Mom and a Coke for Electra. They sat on the big wrap-around porch, waiting for the charcoal to heat.

Electra couldn't help but chatter away. "Apache looks so much better already, doesn't he? I think he walked smoother today, not quite so stove up."

"I see you've picked up some of Clyde's lingo already." Sam grinned. "I think you're right. He seems happier."

"Yeah, I can see a light in his eyes. Did you notice, Mom?"

"Um…" Her mother hesitated, but before she answered, a red sports car roared up the drive.

"It's Teresa." Sam stood. "Good, we can put the chicken on."

The four women ate with gusto, Mom shared stories of the city, and Teresa talked about strange real estate clients. Electra chimed in with comments about Apache, basking in the warm glow of camaraderie. For the first time in months, she belonged somewhere…almost.

The sun hovered above the low horizon, painting the sky with gold and crimson.

"Ah, this is the life." Mom leaned back in the wicker chair and put her feet up on the porch railing. "I envy you this, Sam."

Teresa held her glass up in a toast. "Here's to the good life." They clinked glasses and drank.

As Electra sank into the cushions on the porch swing, a truck ground its way up the road toward the house. A pea-green pickup with a light-bar on top came to a stop in front of them. She sat bolt upright. *Now what? What's the fuzz doing out here?* She snorted. *Just like the sheriff you'd see on TV westerns.* Worry flickered in her chest.

"Lots of company today." Sam stepped off the porch to meet the uniformed man as he disembarked. "Hello, Sheriff O'Conner. What brings you out this way?"

He touched the brim of his hat. "Howdy, Sam." He waved at their group on the porch. "Ladies."

He hitched up his pants and heavy gun belt, then shuffled his booted feet. "Well, Sam. I got a call from the Custer County Sheriff this afternoon. Something about a stolen horse."

"Huh?" The cowgirl stood with feet planted wide. "No. There must be some mistake."

Electra's stomach swooped like a bad rollercoaster ride. *We didn't steal him. Could we get arrested and go to jail?*

"Did you remove a horse from a pasture outside Miles City a few days ago?"

"Yes." Sam's face paled. "Yes, I did, but I bought that horse."

O'Conner nodded. "The owner, a Mr...." he consulted his notebook, "Mr. Smythe said he'd been traveling in Europe, and when he came home, the horse was gone."

Sam planted fists on her hips. "Why, that...that slimy little snake took my money and turned in a stolen report."

Ohmygosh. Electra's mouth hung open. *That jerk put one over on us.* She jumped up. Her mom put out a hand to restrain her, but she ignored her and leaped down the steps to join Sam. Fear iced her chest.

"I know you, Sam. I knew your great-grandparents when I was a bitty kid. Let's hear your story." The sheriff leaned against the railing in a soft stance. His calm, soothing voice matched his kindly expression.

Letting out her breath in a whoosh, Sam licked her lips. "That horse was in terrible shape from neglect. Did the sheriff tell you about the complaints Teresa and I filed?"

O'Conner shook his head. "Guess he forgot about that."

The muscles in Sam's jaws quivered. "Teresa, come here and tell the sheriff what happened with Apache."

Together, she and Sam related the story to Sheriff O'Conner.

"He was almost dead!" Electra threw in. *That has to count for something.*

"And, I have a bill of sale." The cowgirl ran inside to retrieve it and the copy she'd made.

He studied the handwritten note for long minutes, then scrubbed a hand over his face. "Well, ladies, this is a bit unorthodox, but it is signed by both parties, and it's notarized." He twisted his weathered face into a frown. "If you don't mind, I guess I'll have to take this copy with me and fax it to the Miles City office."

Yeesh, glad she made the extra one. We gotta keep the proof. Nerves fluttered in Electra's stomach.

Sam's shoulders slumped. "Let me know what you find out right away, in case I need to get a lawyer."

"You bet." The sheriff touched his hat, got into his truck, and drove away.

The buoyant evening had deflated like a month-old birthday balloon.

Fear electrified Electra's body, and she fought to keep her voice from quavering. "What's gonna happen to Apache now?"

"All the signatures are there." Teresa's pat on her arm meant to reassure. "It's perfectly legal. Don't worry about it."

"I hope you're right." Sam trudged up the steps and picked up the dishes. "I'm going to clean up—no need to help. If you guys don't mind, I'd just like some time to myself now."

Electra rode back to the dude ranch with her mom, unease clinging to her like a mist. *If Sam is so discouraged, what hope is there? Am I going to lose my friend Apache? I can't lose somebody else—I need him.*

CHAPTER FOUR

Electra spent the next couple of nights tossing in her bed, worrying about Apache and rewinding the sheriff's visit. What would happen to the horse if he took him? What could she do to stop him? Feeling like a tiny twig in a flooded stream, she punched her pillow. *Nothing. There's nothing I can do.*

When Sam came back to work at the dude ranch, she spoke in short, curt half-sentences to her and Mom and the other women who wanted to get in one last ride before leaving.

What's eating her? Electra rode in silence, not wanting to risk the cowgirl's sharp tone. She grimaced. *Probably worried about Apache too.*

After the ride and unsaddling, she approached hesitantly. "Well, tomorrow I get to come home with you and be with Apache." She gazed at Sam for a moment when she didn't answer. Her stomach flip-flopped. "Don't I? Did you change your mind?"

"Oh. No. No, I haven't changed my mind. I was just...preoccupied." The woman shook her head. "We still have a deal. Be ready to work. We've got lots to do before the next bunch of dudes show up and I have to come back here."

"You bet."

***

Electra left the truck door open and sprinted ahead of Sam to the barn, yelling, "Apache, Apache, I'm here."

As she entered the dim, musty stalls, the gaunt horse pricked its ears forward at the sound of her voice. He ambled to the gate and greeted her with a low rumbling whicker. She breathed in, his scent growing more familiar and pleasant each time.

Sam led Sugar into the barn. "What do you think? Is he strong enough for a short ride?"

Her heartbeat sped up, and she widened her eyes. "Oh, do you think so? I'd love to."

"Let's try. We won't go too far."

While Sam tacked Sugar, Electra grabbed another saddle. With a soothing voice, she murmured to him as she hoisted it to his back. "I don't even need any help now, do I, Apache?" She allowed herself a small grin.

The horses walked out into the prairie, littered now with a riot of pink, yellow, and blue wildflowers. The evening sun burnished the horizon, and Sam let out a long sigh. Electra threw her a sideways glance. *I think she needed this. She's been pretty stressed.*

Apache plodded slowly along. His appearance was a lot better. Still awfully thin, but his ribs weren't showing so prominently, and his coat was getting smoother with her grooming. "He's happy to be out here." She swung her face toward Sam. "So am I. Thanks."

"Well, it's obvious you've been good for him. He's a one-woman horse now."

Pride welled up inside and filled the hollow spaces in her chest.

She settled into a comfortable silence, listening to the crunch of the horses' hooves on the grass, the trill of meadowlark, the ratcheting of an insect. She was beginning to understand why the cowgirl loved this place. *It's peaceful. This feels good.*

As they rounded the corner back home, Sam gasped and drew up her reins sharply. Sheriff O'Conner's rig was parked by the house, and down by the barn was another vehicle with a horse trailer. "Oh no." She nudged Sugar forward.

"What? What's going on?" Electra's voice came out quavery. She slipped out of the saddle, dread turning her knees to water.

Sam dismounted in front of O'Conner. "It's…?"

The big officer scrunched his face into a rueful frown. "I'm sorry, Sam." He withdrew a piece of paper from his breast pocket and handed it to her. "I'm afraid Smythe got a court order to return the horse. The nephew had no legal rights to sell it, and Smythe wants him back."

Electra's chest pinched, her worst fears coming true. "N-o-o!" She choked back tears and anguish.

Sam dropped the paper and reached for her hand. "Sheriff, this is terrible. Isn't there anything we can do…contest it? Keep him until…?"

O'Conner shook his head. "I'm sorry. The Custer County animal warden has instructions to take the horse back immediately."

Electra and Sam stared toward the barn where the pudgy warden leaned against his truck, chomping on his gum, and studying his fingernails like they were the most fascinating things in the world. Then he glanced up and sauntered toward them.

"You saw the order. I gotta take 'im." He reached for Apache's bridle.

Electra threw her arms around the horse's neck. "No. Please! Please don't take him. He was near-dead. I helped… He's better now… Please…"

The animal control officer merely huffed and led Apache toward the horse trailer. She hung on for dear life, sobbing and pleading, her feet dragging in the dirt. The horse balked and curved his head toward her as if to give comfort.

The warden jerked on the reins. "C'mon now, git on in here."

Sam strode to Electra and put gentle hands on her shoulders. "My dear, we have to let them take him. For now." Her voice was husky. "But we'll get him back. We're going to fight this, I promise."

She collapsed into Sam's arms. "Noooo." The cowgirl's chest trembled against her face. The men loaded Apache, tossed the saddle and bridle aside, and then drove away. Slowly the two slid to the ground, holding onto each other, their tears mingling in the dust.

***

Horace and Clyde sat at the kitchen table, one hunched over, the other leaning back in his chair. With shaking hands, Sam poured coffee.

Electra hiccupped a sob now and then. *Apache is gone! What'll happen to him back in that pasture all by himself with no one to care for him?*

The old man wrapped big hands around his cup. "Well, there's no doubt about it. You're gonna have to get yourself a lawyer."

Sam slumped into her chair. "I have no money for a lawyer. I spent the five hundred I had saved to buy Apache from that…that conniving little scoundrel. And now it looks like I won't even get that back."

Clyde shook his head. "This is outrageous. The owner obviously didn't care a whit about his horse, leaving him for months like that and not even checking to see if the nephew was caring for it." He sipped his coffee. "Seems to me, you have a clear-cut case of animal abuse."

Sam let out a long sigh. "Yeah, you'd think so. But that Custer County warden didn't seem to care one way or the other that Apache was almost dead."

Electra sniffled. "We have to get him back. He's going to die." Her insides churned.

"Listen." Clyde set his cup down with a thump. "Let me give my lawyer a call—see how much he'll charge to take this on. I'm willing to give you an advance on your wages. I don't want to see you gals lose this horse."

Oh yes. Perfect. Hope blossomed in her mind.

"Oh, Clyde." Sam's eyes glistened. "I can't let you do that. I'll be in debt to you for the rest of my life."

Horace made a growling sound. "I've got some set aside—I'll chip in."

Electra jumped to her feet. "Sam! Oh, Sam, will it work? Can we do this? We gotta do this—pleeeeease!"

The old man grinned. "Don't worry about it, little gal. We're gonna get this thing solved."

She stared at these old men in wonder. *Wow. These guys… They're not family, but they're coming together to help Sam out. Sheesh. We barely know our next-door neighbors at home.*

***

She lay wrapped in unfamiliar sheets in the loft room at Sam's house. After an afternoon spent with busy work, both trying to ignore the empty stall in the barn, the cowgirl asked if she'd like to spend the night. Mom said it was okay, so here she was.

Clouds flying over the moon cast moving shadows on the floor. Her eyes refused to close. She couldn't get the image out of her head—Apache being dragged into the horse trailer, his head hung low. He knew he was going back. Back to a bare pasture with no feed and no water and no love. Would that Smythe guy take any better care of him than his stupid nephew? Now that the horse was gone, would she have to go back to New York with her mom?

The pain began low in her stomach and radiated upward through her chest. Her breath pushed tiny sobs through her constricted throat. Emptiness and loss swirled around her like those "dust devils" Sam called the wind gusts. She buried her face in the pillow, trying to shut out the images, the voices telling her she was all alone, she was a nobody, and no one cared.

If someone reached in and yanked her heart out through her chest, it couldn't be more painful than this. She dug her fingernails into the flesh of her arms, pressing harder and harder, raking them across the skin until she felt the slick warmth of blood.

***

A knock woke her. For a moment, she forgot where she was, who she was, and why she was all tangled up in the sheets.

Another knock. "Electra, are you all right?"

Oh man. It's Sam. The image rushed back. *Apache. He's gone.* She groaned.

"Electra? Please answer me. I'm coming in."

"Okay. C'min." Her voice rasped.

Sam opened the door, and stood still for a moment, staring around the room. Electra burrowed under the mound of bedclothes.

The cowgirl sat on the edge of the bed. "Honey, are you sick?"

"No."

"Then why are you still in bed?"

Electra huffed a snort. *Why do you think?*

Sam tugged the blankets away from her face. "You're quite upset about Apache, aren't you?"

She buried her face into the pillow.

"Electra. We can't give up on him. We're going to fight this. You heard Horace and Clyde yesterday—they're going to help us. And Teresa too."

"Won't matter." The sob erupted before she could stop it.

"That's not true." Sam's voice held a note of anguish.

"Wanna go home."

A gentle hand on her shoulder. "We can't just let them do this. I'm not going to. I'm going to fight this… And I need your help."

Her shoulder twitched, all on its own.

"I can't do this without you." Sam prodded her side. "C'mon. You've got to get up. Let's do this—together." She stood, threw open the curtains and blinds. "I'm going to fix breakfast, and then we'll strategize. Okay?" Her boots clumped on the stairs as she went down to the kitchen.

Electra groaned and rolled to her side. *I never want to get out of bed.* The smell of bacon finally tantalized her grumbly stomach, and she dragged her legs over the side of the mattress, as if each one weighed a thousand pounds. Seeing the spots of blood on the sheet, she covered it with the blankets. She rummaged in her backpack and found the familiar black baggy clothes. Peering into an ancient wavery mirror, she applied white makeup to cover her blotchy face and spiked her hair with gel until it stuck out in every direction.

Pancakes and bacon were on the table when she plodded into the kitchen. Sam spun to greet her and winced.

She doesn't like my Goth look. Meh. Who cares? She sat at the table and stared at the food.

With a smile that appeared forced, the cowgirl sat. "Now, what we're going to do…"

CHAPTER FIVE

Sam stopped at the Dairy Queen in Forsyth for lunch before their appointment with Clyde's attorney. Sitting outside on the picnic bench, Electra tried to let the warm sun soak the tension out of her back. She took a sip of her Coke. "Do you really think we'll be able to get Apache back?"

"Well, that's what we're here to see this lawyer about. I have hopes—I honestly do. We're going to do whatever we have to, to get him back."

"Ah, if it isn't Samantha Moser." A deep voice spoke from behind them.

She turned to see a tall, dark-haired man in a charcoal suit.

"Jack Murdock. Are you slumming?" Sam pointed at his burger and fries.

He chuckled and sat next to Electra on the bench. "Oh, I enjoy my quota of grease now and then." He focused on her. "How are you, young lady?"

She shrugged and averted her gaze.

"Electra, Mr. Murdock is the owner of my ranch." Sam introduced them. "We're here to see a man about a horse."

"Oh yes, the allegedly stolen horse."

Sam bristled and braced her hands on the table to stand.

Ohmygosh. He owns the ranch where Sam lives? She ground her teeth. *I don't think Sam likes him.*

"Now, now." Jack held up his hand, palm out. "Just ribbing you a little. I know you like to rescue abandoned ..." he glanced at Electra, "...things. I'm not making any judgments."

Electra shifted farther from him on the bench. *This guy is like an oil-slick.*

Sam's face pinched tight.

Jack put a couple of fries into his mouth and chewed. "In fact, I might be able to help you with that little problem."

Sam cocked her head. "You might?"

The man wiped his lips with a napkin. "Yes, I might. Why don't you let me put you in touch with my attorney?" He reached into his pocket for his wallet.

"We already have an appointment with one, in just a few minutes." She checked her watch. "But thanks anyway."

"No, no. This guy's the best. If you've got him working on your side, you're assured success." He handed her a card.

She stood. "Well, thanks, Jack. Let me go ahead and meet with my guy, and if he doesn't think he can take the case, I'll give yours a call." She took the card and stuck it into her purse. "C'mon, Electra. We don't want to be late. See you, Jack."

He upsets her. The grease from her lunch congealed in her stomach. *He's not a nice man. His offer is bogus.*

***

Clyde's attorney had a one-man office on the second floor of an old brick office building just off the main street in Forsyth. He greeted them with a handshake and ushered them into his dimly-lit office—forest green walls and drapes and a dark walnut desk. She and Sam sat on brown upholstered, straight-backed chairs. Electra blinked, letting her eyes adjust. It was like a dark cave. It didn't give off any vibes of hope. She squirmed. *Not a very cheerful place.*

"Clyde filled me in a bit on what's happened." The gray-haired man steepled his fingers. "Why don't you tell me in your own words."

Electra added comments as Sam related the story.

The lawyer nodded occasionally and jotted a few notes. "Did you happen to take any pictures of the horse in his original condition?"

The cowgirl grimaced. "Gosh, no. I sure wish I had. But I do have some I took not too long after we brought him home and some more recently that show how much improvement he'd made." She reached into her purse. "I also have the vet and feed bills. And the bill of sale I made out if you want to make a copy."

The attorney scanned the papers and bobbed his head again. "Um-hmm. Well, let me do a little research. I'll let you know if I think you have a case." He stood and held his arm out toward the exit.

Electra followed Sam out the door.

"I don't know. He didn't sound very encouraging, did he?" In the bright sunlight, she squinted at Sam.

Sam shrugged. "I don't have any experience with lawyers. Maybe that's normal. I suppose they have to look into similar cases, see if we have a leg to stand on." She patted her shoulder. "I'm sure it'll be okay."

In the truck, Sam called Teresa on her cell and recounted their experience. When she disconnected, she said, "Teresa said she took pictures the day she found Apache, and she said if we have to go to court, she'll testify."

"That's good, isn't it?"

"Yeah. I hope so. But I sure don't want to have to go to court." Sam sighed.

No, that doesn't sound like fun. She scrunched her face in a grimace. Her stomach roiled.

Then a cold thought froze her. "Sam. Do you still want me to stay here if Apache is gone?" *I have to be here to help her get him back. We have to do this. Together.*

The cowgirl gave her sidelong glance. "Yes, I certainly do. I'm still going to need your help. If you want to, that is."

She smiled then. "Yes. I do."

***

"I've got ten kids from a group home in Billings coming this weekend," Clyde told them the next day. "They're teens who've been in some kinda trouble or were homeless, and the leaders want to expose them to horses and the ranching lifestyle." He rolled his eyes. "Electra, d'you think you'd be up to helping? I think we're gonna need more than just me and Sam."

"I guess." She stubbed the toe of her Martens into the dirt and shrugged. "I gotta go help Mom pack. See ya." She spun on her heel and trudged toward the cabin.

Clyde's questioning voice followed. "What's got into her?"

She slowed to hear what Sam would say.

"It's losing Apache. She was doing so well, but now she's retreated into the dark again. I don't know what to do with her. I keep trying to get her to show some fight, to help me get Apache back, but she seems to have given up."

An arrow of guilt zinged through Electra's chest, and she stumbled.

Clyde again. "I can't figure out kids these days. When I was a kid, my dad kept me so busy I never had time to get depressed."

You never had your brother get killed and your dad leave, did you? She almost changed direction to give that guy a piece of her mind. Her shoulders slumped. *Nah. He wouldn't understand. Nobody does.* She continued to the cabin and opened the door to her mother's room.

"Hi, sweetheart, I'm glad to see you. I need help getting ready." Mom's eyes were shiny and wet.

"Okay." She opened a dresser drawer, keeping her back turned to hide her own threatening tears.

Her mother kept a running patter as they stuffed her suitcases, recounting all the "fun" they'd had on this vacation.

Maybe you *had fun.* She snorted.

"What? Didn't you have a good time helping with Apache?" Mom straightened from stooping over the luggage. "I thought you really liked doing that."

She huffed again. "Well, yeah. But now he's gone."

"I know, honey, and I'm so, so sorry." Mom clasped her in a hug. "Do you want to come home with me then?"

"No!" Her lower lip jutted forward, and she pulled it back between her teeth to keep it from trembling. She blinked in surprise at her quick answer. Only a few days ago she was ready to go home to her friends. But then, Apache happened. *I can't be in New York when Sam gets him back.*

"Okay. That's fine. Just checking. If I know Sam, she's going to put up a fight, and she's going to get him back, and she'll need your help more than ever." Her mother's eyes went soft. "Plus, Clyde needs more help too. Did he tell you about the group of kids coming out?"

"Yeah." She lowered her gaze to the floor. "But I dunno how *I* can help with them."

"Clyde and Sam will let you know what to do. You might be surprised."

She shrugged and went back for more clothes in the dresser.

***

Sam drove Electra and her mom to the airport. No one seemed to want to talk much. *Fine with me. Mom'd just say how much* fun *we had, and how I'm going to be a cowgirl and all that crap.*

But after the last teary hug and when the plane had disappeared into the clear turquoise sky, second thoughts scampered through her head. *Why did I stay? Nobody here "gets" me like my Goth-girls. I should've gone. Especially since Apache isn't around anymore. What good am I here? And Mom's going to be all alone in that dark apartment.*

She climbed into the old, beat-up pickup, and Sam gunned it down the highway.

Hunched against the door, she stared out at the passing prairie.

The cowgirl made several attempts at conversation. "I know you miss your mom already. But we're going to work hard, have fun, and get Apache back."

The empty hole in her middle grew larger. *Yeah, right. As if...*

Sam finally gave up when she didn't answer.

When they got home, she immediately went up the stairs to her room, shut the door, and buried herself in the blankets on her bed.

As the afternoon shadows lengthened, Sam knocked on her door. "Supper is ready."

She turned her face to the wall.

"C'mon, Electra. Come downstairs and talk to me."

No. I don't want to talk. I just want to go to sleep and never wake up. She dug her nails into the still-raw scratches on her arms. The pain relieved her heartache...for now.

***

Pounding on the door brought Electra bolt upright. Sun filtered through the curtains. *Morning. Ugh.*

"C'mon, girl. You gotta get out of that bed and help me today. We've got a bunch of people coming to Clyde's."

She groaned.

Sam pounded again. "Electra. Come on out. Now."

She fluttered a frustrated breath. *Aw, geez, she's not gonna give up.* Finally, she crawled out of bed and opened the door a tiny crack. "I don't want to."

Sam swallowed. "Electra. You've got to snap out of this. Clyde and I need your help today."

Hmm. Maybe she will *give in. She's not my mother.* "No, you don't. You can't make me."

"Yes, we do. We have ten kids coming today, and we need you to be there."

Electra glared. "No."

The cowgirl had a *don't mess with me* expression on her face. "You *are* coming to work with me today."

Crud. She flashed the woman another sullen glare and stomped back into her room. Applying her white and black makeup, she spiked her hair, and tugged on her now-crusty black outfit. Slamming her bedroom door, she stomped down the stairs. "Okay, I'll come. But you can't make me like it."

Sam hissed a breath from between clenched teeth and opened her lips in a fake-looking smile. "Great. Hop in the truck."

***

About 11 o'clock, two minivans arrived, loaded with jostling, scuffling teens and pre-teens. Four adults disembarked and herded the ten kids into the yard, where Clyde had set up picnic tables. Boys with shaved heads and baggy pants sauntered from the vehicle; others with long hair or dreadlocks slouched behind. The girls—some with lots of cool makeup, some with dreds, some tattooed and pierced— giggled and whispered.

Electra raised her brow. *Hmm. Maybe a Goth-girl or two.* She tittered as Clyde stopped in mid-stride and stared openly at the low-rider, crack-of-dawn pants one boy sported.

During lunch, the rancher talked to the group, explaining how ranch life worked and what they'd be doing over their weekend stay. "Today, we'll introduce you to the horses, let you get acquainted, maybe feed or brush them. And tomorrow, if you want to, we'll go on a little ride. It's not mandatory, so you do what you're comfortable with."

One boy sporting a black leather jacket elbowed the one next to him who wore Levis and a western-style shirt. "Awright, just for you, Tex. Ride 'em, cowboy." The second kid glared and moved away. The rest of the group snickered and made scoffing noises.

"Settle down, kids." The man in charge sent them a warning glare.

Electra smirked. *Good luck with that.*

Clyde spoke to the would-be cowboy. "How 'bout I let you ride LeRoy?"

The boy's face lit up with a huge grin.

Maybe he already knows about horses. If it's anything like me and Apache, well…maybe he's okay.

When they'd finished eating, the counselors made sure the kids cleaned up the tables, put their paper plates in the garbage and soda cans into a recycling bin. Then Sam, Clyde, and Irene led the group to the corrals where the horses stood, some dozing, some hanging their heads over the fence.

Clyde grabbed a halter and demonstrated how to catch one of the horses. Sam and Irene did the same, then led their charges out of the corral to the group.

Electra sneaked away to the barn where Ginger greeted her with a low, rumbling nicker. She stroked the mare's face up to the forelock. "How do they think I'm going to help out with this bunch of misfits, huh?" She snorted. "Is it like the blind leading the blind?"

Leaning her forehead against the horse's neck, she drew in deep breaths of the horsey scent she was now beginning to appreciate. Then, with a shrug, she clipped a lead rope to the halter. "Well, if *I* can learn to ride, maybe they can too."

She led Ginger from the barn. Sam talked to a group of girls clustered around her and showed them how to approach the horse, quietly from the front or side and not from behind. "You could startle him, and he might kick, in self-defense."

Standing with the mare off to the side, Electra scowled and crossed her arms over her chest. *Who am I kidding? Me, a leader? Huh.*

Then a girl—maybe a little younger than her—dressed in black, wearing white makeup and spiked hair, ambled toward her and Ginger, intent on the ground. Electra's heart jumped, knocking at her ribs. *Yeah. A Goth-girl. Hmm.* The young teen stopped and glanced around as if to see who might be watching her, then moved forward again.

In silence, Electra combed the mare's mane with her fingers. The girl put out a hand, then quickly withdrew it as the horse fluttered her nostrils.

"It's okay. She won't bite." She took the girl's hand and guided it toward the horse's face. The hand trembled, but when she touched Ginger's velvety nose, she raised her head, her black-rimmed eyes opened wide. Electra put out her hand, flat-palmed, with a carrot. Ginger ate the treat and nuzzled her pocket for more. She handed the girl a carrot. The teen copied the open-handed offering and gave a little gasp when the horse lipped it into her mouth.

Smiling, she slowly, deliberately stroked the contours of the mare's face, as if she were a blind person memorizing someone's features. She lifted her gaze. "She's cool."

A cottony cloud of rapport enveloped her. "Yeah, she is. I'm Electra, by the way."

"Sapphire. How'd you get to be a horse person?"

She huffed. "I'm not, really. I live in New York. My mom brought me out here for this lame 'bonding' vacation." She glossed lightly over Jimmy's death and slid into Apache's story.

"Wow, sick. D'you think you'll get him back?"

A shrug. "I hope so. Sam thinks we will."

As Sam and Clyde demonstrated to the kids how to brush and currycomb the horses, Electra picked up a brush to show Sapphire. "Work front to back, like this. Sam says 'cause that's the way the hair grows."

The girl took the tool and gently brushed Ginger's neck. The mare blew soft flutters through her lips and curved her neck around the two. Sapphire's tight shoulders visibly relaxed. Electra allowed a tiny smile. *Yeah. I can identify with that.*

CHAPTER SIX

The next day, after a successful ride for several, the group home kids unsaddled and brushed their horses before heading back to Billings.

Electra and Sapphire tended to Ginger. The girl's expression softened as she caressed the soft nose and ran her palm up to the forehead. Then she took the golden mane in her hands and buried her face. Electra met Sam's gaze. A bright beam of pride shot through her chest and heated her cheeks.

As the group boarded the vans, Sapphire spun around toward her, but stopped short. "'Bye….uh…thanks…" Then she ran to the vehicle.

Warmth suffused her body. *Wow. I did* do something good.

On the drive home, she quietly stared out the passenger side window, replaying the feelings of almost-kinship with Sapphire and satisfaction of introducing her to the peacefulness of a horse.

Sam touched her shoulder. "You did a really good job with that girl this weekend."

She swiveled her head toward the cowgirl, blinking back the sting of tears. "Yeah. I think I helped her a little." She bit her lower lip. "She lost both her parents. Ended up on the street, stealing, an'…" Her throat tightened and her own sorrow threatened to surface. She diverted her eyes from Sam and stared out the window again.

Sam squeezed her arm. "I'm proud of you."

Her heart made a funny little jump in her chest. *I did okay, didn't I?*

When they drove up the rise toward the house, a white pickup was parked out front. Sam pulled beside the logoed truck door and sighed.

"Who's that?" Electra asked. "I saw him at Clyde's yesterday."

Sam pushed out a forceful exhale. "That's Brad Ashton. He's a film-maker. He took footage of me to include in a documentary without permission. I wish he'd just go away." She opened her door and stalked around the front of her pickup to meet the dark-haired man who already stood outside, smiling broadly.

"Now what?" She stopped, her fists on her hips.

Electra got out of the truck and leaned on the front, watching with hooded eyelids.

Ashton chuckled. "Just like a bad penny, huh?" He reached into his shirt pocket and drew out a sheet of paper. "A release form for the documentary." He offered it to her. "That is, if you want to. If you don't, then I'll take your scene out."

Sam seemed to hesitate.

"But I'd really like to keep the footage in. You sit a horse so pretty." Ashton continued to extend the paper. "You don't have to decide right now. Think about it if you want."

"Well, it's about time." Grinning, Sam took the form and put it in her pocket. "Nice to meet a man who can admit he was wrong."

Brad quirked an eyebrow. "Wrong? Me? Never."

Sam snorted. "Yeah, right."

What? What is this? Electra cleared her throat. "You want me to start the chores?"

Sam stared. "Chores. Yeah." Then to Brad. "This is my friend, Electra. We have to feed my horse and exercise her a bit. You wanna come along?"

"Sure." Ashton touched two fingers to his hat brim.

Electra frowned. *Who is this guy, and why is Sam suddenly all smiley with him when she just told me she didn't like him?*

At the corral, Sugar trotted to the fence and whickered when they approached. Her heart tripping, Electra rushed forward and threw her arms around the horse's neck. *Horses seem more real than people sometimes.* Sugar nuzzled her pocket for a treat.

Ashton walked slowly forward, holding his hand out for the mare to sniff, then rubbed her face, talking in a quiet voice. "Easy there, girl. Do I smell all right? Huh? Okay then." He reached out his other hand to Electra who gave him a cake pellet, and then he let Sugar eat from his palm.

She watched open-mouthed. *Hmm. He seems to know what to do.*

"You don't act like a city boy," Sam blurted.

"I've rode a green horse or two." Brad exaggerated a bow-legged stance.

Electra took a step back. *He's full of surprises.*

"Where?" Sam asked.

"Livingston."

"Ah, wind country."

Brad chuckled. "You could say that. All our cows were shorter on one side from leaning into the wind."

"What? Really?" When she saw his grin, Electra rolled her eyes.

Sam laughed. "So, why did you leave?"

"Dad lost the place." He stared at the horizon, a faraway look in his eyes.

"Oh. I'm sorry. That's happened to a lot of ranchers."

"Yeah." His voice sounded sad.

The cowgirl rested an arm on a fencepost. "You want to

stay for supper?"

"Depends… Whatcha cookin'?" The twinkle returned to his eyes.

Sam gave him a mock glare. "Leftover spaghetti. Take it or leave it." She spun around and headed to the house.

"Spaghetti—always better the next day."

This conversation was ridiculous. Electra frowned and tromped to the house, giving Brad dark, sidelong glances.

It didn't take long to reheat the food, and Sam set the steaming bowl of spaghetti on the table. "Wash up, sit down, and eat." She pointed to the bathroom.

"Yes, ma'am." Ashton saluted and headed for the hallway.

Sam started dishing up plates.

"Why'd you ask him to stay?" Electra sat at the table, pushing her lower lip into a pout.

Sam stopped in mid-ladle. "Well, that attorney we saw left a message that he couldn't take the case. Brad said he might be able to help us get—"

The young man appeared, wiping his hands on his pants. "Mmm, that smells good. Let me at it." He sat, tucked a napkin into his shirt front, and picked up his fork and knife, striking a comical expectant pose.

Sam set his plate in front of him.

"Ah, a woman who serves." He twitched his eyebrows.

Sam laughed. "Oh no. Don't you be getting used to it."

"So you're just being nice 'cause I'm company."

Electra glared at the two. *Lame-O.*

"Something like that." Sam ignored her and sat down to eat.

He raised a forkful of spaghetti high in the air, leaned his head back, and slurped down a long strand. He winked at Electra. "Bet you can't do that."

She curled her lip and hunched back over her plate, deliberately cutting her noodles into small pieces.

"Sorry." Brad straightened in his chair. "I should mind my manners when I'm with ladies."

Electra snorted.

Sam grinned. "So, you do a lot of riding on your dad's ranch?"

"Fair amount. Helped with branding, fall roundup, stuff like that."

She twirled her spaghetti around her fork. "Ever do any rodeoing?"

"Naw. Not really. Just around home when a horse suddenly decided to get feisty. Did my share of hittin' the dust."

Electra sneered. "Didn't wanna get bucked off in front of a crowd, huh?"

"That's right." He snickered and ran his gaze over Sam. "How 'bout you? I'll bet you'da looked cute running the barrels."

A flush crept up the cowgirl's neck. "Don't know about that. Did a little when I was about ten."

Oh brother. He's flirting with her. And she likes it! The spaghetti rested like a clump of worms in her stomach.

"You oughta try it again. You got the build."

With a long, exaggerated sigh, Electra pushed back her plate, got up, and stomped upstairs to her room. Grownups! She'd never figure them out. First, Sam says she doesn't want to see this guy, then she invites him to eat and plays all silly with him… *Blech.* She slumped onto the bed. She missed her mom. She missed her friends. She missed Apache. And now that attorney wasn't going to help. Maybe they'd never get him back. Loneliness crept into her soul like a thief. She bit her lip to stop the trembling.

When she heard a car pull up, she glanced out the window

to see Teresa get out. Sam's friend carried a manila envelope and a bottle of wine. *Might as well go down. Maybe I can at least talk to* her. She slouched down the stairs. "Hi, Teresa."

"Hi there. Nice to see you again."

"You should have been here fifteen minutes ago," Sam apologized. "We just finished off supper."

"No, that's fine. I ate in town." Teresa handed Sam the bottle. "But crack this open, and I'll have a glass." She shuffled into the kitchen, where Sam introduced her to Brad and retrieved goblets.

He stood and held out a hand for her to shake. "Pleased to meet you. I understand you've been helping Sam try to rescue a horse."

"Yeah, that's right. And that's why I stopped by tonight. I have those pictures of Apache when I first found him." Teresa opened the envelope and spread them on the table.

Electra gasped as she saw the photos of the emaciated animal, ribs protruding through his hide, his head hung low to the ground. She'd nearly forgotten how horrible he'd looked. And how much he improved over the few weeks they had him. She choked back a sob. "We've got to get him back."

Teresa gave her a sympathetic glance. "I talked briefly to our real estate attorney this afternoon, and he suggested we check into civil court. We have the signed, notarized bill of sale and these pictures. Maybe we'll get lucky and draw a sympathetic judge."

"Oh man, getting up to present a legal case in front of a judge." Sam's face went pale. "I don't know if I can do that."

"Sure, you can. I'll be there with you, and I'll testify too." Teresa peered earnestly at her.

With a grimace, Brad put down the photos. "Before you do that, why don't you let me nose around a little. I've been filming all over this country, and people are pretty used to seeing me by now."

Teresa met Sam's gaze. "Really? That'd be great."

"What's the owner's name?" he asked.

"Richard Smythe." Teresa returned the photos to the envelope.

"Okay. I'll see what I can find out." He stood and retrieved his hat. "Well, I better be going. Thanks for supper, Sam. Day-old spaghetti. Very tasty." He winked.

"Don't get used to it."

Electra let out a breath. *Finally. Good riddance.*

After he left, Sam found a notepad and pen. "Let's make a list."

Grabbing a Coke from the fridge and a cookie from the jar, Electra sat at the table with the two women.

"Okay." Teresa grinned broadly. "Number one. He's cute."

Sam hmphed and bent over the paper, her chestnut hair covering a rising blush. "Okay, we have the photos, we have the bill of sale."

"Number two. He's willing to help you out," Teresa persisted.

Electra scowled. "He's just trying to hit on her."

Teresa giggled. "Number three. He's got a nice butt." She sipped her wine.

"Ugh." Her stomach roiled. *This is sickening.*

Sam rolled her eyes. "Come on, you two. Knock it off and help me out. I don't have a lot to go on here. And if I do have to present my case to a judge, I'd better have more than this."

It was close to midnight when Teresa got up to leave. They'd mulled and discussed and made lists and drafts of speeches until Electra's brain felt like a cache of dust bunnies from under the bed. But they were no closer to a solution than before.

"I think we're going to have to wait and see what Brad comes up with," Teresa said on her way out the door.

"Yeah, I guess so. Because I really don't want to have to go to court." Sam waved goodnight to her friend and then yawned. "I'm going to bed. I'm fried."

Electra stayed hunched over the wads of paper littering the table, a heaviness overtaking her limbs.

Sam frowned. "What's the matter?"

She shrugged. "Nothin'." Her emotions fought against Brad's friendly, helpful face and Teresa's teasing about him.

"C'mon, I know you better than that by now. There's something bugging you."

Electra's hands flattened, then re-crumpled paper. Her black nail polish was chipped and scratched now, her cuticles bitten.

"We'll get Apache back." Sam peered at her. "I'm even willing to get up in front of the judge and talk him into believing our side of the story."

"It's not that." Electra stood, gathered the litter, and threw it into the garbage. She headed toward the stairs, stopped on the first step, and squinted over her shoulder. "Why d'you need *him* to help anyway?" She ran up the stairs and slammed her door shut.

Sitting by the window, she stared out at the few pinpricks of stars in the black hole of a sky. That blackness was her life. Just when she'd found a kindred spirit in Apache, he was taken away. Just when she thought she'd made a friend in Sam, the cowgirl goes all goo-goo eyes at this guy Brad. And Teresa was no help. She dug her nails into her arms. *It's no use. We won't get him back. And Sam doesn't know I exist when Brad is around.* Salt from her tears stung the scratches, intensifying the itch of pain until she crawled into bed and pulled the covers over her head.

CHAPTER SEVEN

The next morning Electra deliberately stayed in bed until she heard Sam go out. Then she got up, applied her makeup, and donned her signature black clothes. She dragged herself downstairs and sat at the table, waiting for the cowgirl to come back in.

With a snarl, she announced, "I'm leaving."

"Electra!" Sam leaned on the door frame. "What's gotten into you?"

She slumped in her chair, mute.

"C'mon, girl. Tell me what's eating at you." Sam sat next to her.

Electra glared through mascara-caked eyelashes.

"I'll let you ride LeRoy at Clyde's today." The woman raised her brows and smiled—fake, like when Mom pretended to be cheerful.

"I wanna go home." Her lip quivered.

Sam's face softened. "Oh, sweetie. Tell me what's wrong. If we can't make it right, you can always go home."

"I always sat next to you." She heard defiance in her own voice.

"You don't like Brad?"

Electra rose from her chair. "I thought *you* didn't like him."

"But why? He may be our only hope of getting Apache back."

"Not *him*." Her voice rose to a shout. "I'm packing." She

strode toward the stairs. "And you can't stop me!"

The door slam reverberated behind her. She threw herself face down on the bed. She wanted to kick and scream and pound on Brad and Smythe and Jimmy and Dad… She threw a punch into her pillow. *It's not fair!*

After a few minutes, Sam knocked softly. "Please don't do this, Electra. Come out and talk to me."

"You don't like me anymore." Her words were muffled by the blanket.

"That's not true. Where did you get that idea?"

"You ignored me."

"When?"

"All the time *he* was here."

Sam turned the doorknob, came in, and sat on the bed. "If I did, I didn't mean to."

"Just like Dad." Electra buried her face in the pillow.

Sam rubbed her back. "Because he left you?"

She hiccupped and gave a slight nod.

"I'm not leaving you, my dear. You're my friend. I like you, and I want you to stay for the rest of the summer."

Electra lay still, holding her shoulders rigid with fear and uncertainty. *Does she really want me to? Will we be able to get Apache back? Have I made a mistake staying here?* The old negativity jabbed at her. *Naw, you're a nobody; you can't do anything right. You'll never get the horse back. You might as well give up.*

"I need you to help me. I don't want you to leave. I can't do this without you."

She peeked an eye out from the pillow.

"Honest, I can't. You're my right-hand girl. You and me together—we'll come up with the ideas, and if we need some muscle, then *maybe* we'll let Brad or Clyde help us."

She allowed a tiny smile of hope. "Can we go see him?"

"See Apache?" The cowgirl paused a moment. "Sure. Why not? Let's drive by there and see if he's being cared for."

"Yeah." Electra sat and wiped her eyes, fingers coming away black. "Bring your camera. If he's not, then we'll have evidence."

"Good idea. Why don't you take a quick shower, and we'll go."

***

Leaving the rough dirt road outside Ingomar, Sam shifted into high gear and sped down the highway, rolling down the side window to create a breeze.

Electra sat silent but leaned forward slightly, peering out the windshield. "Do you think he's all right?" She faced the woman. In a hurry to see Apache, she'd foregone the Goth makeup, even though her eyes reflected from the mirror swollen and red.

"I sure hope so. We may have to be prepared for anything, though."

She slumped against the back of the seat, her mouth quivering downward. *For anything? Like, he might be dead?* Fear iced her chest.

Sam swerved to avoid a road-killed rabbit. "You mentioned your dad this morning. He ignored you?"

She snorted. "Like, ye-ah. Jimmy was the only one who mattered."

"Your brother."

She nodded.

"And," Sam spoke hesitantly, "Jimmy was killed... In an accident?"

"Yeah." The reply came out as a hoarse whisper. Then she sat up straighter. Her words came with force. "And Dad was driving."

"Oooh. So he blamed himself."

"I guess." Electra shrugged. "Didn't take him long to

leave me and Mom."

"I'm so sorry. You've had a lot of loss in your life. I understand a little bit—I've lost some family too. Everyone deals with grief in different ways. Your dad just wasn't as strong as you and your mother."

"Yeah. I guess." She sniffled. "But I think Mom is trying to ignore everything, pretending to be cheerful all the time." *She can't fool me. It'd be easier if she cried or yelled or something…* The old pain bunched in her stomach and burned its way up into her throat. With her right hand, she dug her nails through her pants into the flesh of her thigh. *Stop. Stop. Stop.*

Sam grabbed her left hand and squeezed. "I'm sure she's simply trying to put on a brave front for your sake, to help you get over the sadness."

She shrugged, not trusting her voice.

"Well, I'm here. Anytime you want to talk…about anything." The cowgirl patted her hand and gave her a soft smile.

Nodding, she faced out the side window, blinking back tears. *How come she's being so nice to me? She doesn't really care, does she? Just watch. Next time Brad's around…* She sniffed.

***

Stopping at a drive-through on the edge of Miles City, Sam bought her a soft drink, a cup of coffee for herself, and a giant home-made cinnamon roll to share.

The late morning sun bore down. Low on the horizon, thunderheads gathered. Dust swirled in a long tail behind them on the country road as they drove closer to the ranch where Apache's fate lay hidden.

Up ahead, the windmill blades churned in the increasing wind. Electra's chest tightened. What would they find? "There he is." Her words came in an explosive breath, and she pushed her face closer to the windshield.

Apache stood by a gleaming new water tank, his tail

switching in the breeze. Tears prickled her eyes.

"Oh, thank God." Sam released a breath and parked the pickup.

Electra was out the moment the truck came to a stop, leaving the door wide open. She took a couple of running steps, then slowed to approach the horse cautiously. Apache lifted his head, his ears pricked toward her. He whinnied, trotted to the fence, and stretched over the wire. With a half-cry, half-giggle, she flung her arms around his neck.

Sam joined them, rubbing his face and murmuring, "You're still alive. You're okay. Oh, I'm so glad."

Apache fluttered his nostrils and nuzzled them both. Electra reached into her pocket and offered him a handful of cake pellets. "He's still awfully thin."

"Yes, but he's got water and a feed trough." Sam glanced around, pointing at an open gate. "He has access to a grassier pasture too. Oh, I'm so glad."

Electra sniffled and hugged the horse again. "But I miss you so much." A sob rose in her chest, and she swallowed it down.

The roar of a diesel engine brought their attention to the road. A big black 4x4 pulled up beside Sam's truck. A tall, muscular man slid out, leaving his door open to the view of a shotgun on a rack in the cab. He stood within reach, arms crossed over his barrel-chest. "What are you ladies doing here?"

"We're just check—"

Sam cut her off before she could say any more. "We were just driving by and stopped to pet the horse. My young friend here loves horses."

"Hmm." The big man didn't appear convinced. His forehead furrowed. "Say, aren't you the two who stole this horse a couple weeks ago?"

"No!" Electra's denial was a shout.

Sam put an arm around her. "It was just a misunderstanding, sir."

Glowering, he took a step forward. "Well, that's not what I heard. You gals can just get off this property right now."

"Who are you?" Sam wasn't about to give in so easily.

"Let's just say, I been hired to keep the likesa you away from this horse." He puffed out his chest, uncurled his arms, and reached inside his pickup toward the shotgun.

"We're leaving. No need for threats." Sam grabbed her arm and propelled her into their vehicle. Gravel spun under the tires as she punched the accelerator.

Electra's heart beat nearly out of her chest, and her mouth was so dry she could barely swallow.

As Sam sped down the dirt road, she kept glancing into her rearview mirror to see if they were being followed. Finally, when they reached the highway, she stopped the pickup. Her hands shook when she unclamped them from the steering wheel.

Electra gulped a sob, and tears streamed down her cheeks. She took short, hiccupping breaths.

Sam took her hand. "It's okay. Take a deep breath now. You're hyperventilating."

She wheezed and collapsed into sobs again. "No…use… Never…get…Apache…back… now."

"No. We are *not* giving up. We're going to get him back, I promise." An arm encircled her shoulders.

She closed her eyes in a grimace. Who was the woman trying to kid?

Once home, she stormed into her room, the door slam an exclamation mark on the day.

***

Electra fought the blankets binding her, pummeled the lumps in her pillow. Images ran in a continuous reel: Jimmy in a mangled black SUV; Dad storming through the house, punching a hole in the wall; Apache lying dead, Sam's body draped over him.

She sat up, gasping, and swiped sweat-damp hair from her eyes. The clock's face glowed a red 3:34 a.m. Sam would be pounding on her door in a couple hours, telling her to get a move on, they had to go to work. She groaned.

Even though they hadn't been to church in years except for Jimmy's funeral, something her mom said once flashed into her mind. "Give your troubles to God; He's up all night anyway." She fluttered a breath through her lips. *Yeah, right.*

Gazing out the window at the pale sliver of moon, she took a breath. "Okay, God. If you're up there listening…me and Sam need your help getting Apache back, all right? All right, then. G'night." She blew out a breath. This might take divine intervention all right—a downright miracle.

Setting her alarm for 6 a.m., she crawled back under the covers.

She was up and dressed by the time Sam knocked on her door. "Time to rise, sunshine."

"Okay." Electra opened the door with a grin.

"Wow. Look at you. All scrubbed up and dressed already." Sam tucked stray chestnut tendrils behind her own ears. "C'mon downstairs. Breakfast is ready."

They sat, and Electra attacked her eggs and toast. "Y'know what?" she said around a mouthful. "It might be okay to have Brad on our side. He's been all over the country, talking to people. Maybe he knows somebody who can help us get Apache back."

Sam opened her mouth but didn't speak for a moment. "Uh… Yeah! I mean…yes, he said he'd do some nosing around, see if he could get any information for us." She blinked.

"Yeah. Let him do some of the work."

"Okay then. Let's get over to Clyde's and see what he has

for us to do today." Her friend flashed a thumbs-up. "Thanks."

She ducked her head. "Sure."

***

"You've been a whirlwind of busyness today." Clyde came up behind Electra and Sam as they unsaddled at the end of the day.

The cowgirl gave him a lopsided smile. "I keep mulling over the situation with Apache. I don't know what to do." She told him what had happened the day before.

He raised bushy eyebrows. "Dang. That sounds serious. Why in the world would Smythe hire a thug to protect that broken-down old horse? Against two little gals like you?" He reached into his shirt pocket for a snoose can. "And my attorney not wanting to take your case. That don't make any sense. Somethin' stinks."

Electra brushed LeRoy. "Yeah, but Brad said he'd find out what's going on. He'll help us get Apache back."

"Well, it's good to have people on your side." Clyde grinned at her, then back to Sam. "Ya know, that punk nephew took your money. You oughta at least be able to get that back."

"We don't want the money." Electra's voice rose. "We want Apache!"

Sam shrugged. "They've bonded, and I can't see either one without the other."

"Well, what the kid did was illegal. Maybe you oughta at least write Smythe a letter, see if that'll get him to talk to you about the whole mess." Clyde spat a stream of tobacco at a dirt clod.

"Yeah. Can we, Sam, huh? I'll do it! I'll write the letter. D'you think that'll help?" She hopped from one foot to the other.

"Well, we can try it." Sam sighed.

Her stomach knotted. *She doesn't think it'll do any good. But I gotta try.*

That evening after chores were done and supper dishes washed, she sat at the table with a tablet and pen. "Dear Mr. Smythe… Is that the right way to start?" she asked.

"Well, I think it should be a little more formal. Here's how you'd do a business header." Sam showed her the format.

Electra leaned over the paper, wrote, scribbled out words, and chewed on the pen. "How does this sound?"

Sam read what she'd written.

> *Mr. Smythe:*
> *We found your horse—almost dead—laying in the dirt in 90-degree heat with no water and no food. Miss Samantha Moser bought a tub and gave him water and hay. We met your nephew, Todd Smythe, and he said he called you to get permission to sell Apache to us. ~~Sam Samantha~~ Miss Moser wrote him a check for $500 and wrote out a bill of sale and he signed it. We took your horse to the vet, gave him medicine and special food, and we loved him. He was getting better, but you took him away. Please, can we have him back?*
> *Sincerely,*
>
> *Electra Lucci*

CHAPTER EIGHT

"You've written a very impassioned plea. I'm proud of you." Sam corrected a couple of grammatical errors. "Do you want to type this up on my computer? I'll print it out, and we'll send it off."

"Thanks. You think it's okay?" Electra chewed her lower lip. "Really? Then, let's do it."

The next day, they mailed the letter, Electra pushing the envelope through the slot with a determined exhale. *Will this work? This* has *to work.* "So, if it takes two days to get there and maybe he thinks about it for a day, and then two days to get an answer back..." She ticked off the days on her fingers. "Maybe we should give it a week, just to be sure."

Sam lifted her brow. "We can hope for that anyway. That would save me from having to go to court."

She could hardly wait to hear back, needles prickled under her skin, and before the week had passed, she badgered her friend to stop at the post office every day after working at Clyde's. Every time Sam opened the box, she crossed her fingers and held her breath. But no letter came. One week became two and then three. Disappointment shrank the bud of hope that had sprouted when she wrote the letter.

One evening, they sat in the living room after supper, Electra on the sofa, her shoulders heavy with the weight of defeat, her head bent to her chest, trying not to feel sick to her stomach. "He's not going to answer, is he?"

"Who?" Sam glanced up from her book.

"Mr. Smythe."

A sigh. "It doesn't look like it. I guess I'm going to have to bite the bullet and look into the court angle." When the phone rang, she jumped. "Wonder who that could be."

"Maybe it's him." Electra leaped up from the sofa, suddenly alive with expectation.

Sam answered. "Oh, hi, Brad. Long time-no see."

Oh, it's only him. Electra slumped back on the couch with a sigh that wrenched her very soul.

Brad's voice boomed over the speaker on the wall phone/message machine. "Yeah… Sorry 'bout that. Boss is keeping me busy. I just wanted to touch base with you. You guys doing okay? Anything new on the horse?"

"No, we're just sitting and waiting." She told him about the letter.

"Good idea, but I wouldn't hold my breath." Brad paused. "I've been checking into Mr. Smythe a little. He's from back east and is a foreign investor, apparently quite wealthy. He's a big landowner over in Custer County, and apparently, he is in the process of stocking his ranch with buffalo. He's a big proponent of 'economic viability with ecological sustainability,' to quote his website, and talks about returning the land to the wild."

"Hmm. I wonder if he knows Jack Murdock and Scott Roberts with the Big Open."

"I'd bet they probably do run in the same circles."

"Well, thanks for the information, Brad."

"You bet. See you soon."

"Okay, thanks." She hung up.

"We're not getting Apache back." A tear rolled down Electra's cheek. *He'll die without us. And* I'll *die if he does!*

"Well, I don't think we should give up." Sam sat beside her.

Electra didn't understand all that stuff Brad was talking about. But she did understand they were not getting Apache back. *It's no use. What can Sam and I do?* Her chin sank to her chest. Her limbs too heavy to move.

***

The following weekend, two counselors brought a vanload of kids from the group home in Billings—some who had been there before plus a couple of new faces. The woman counselor, Robin Johnson, greeted Sam and Electra with a wave. "They had such a good time here before, we thought we'd try it again."

This time, the kids responded with more enthusiasm. "Can we ride?" "Let me brush the horse." "What can I do?"

Sapphire approached Electra shyly. "Hi. Can I pet Ginger again?"

She nodded. "C'mon, we'll go get her."

The younger teen, again clad in her Goth-girl attire, sidled up to the mare, hesitantly putting out a hand to pat her neck. "She's so soft. So pretty."

Electra gave her pellets to feed, and soon they were petting, brushing, and talking.

"You're not dressed Goth today." The girl gave her a sideways glance.

"Nah. It's too much work…all the makeup and hair gel and stuff." She ran a hand over her smooth hairdo. "I…guess I just got busy helping Sam…"

"Sure. I get it."

"Is there a group at your school?"

Sapphire shook her head. "Not really. A couple of girls. But they're more into the fashion statement. I thought we could be friends, but…" She shrugged. "You? Back in New York?"

"Yeah. A group of us 'misfits'—none of the other groups accepted us, so…" *Wonder what they'd think if they could see me here, working with horses? Will they still be my friends?* A flutter of doubt tickled her ribs. "You want to try riding today?"

A flash of fear crossed the teen's face. "Um. I dunno." She raised her gaze to Ginger's back. "It's pretty high up…um…if I fall off."

"You won't fall. Let me get Sam. She'll help, an' we'll both be right here beside you."

As Sam and Electra led the mare around the corral, Sapphire broke into a huge grin. "Look at me, Miss Robin. I'm riding."

"Way t' go, girl. You're doing good," the woman called out and then strolled next to Sam. "This is so good for these kids. I couldn't believe the difference in this group after last time. They've all been clamoring to come back."

Before they left, the counselors met with Clyde and Sam and worked out a schedule to bring kids to the ranch once a month.

"Cool." Electra hopped into the pickup. "Let's stop in Ingomar and check the mail."

No letter from Smythe. "What should we do?" Defeat weighed like a heavy saddle on her shoulders. "Brad sure hasn't come through for us either."

"I know. I hoped he'd have some ideas. Other than how 'big and powerful' Smythe is. I think I do need to pursue charges against his nephew though. We can't let him get away with what he did." Sam patted her knee and changed the subject. "You did such a good job with Sapphire both times the kids visited. You're a natural. I'm really proud of you, and I'm so glad you decided to stay and help me out this summer."

Electra's face warmed, and she allowed a small smile. *I'm glad too.* "I like her. She reminds me…"

"Of you?" Sam raised her brow.

"Yeah, a little. But she had a really bad life. She lost both parents, and the uncle she went to live with didn't want her, treated her really mean. She got in some trouble, and when she got out of juvie, he wouldn't take her back." She gazed out the window for a moment, wondering how Sapphire could find happiness. "She needs an Apache." An ache grew in her heart. I *need my Apache.*

***

After chores, Sam cracked eggs to scramble for supper. "We need to stop for groceries next time we're in town."

"Whatever." Electra couldn't bring herself to care about what to eat next. The photos of Apache's thin form hovered in her periphery.

The sound of a car pulling up to the house broke the dark spell.

"It's Brad," she announced with a sneer in her voice. "Nice of him to show up now. Just in time for supper."

She opened the door. There he stood, grinning, a dark lock curling over his forehead. "What are you doing here? We haven't heard from you in weeks."

"Hi, Electra. Nice to see you too." He stepped inside. "Hi, Sam."

The cowgirl's face lit up. "C'mon in."

Electra turned away and tried to ignore him as she popped bread into the toaster.

"Well, I had some more work to do on the documentary, so I was in the neighborhood." He took pre-made salad and tomatoes from a grocery sack and handed them to Sam. "Since I seem to be crashing your supper, maybe I can contribute something."

Her friend huffed a little laugh. "Well, thanks. All we're

having is scrambled eggs, so if you want to fix the salad, you're welcome to join us."

Electra gave him sidelong glances as they sat down to eat.

Brad grinned at her. "Am I still on your 'list'?"

She rolled her eyes. "I thought you were going to help us get Apache back. Where've you been?"

He took a bite of salad and set down his fork. "I'm really sorry. I've been running all around the state with work, and I haven't been back here at all. It's been crazy." He swiveled his head toward Sam. "Anything more on the horse?"

She shook her head. "No. But everybody keeps telling me I need to file charges against the nephew. At least get my money back."

Brad nodded. "I agree."

"How do we go about doing that? Do we have to go to a judge?" Sam pulled a long face.

"But I don't want the money back," Electra wailed, yearning spiking her chest. "I want Apache."

"Well, I do, if we can't get the horse. That was all my savings." The woman's eyes sparked.

Electra grimaced. "Yeah, sorry. I know." *But I need my horse.*

"Tell you what," Brad said. "I'll go with you. Let's go talk to Sheriff O'Conner in Forsyth tomorrow. He should be able to tell us what steps we need to take."

Sam inhaled deeply. "Okay. Thanks. I'd appreciate your company." She squeezed Electra's shoulder. "We'll work on this. Together. Okay?"

"O-kaay," she mumbled and dropped her gaze. *Worth a try, I guess.* But she wasn't going to hold her breath.

***

The next morning Brad roared up to the house. Electra let Sam scoot into the front seat with Brad before she piled into the backseat of his pickup.

"So, this Smythe is a big money mogul, huh?" Sam asked. Brad curled his lip and nodded.

"Is he part of this 'Big Open' movement?"

"I've only dealt with Roberts, doing this documentary. Hadn't heard Smythe's name before this. But he sure sounds like he'd fit right in, with his buffalo herd."

Electra leaned over the seat back. "Well, if he's such a big ranch owner, why did he abandon Apache, and why does he care if we wanted to buy him?"

Brad shook his head. "That's a really good question. I'd like to know the answer myself."

"Me too." Sam peered out the window. "Me. Too."

The visit with Sheriff O'Connor at first seemed unsatisfactory, as the lawman stroked his gray-stubbled chin with his thumb and forefinger for long minutes, a frown creasing his forehead. "W-e-l-l," he finally spoke, "the horse does belong to Mr. Smythe, and if he doesn't want to sell, I'm afraid there's not much we can do about that."

Electra stiffened. Anger coursed hot through her veins. Sam put a gentle hand on her arm.

"But…" the sheriff said again, in his slow, contemplative way, "you can charge this kid with fraud."

"How do I do that?" Sam asked. "I don't have money for an attorney. I gave my last five hundred to him."

The sheriff's advice was to file a small claims complaint in justice court in Miles City. He told them this was civil court, with no lawyers, just a judge. "Good luck to you."

"Thank you, Sheriff." Sam stood and gestured to her companions. "Well, wanna go on in to Miles City?"

***

After they left the courthouse, Sam exhaled a sigh. "Whew. I'm glad that's done."

"What happens now?" Electra asked.

Sam shrugged. "We wait. The clerk said Smythe can decide to settle out of court or show up on the court date, and we'll go from there."

Brad reached out his hand to shake hers. "Good job. The first step taken. Let's go to the 600 Café to celebrate. I'm buying."

Electra, more relaxed than she'd felt all day, found a smile. "Yeah! Can we, Sam, huh?"

"Sure. Sounds good to me."

CHAPTER NINE

Nightmares plagued Electra's sleep. Dreams of skinny Apache, of horse skeletons lying in the pasture, flashes of Jimmy in a crumpled SUV, sometimes of him riding a ghost horse. During her waking hours, she bit back her pain, trying to be like her mom and ignore it. Settling into the routine at Sam's and working at Clyde's, she helped prepare for the next visitors. She and Sam were kept so busy neither had the energy at the end of the day to talk, much less think about what might happen with the court and Apache.

The following weekend, the group home kids were scheduled. "I think we'll take Sugar along today. We might need an extra gentle horse." Sam backed up Horace's trailer to the chute and loaded the Thoroughbred rescue.

Sapphire was the first out of the group home van. "Hi, Sam! Hi, Electra! Gotta go see Ginger." Without further conversation, she sprinted toward the corrals, leading the group of eager kids. Electra giggled at the girl's excitement. *She's just like me.*

The counselor, Miss Robin, exited the van, stretching. Two new teens stepped out behind her.

"Welcome back," Sam greeted her.

"Good to be here." The woman gestured to new visitors. "This is Justin and Wendy. They'd like to meet your horses."

Justin, like several of the other boys on their first visit, stood with a defiant stance, thumbs hooked in the waist of low-riding pants, eyes mere slits, slowly chewing a wad of gum. *Tough guys.* Wendy was a tiny, fair-haired waif who stood behind Robin, head down, shoulders hunched.

Electra's heart wrenched at the little girl's defeated posture. She glanced at Miss Robin, who lifted one corner of her mouth and shook her head.

"Well, Justin, Wendy, I'm glad you've come to visit us." Sam gestured toward the corral. "Do you want to go see the horses?"

The boy merely shrugged, but Wendy's gaze lifted for a fleeting moment.

"C'mon then. Let's go." Sam led them to where Sapphire already stood caressing Sugar's neck.

"C'mere, Wendy. Come help us." Sapphire put out a hand.

The little blonde glanced quickly at Robin who nodded, and then she scuffed over to the horse. Electra joined them, and with Sapphire, flanked Wendy as she hesitantly approached Sugar. Her head rose in tiny, halting movements until she came face to face with the mare. Sugar's liquid brown eyes held hers, and time seemed to stop. Electra dared not breathe, waiting for a sudden movement to startle either one.

She lifted her hand. Sugar lowered her head to meet the touch. For long moments, Wendy stroked the velvet muzzle. Then she suddenly darted forward to wrap her arms around Sugar's foreleg.

Aww, look at that. How cool. Electra's limbs tingled.

Behind them, Sam gasped and stepped forward, but Sugar stood perfectly still.

Electra smiled. *Yup. She needs this.* The mare curved her head around the tiny girl. *Ohmygosh, she's giving her a hug.*

On the way home, Sam braked as they approached her neighbor's driveway. "Let's stop and visit Horace for a minute. We haven't seen him in a while. Sugar will be okay in the trailer for a little bit."

"Yeah, let's."

The gray-haired man opened his screen door with a flourish. "Come in, come in. So nice to see you. I have some iced tea if you'd like to wet your whistles."

Electra giggled at his phrasing. *He's kind of cool, for an old dude.*

Sam gave him a hug. "Sounds great. How you been, Horace? You haven't been by lately."

He held out a hand to shake Electra's "I'm a doin'. Every day I wake up on the right side of the sod, I figure that's a blessin'."

She and Sam laughed and followed him into the kitchen where he retrieved glasses and the tea.

"How's the dude-bustin' goin'?"

"Good." Sam peered at her. "You want to tell him about today?"

"Okay." At first, she hesitated. It had been such a special moment. *Will he think I'm bragging?* But then a surge of excitement coursed through her body. "Yes. Ohmygosh yes. You aren't going to believe this. We took Sugar over to Clyde's and there was this shy little girl—Wendy—who would hardly look at anybody and then she petted Sugar and ohmygosh it was a miracle ..." She paused her rush of words and a tear trickled from the corner of her eye. "It was awesome," she whispered.

Horace's leathery face beamed with his grin. "Now, that's what I like to hear. You're doin' good things there." He nodded. "Yup. Good things."

A flood of satisfaction washed over Electra. Yes, it *was*

good. She liked helping other girls who needed their own "Apache experience." It took her mind away from her own troubles, for a little while anyway.

Moving into the living room, they talked more about horses and Apache, and then Sam asked if he'd heard any more about the offer from the Big Open people on his ranch.

"Oh yeah, I had a coupla calls and a letter or three. When the last guy showed up, I told 'im if they didn't 'cease and desist' they'd be hearin' from ol' Bertha." He glanced over at the rifle hanging on the wall. "I think maybe they got the message."

"Well, good." Sam smiled. "I hated the thought that you'd be moving away."

"Naw. The fancy life of leisure ain't for me. I'll be here till I die."

***

After chores and supper, Electra finished wiping down the table and countertops.

Sam settled into her rocking chair with a book. "Wanna come join me?"

"Can I use your phone and call my mom first?" She leaned against the living room doorway. "I gotta tell her about Wendy and Sapphire."

"Sure. Go ahead. Tell your mom hello for me."

"Okay." She spun into the kitchen and punched in the number. "Mom, hi, it's me, you'll never guess what we did today!" She blurted the story again in an excited rush of words.

Her mom's voice oozed praise and approval. "Sounds like you're doing great things there. Keep up the good work."

"Thanks." A glow lit her insides. *Mom is actually proud of me.*

"Well, I can't wait to come out and see you again. I love you."

"'Kay, Mom. Love you too. 'Bye." She floated into the living room and plopped on the couch. "Oh, Sam, I don't want this summer to end. That was just too cool today."

"It was, wasn't it?" Sam set down her book. "I couldn't believe Sugar was so quiet and so patient. I knew she was a sweet, loving horse, but I had no idea she had such a compassionate heart."

"I know. It was like she knew how sad and lonely Wendy was… Like with Apache and me." She swiped at her eyes. "Oh, I miss him so much."

Sam's face held a soft expression. "One day at a time, huh? Well, I'm beat. Shall we head for bed?"

*****

Several days later, when Sam and Electra got home, the answering machine blinked furiously in the kitchen. *Uh-oh, wonder who called. Is it good news or bad? Maybe we're getting Apache back.* A yearning permeated Electra's body so strong she could barely move.

The first message was from the clerk of justice court in Miles City. "We have set a court date for July 21 at 10 a.m. If you have any questions, please call…"

Sam's face went pale. "I'm really going to have to do this." She swallowed and punched the button.

Electra's stomach flip-flopped in sympathy. *Glad it's her and not me.*

The next message played. "This is Sheriff O'Connor. The Custer County Sheriff's office has given us a heads up that Mr. Smythe is trying to file charges that you took his horse without permission…"

"What?" Sam slammed a fist on the counter. "He can't do that!"

No! Electra scowled. *Ohmygosh, what now?*

The message continued, "…but I've advised them of the circumstances and that I was there personally when the horse was returned. Give me a call…"

"Aarrgghh!" Sam punched the message button with a force that made the phone ding.

Charges? Theft? Angry bees buzzed in Electra's tummy. What was going on? She stared at her friend with widened eyes. "What does that mean?"

Sam shook her head. "I don't know for sure. I'll have to call tomorrow and see if I can find out more." She hit the button for the next message. "I can't believe that man."

"Hey, Sam, it's Robin. I have an interesting proposition for you. Give me a call."

The cowgirl dialed the counselor's number, putting the phone on speaker as she opened the cupboard to take out noodles and a can of tuna for a casserole.

Miss Robin's voice wafted over the speaker. "I'm glad you called back. Listen. My daughter has a neighbor, an older woman who is going to move to an assisted living facility."

"Okay?" Sam frowned.

Electra leaned forward, head cocked.

"Turns out the lady was a trick rider up until just a few years ago, and she has a horse she would like to rehome. My daughter says it's a sweet, older mare, and I thought of you and how well the kids respond to your horses at Clyde's. I know he's going to need all his stock during hunting season, so I thought maybe…"

She gasped. Could Sam adopt another horse?

"Oh. Uh…that sounds really great…but I don't have any money to buy the horse." Sam wagged her head "no" at Electra's pleading look. "I dunno, maybe Clyde would, but if it's an older horse, he probably won't want her for his string. He's been very generous with me, but I don't want to owe him money either."

"I thought about that," Robin said, "but I think it might be kind of a rescue situation. This lady has no relatives to take the horse, and she told my daughter she might have to send her to auction. She's heartbroken at the thought."

Oh no, not another horse lost! Electra's heart squeezed so tightly she could hardly breathe.

Sam's face drooped. "Oh dear. I'll bet she is."

"Well, why don't you do this—can you come to town sometime this week and meet her and the horse? Maybe we can work something out."

"Okay, yeah. I'll talk to Clyde tomorrow and see if I can get a day off. I'll let you know… And, thanks for thinking of me."

Electra's forehead pinched. "We can't let that horse go to auction. That means…?"

"Probably would be used for dog food." Sam winced.

What? Horror pressed against her heart. She groaned with pain. "No! That can't happen."

"Well, I'll see if Clyde will let me off tomorrow, and we'll drive to Billings and take a gander at the situation. I can't make any promises though." She shook her head. "I don't know where on earth I would get the money for another horse and for the feed." She sagged against the counter.

Electra's thoughts raced. What could she do to help? Surely Sam wouldn't let that horse be killed…for *dog food?* Her breath came in gasps as horrific images ran through her mind.

CHAPTER TEN

When Electra came downstairs the next morning, Sam was on the phone with the sheriff. "I got your message. Can Smythe do that?"

"Naw, I don't see that he can. The horse was returned, plus he's still got your five hundred." The sheriff's mellow baritone boomed out of the speaker as Sam poured a cup of coffee.

Electra moved next to her friend, put a hand on her arm, and gave her what she hoped was an encouraging smile.

Sam fluttered a breath. "I guess he got the summons for small claims court. C-could you come as a witness for me?"

"Uh, let me check my calendar." Paper rustled. "July 21? Yeah. Yeah, I can be there."

"Thank you, Sheriff. I really appreciate this."

"Sure." He paused for a beat. "Say, might not hurt to get that animal warden to come too. He's another witness."

"Well, he was there at the beginning when we found Apache, and he picked up the horse to take it back. But he wasn't very cooperative. I don't think he'd be a willing witness."

Electra snorted. *That fat, lazy slob? No way.*

O'Connor chuckled. "Yeah, I gathered that. Let me make

a call, see what I can do."

"Thanks again, Sheriff." Sam hung up, her face bloodless. "Oh man, I'm going to have to prepare for this court thing in two weeks." She grabbed a dishcloth and twisted it in her fingers. "Oh dear, what else do I need to do?"

"How about Teresa?" Electra suggested. "She could be another witness."

"Yes. Yes, she could." Sam dialed her friend and filled her in.

"Of course, I will," Teresa said immediately. "You want to get together again soon and go over some more plans?"

"Oh, could we?" Sam swallowed. "I'm so nervous already, I don't know what I'm going to do."

"It'll be fine. You've got at least three witnesses, maybe four if the warden cooperates, plus the photos and bill of sale." Her friend's cheerful voice sang over the line.

Yes! Electra pumped her fist in the air.

"Thanks, Teresa. You're the best." Sam hung up from the call and leaned against the wall. "Thank goodness. She'll help."

"That's great." Electra cleared her throat when the cowgirl made no further moves. "Are we going to Billings today to see that horse?"

Sam jumped. "Oh. Almost forgot. I'll call Clyde right now."

Oh good, at least we're going to see the horse. She released a breath. *When Sam meets her, she surely won't be able to let it go to auction.*

Electra slid onto the passenger side of the pickup. Sam, already behind the wheel, fired it up and headed to I-94 toward Billings. For the first several miles, Electra sat quietly, staring at the passing empty prairie. Just a few weeks ago, she'd fallen into a deep funk with the loneliness of this land.

But then… Then came Apache…and Sam…and the group home girls… And maybe now they would be getting a new horse.

She couldn't contain herself any longer, and the words gushed out of her. "Oh, Sam. I'm so excited to meet a real live trick rider and her trick horse. How does that work? What do they do? How do they train them? Would we be able to do that too?"

"I dunno." Sam gripped the steering wheel until her knuckles went white. "I dunno how to do it… Money for this horse, go to court, get Apache back…" Her breath came in short heaves. She slowed the truck and pulled to the side of the road.

"What's the matter?" Electra peered at her. "Why are we stopping? Are you all right?"

Sam eased out of the vehicle and bent over, taking deep gulps of the fresh air.

Ohmygosh, what's happening to her? A wave of cold panic rising, Electra flung open her door and ran around the truck. "Sam? Sam, are you okay?"

The cowgirl gave her a smile that was more like a grimace. "Yeah. I am now. Just got a little dizzy, that's all." Breath whooshed from between her lips, and she fanned the air in front of her face. "All right then. Let's get back on our way and go see a lady about a horse."

"Okay!"

As they picked up speed again, Sam's cell phone rang. Electra checked the display. "It's Bra-a-d."

"Answer and put it on speaker, please."

Electra punched the buttons. "Hi, Bra-a-d. We're in the truck, but you're on speaker. Talk to Sam." *That poser. Why does Sam keep encouraging him? He promised to help, but what has he done—nothing.*

"Hey there, how are my favorite cowgirls today?"

Electra rolled her eyes.

"Hi, Brad," Sam said. "We're okay, on our way to Billings. What's up?"

"Oh, you are? That's great. I'm working in town today. Are you coming in for supplies?"

"No, we're going to check into a possible horse rescue situation." She told him the story.

"Cool. Can I meet you there? I'd like to meet this horse too."

"Um, sure, why not." She gave him the address. "We'll be there in about forty-five minutes."

Electra snorted. *Now he's butting into this deal.* Then she brightened. *But…maybe he'll help convince Sam to rescue this trick horse.*

At the outskirts of Billings, Sam steered onto a secondary road that led into a more rural area with small ranches and homes with acreage.

"This is pretty." Electra stared out the window. "It'd be nice to live closer to a town."

"Yeah, it would be handy sometimes. But I do love my place, even if it is isolated."

Yeah, more like out in the middle of nowhere.

Sam pulled into the driveway at the address Robin had given.

"All right—let's go see this trick horse." Electra bounced out of the truck, excitement rushing through her body like a waterfall.

The counselor's SUV was already there, and she exited the vehicle when they approached. "Hi there. Ready to meet Miss Ellie and her horse?"

Electra beamed at her. "Yeah."

Sam gave a thumbs-up, and they followed Robin to the house.

A snowy-haired woman, possibly in her seventies or even

eighty, opened the door. "Hello, dear. I see you brought your friends. Come in, come in." She maneuvered her walker to the side to let them by.

They entered a tidy living room where the walls were covered with pictures of Ellie as a young woman in various poses—standing atop her horse, hanging sideways, and over the horse's rump, even one under the belly of the horse.

Wow. How cool. Electra leaned close to study the photos. *That looks like fun.*

"That's me with my Trixi." Ellie's voice held a note of pride as she pointed to a more recent photo. "I've had her for twenty years, since she was a foal."

Electra glanced from the pictures to the woman. *Maybe she's as not as old as she appears.*

The woman continued. "Named her after Trixi McCormick, Montana's own famous trick rider from the 1940s and '50s."

"Cool." Electra's voice came out breathy with excitement. *I wonder if I could do it.* "How did you learn to do all that?"

Ellie chuckled. "Lots and lots of practice and many, many falls."

The doorbell rang. "I'll get it for you," Robin offered.

Brad entered, holding a camera.

"Hello, ladies." He took off his hat, and Robin introduced him to Ellie. "This is Brad Ashton. He's a videographer and may be doing a documentary on Sam and her rescue horses and her work with the group home kids."

He shook her hand. "Do you mind if I do some filming?"

"That would be just fine, young man."

He raised one eyebrow at Sam. She shrugged and gave him a slight nod.

"Would you folks like to meet Trixi?" Ellie gestured toward the picture window in the back of the house, which overlooked a nearby red and white barn and a green pasture.

Standing by the fence was a light tan mare with a lighter colored mane and tail.

"Oooh." Electra pressed against the window. "Is she a palomino?" She squinted at Sam. "Is that the right word?"

Ellie opened the back door. "No, actually she's a light-colored chestnut. But she's beautiful, isn't she? We made a good pair back in the day." She stepped her walker onto a porch. "I can't trek all the way out there anymore with this thing, but you folks go ahead and meet her. She's very friendly."

Sam gave a low whistle. "She is gorgeous."

Although she tried to walk like a lady, Electra couldn't restrain herself and charged ahead. First one to the fence, she held out a hand for the mare to sniff. She could almost picture herself on Trixi's back, executing some glamorous trick. She ran her palm up the horse's face and rubbed behind her ears.

Sam joined her and stroked Trixi's neck and combed her fingers through the almost-blonde mane. The horse nuzzled her arm. She took a cake pellet from her pocket and fed her the treat.

"Go on in the pasture with her," called Ellie. "I'll show you something."

When she and Sam stood by the mare's side, Ellie gave a couple of sharp whistles and motioned with her arm. Electra jumped when the horse bowed, then folded her front legs under, followed by her back legs. Trixi turned her head as if expecting something.

Wow. What is she doing? Her mouth dropped open.

"Go ahead, climb on." Ellie had a big smile.

She raised her brows. "I can?"

"Yeah, you sure can," the older woman called from the edge of the porch.

"Go ahead," Sam encouraged. "I'm right here. It'll be

okay."

Electra straddled the horse, Ellie gave a signal, and Trixi rose to her feet. With slight heel pressure, the horse ambled forward, alongside the fence.

"Wow!" Brad spoke from behind Sam. "That's awesome." He had his camera trained on them.

Electra sat taller, like a celebrity. *I can totally see myself doing this.* When Trixi came back to where Sam stood, she slid off.

"You try it, Miss Samantha," Ellie called.

Once again Ellie whistled and made her hand gesture. Trixi kneeled, and Sam mounted. In a smooth motion, the horse got up and walked toward the barn. Electra saw Sam use slight pressure with her left knee, and the mare turned to the right. Pressure from the right and she went left. They rode back to the group, Ellie whistled again, and Trixi lay down so Sam could get off.

"Isn't she awesome?" Electra followed her friend back to the porch.

"This is one amazing horse, Miss Ellie," Sam said.

She is *amazing.* Electra held her breath. *Will she adopt Trixi? Please, Sam, please. I want this horse.*

"Isn't she?" Ellie's face was lit with a proud glow. "We had a good long ride together, but now…" Her blue eyes misted, and she stared off at the rolling hills in the distance.

Electra caught Sam blinking back tears too. "Miss Ellie, I—"

"Yup. I can't get around anymore without this thing." The older woman smacked her hand on the walker. "Can't take care of my baby anymore. Dadgummed stroke." She shook her head. "You and your girl there would be perfect for her."

Oh please, please, please! Electra flashed a hopeful, wide-eyed look at the cowgirl.

Sam took a shaky breath. "I would love to own her, but…"

"Only five hundred." A determined expression came over Ellie's face. "She's worth a lot more, but I want her to have a good home. I had one guy interested, but she's too old and not trained to work cows. The second family had a troop of hellion kids. Not letting Trixi go to them. I could use the money though, and if I can't sell her to someone worthy, she'll have to go to auction."

Horror dropped Electra's jaw, locked her chest, and she couldn't breathe.

Sam squared her shoulders and turned away. "Miss Ellie, I don't have any money." She stared down at her boots. "I'm sorry I got your hopes up"—she faced Electra—"and yours too, honey. I don't think this is going to work out." She changed direction and strode around the side of the house to the pickup, wiping her cheeks.

Electra's boots crunched on the gravel as she ran behind her. "Wait. No! Nooo." It came out in a wail. Her face scrunched into misery, and tears cascaded down her cheeks.

Sam opened her arms and gathered her into a hug. They rocked together, their tears mingling. Finally, Sam disengaged and blew her nose. "I need to thank Miss Ellie and tell her good-bye. You can wait here if you want to."

Electra sniffled. "No, I'll come along." *Will we lose this horse too? Nothing ever goes right. Why do I even hope?*

They went back into the house, where Ellie sat in her recliner, her wrinkled face in a hangdog expression. Brad and Robin sat nearby, concern etched on their faces.

Sam knelt beside the chair and took the woman's hand. "I'm sorry, Miss Ellie. I'm not sure if I have any options, but let me think about this, and see if there's anything I can come up with. I really like Trixi and would love to have her."

Ellie nodded. "You'll be able to. I believe you're the one."

"Bye, Miss Ellie." Electra gave her a hug. "We'll be back. I know we will."

They all said their goodbyes and headed to their vehicles. Robin rolled down her window. "See you at Clyde's in a couple weeks. I'll be thinking about this too. Hang in there." She drove away.

Brad paused beside Sam's truck. "May I buy you ladies lunch?"

"Sure. That would be nice," Sam responded.

Hunger pangs suddenly erupted. "Yeah, I'm starved."

They met at the Pays Café near the stockyards. The waitress offered them menus and poured coffee. Electra silently stared at her menu, chewing on her lower lip. *How could Sam let that horse be sold for dog food? There's no way she can do that.*

Brad took a sip of his coffee. "You know what I'd like to do, with your permission?"

Sam shook her head. "What?"

"I did a bit of filming at Ellie's, and I got to thinking. She's a pretty well-known person in Montana. I'd like to do a feature on the fact she has to give up her horse, that you would like to rescue Trixi, and also bring in what you've done to try to rescue Apache."

"Me?" Sam raised her eyebrows. "I haven't done anything. I've failed at all of it."

"No, you haven't. You saved Apache's life, and you're also trying to save Trixi's. I think it would be a dynamite story."

Electra's heart sped up. "That'd be so cool, Sam."

"I dunno." She scrunched her mouth to one side. "I don't know what good it would do, and I… I don't think I want to be on TV for everybody to see."

"I know you're basically a shy country girl." Brad grinned. "But I already have some awesome footage of the two of you on Trixi. Not to mention that scene of you riding down the hill when we first met. I'd like to show the before and after pictures of Apache. I think people would really like this story."

"Yes!" Electra bounced in her seat. "Please say yes, Sam. It would be so cool to be on TV." Then she sobered. "Maybe it would help get Apache back… And maybe save Trixi too?"

Sam leaned back against her chair and exhaled. "I'm not sure… Let me think about it. There's so much to digest, and I'm going to have to make some decisions. If I get a loan from Clyde to buy Trixi, I'm going to be in debt, and I really hate that. I saw what that did to my folks."

On the way home, Electra sat quiet for a while, staring out the window. *What would convince her? What can I do?* Then she had an idea. "You know what? I have about seventy-five dollars saved from my allowance. And maybe my mom would pitch in something too, and that would be a start toward buying Trixi."

The cowgirl cocked her head toward her. "Oh, my dear, that is such a generous offer. I appreciate it, I really do. But I can't take your money. I have to figure this out on my own."

"If I did, then I'd be a part-owner of a horse." Electra giggled. "Hey, I could call Mom tonight—maybe she would buy Trixi."

"But even if your mom could come up with the money, where would you keep a horse in New York City?"

"Well, there are some stables not too far away where Mom took me to ride a few times."

"That costs quite a lot though."

Hmm. Hadn't thought of that. But, I want Trixi—at least for Sam. Maybe I could earn some more money when I go home. "Okay, but if you need it, I'd really like to contribute. Trixi deserves a good home, and she would be so good for us—for you, like when you're working with the group home kids."

Sam blinked rapidly. "Thanks. You're so sweet to offer, and I appreciate it." She glanced at her watch. "It's early enough yet. Let's stop at Clyde's and see if he needs us to help with anything this afternoon."

"Okay." *At least that'll keep my mind off Trixi. Oh, I hope we can still save her.*

CHAPTER ELEVEN

The fourth of July dawned bright and warm with a tangerine wash outlining the horizon in a clear blue sky.

By 7 a.m. Sam's blue pickup wended its way on the dusty road to the dude ranch. Electra sat, her shoulders slumped, eyes half-closed, miffed at the early hour Sam had roused her. *For a rodeo? What's the big deal about that?*

They were greeted by a cacophony of bawling calves, bellowing steers and bulls, and whinnying horses. Clyde met them when they pulled up. "Mornin', ladies. Ready for the big rodeo?"

"You bet we are." Sam grabbed a tray of cookies and headed toward the house.

Electra's curiosity piqued. "What is a rodeo, anyway, and where did all these animals come from?"

"Well, these contests have been going on for many years." Clyde spat into the dust. "Used to be that cowboys from the neighborhood would get together on Sunday afternoons to see who could stay on the back of a bucking bronc the longest. It evolved from there into organized events, like this one."

"Oh, okay." She couldn't understand why they'd want to do that, but... *whatever floats their boat.*

"The animals are donated by a rancher from Miles City who raises stock especially for rodeos. He came last night with bucking stock for the competition."

"Okay. I've never seen one before."

"You'll have a good time, I know you will." The rancher touched his hat brim and headed off toward the corrals.

All morning, neighbor women arrived with more cookies, cakes, and pies, salads, rolls, and condiments. Electra stared in curiosity as Irene set up a tub of ice and small barrel with a handle. "What is that?"

The ranch wife grinned. "That is an old-fashioned ice cream maker. A little later, I'll put some cream and sugar and vanilla in the container and maybe you'd like to help crank the handle and make ice cream."

"Whoa! Really? *Make* ice cream? Right here?"

"Yup. That's the way everybody used to do it—before the supermarkets came along and started carrying the factory-made stuff in cartons. This is *so* much better."

"Wow. Yeah, I want to help make ice cream. Ohmygosh, I can't wait to tell Mom."

She followed Sam around the yard and corrals, barely able to take it all in. "Ohmygosh, Sam, this *is* a BIG deal. I had no idea."

"Yup, it sure is, for this community, anyway."

Cowboys and cowgirls stood in line to sign up for events, and more neighbors and tourists arrived to watch. Even the vans from the group home joined the crowd.

At 2 p.m. Clyde mounted a platform above the chutes with his bullhorn. "Ladies and gentlemen, welcome to the annual Ingomar July Fourth rodeo."

The Forsyth High School marching band stepped out into the arena, playing a rousing Sousa march. Then they stood back with the opening notes of "The Star-Spangled Banner." The crowd rose from their lawn chairs and seats on vehicle hoods, hats in hands over hearts as the Custer County Rodeo Queen rode out with the American flag. Her attendants carried the Montana flag and other colorful banners as they galloped around the arena. When they came to a stop in the center, all the horses bent one knee and bowed.

Electra stood beside Sam and sang the few phrases she remembered along with the audience. She'd never seen anything like this. As she listened to the words, a lump formed in her throat, and her eyes stung. *This is so cool.*

As the last notes died away, the crowd erupted in applause. Electra waved her hat in the air. "Woohoo!"

Clyde took up the bullhorn again and announced the first event. "Give our youngest cowpokes a hand as they try mutton-bustin'."

The first sheep lumbered out of the chute and broke into a run, a helmet-clad boy of about five clinging to its wool as the creature zigged and zagged toward the center of the arena. Electra giggled.

In a couple of seconds, the little cowboy was picking himself out of the dirt. Several more girls and boys followed, some spitting out dirt, others rubbing their backsides, some bursting into tears.

Aww, poor little kids. I hope they're not hurt.

Sapphire and Wendy joined her, and the three hooted and giggled at the sheep and kids' antics. "That's looks so fun," she said wistfully. "I wish I could've done that when I was little."

Sam laughed. "I tried it a couple of times. Never could get the hang of staying on. It's harder than it appears."

"I'll bet you were the cutest little mutton-buster though." Brad's voice came from behind them.

Electra made a gagging sound in her throat.

Sam rolled her eyes. "Oh yeah, sure, after I fell off and

rolled around in the dust and manure. I was real cute. Uh-huh."

Electra laughed and punched Sam's arm.

Only two stayed on their sheep's back for the six-second ride. Then the six-year-old girl and seven-year-old boy ran out to share the applause as Clyde announced a tie.

"Lots of people seem to know about this little rodeo—got a big crowd here today." Brad swept one arm over the scene, his video camera in the other hand.

"Are you filming, Brad?" Electra asked.

"Yup. Always on the job, ya know. Besides, I'd like to do a little interview with you and Sam."

He fixed his chocolate eyes on the cowgirl. "I'm still hoping you'll let me do the story."

Electra caught a breath. *Yes!*

Sam's face flushed pink, and she blew out a breath.

"C'mon, Sam," Electra prodded. "It's for a good cause."

Brad nodded. "Yes, it is. If nothing else comes from my video, maybe someone will step up to rescue Trixi."

Sam pressed her lips into a thin line. "Well…okay. Let's do it."

"Yes!" Electra high-fived Brad. She squealed and faced the other girls. "We're gonna be on TV. We'll be famous."

"Yeah, you will." Brad chuckled. "And, if I can get permission from your group counselor, I'd like to talk to you young ladies too."

Wendy stood slightly behind the older girl, eyes downcast. Sapphire's eyes widened. "Really?" She grabbed Wendy's hand. "Let's go find Miss Robin."

Robin and the girls showed up just as the barrel racers began their competition.

Fun. Electra hopped up and down. "Sam! Sam! Could I learn to do that? That is so cool."

The cowgirl grinned. "Well, first you need a good horse.

And remember, they cost a lot of money. Then, you'd have to work really hard and practice every single day."

Electra's euphoria deflated. "Oh. Yeah." But when a vision of the trick pony popped into her head, she smiled again. "If we get Trixi, I could at least start practicing, and when I go home, I'll go to the riding stables every chance I get, and when I come back here next summer you can help me some more."

Sam's mouth quirked up at one corner. "That's a good plan. Let's wait and see what happens."

Sapphire joined in. "Yeah, me too. Can I learn barrel racing too? Will you teach us?"

"Hold on, hold on." Sam held up her hands in mock surrender. "You're ganging up on me here. One thing at a time, okay?"

Brad introduced himself to the counselor and talked to her about the interview with the girls.

She thought a moment. "Sure, why not. It'll be good publicity for what Sam and Clyde are doing here as well as the rescue horse aspect."

Electra and Sapphire joined hands and jumped up and down. "Yes! We're gonna be on TV. We're gonna be on TV! Can't wait till Mom sees me on TV."

"All right, girls, calm down now," Sam admonished. "Act professional and answer Brad's questions politely."

Electra immediately sobered and stood straight, and Sapphire followed suit. Brad lifted his hand-held camera and began asking questions. At first, Electra's tummy fluttered with nervous butterflies. *What if I mess up, say the wrong thing?*

"I'm with Electra Lucci, from New York City. Electra, tell me how you came to be in Montana?"

She snorted, but then caught herself and spoke softly. "Well, it was Mom's idea to come to a dude ranch..."

Brad was so patient and so nice, she soon warmed to the interview and remembered to think before she answered. *This is fun. I hope I did okay. I hope Mom will be proud of me.*

He also interviewed Robin and Sapphire and then lowered the camera. "Thank you very much, ladies. I appreciate it."

"Thank you, Brad," the girls chorused and ran off, giggling and squealing again.

Clyde announced saddle bronc riding next, and Electra stood beside Sam to watch the cowboys try to stay on the back of the bucking, kicking broncs. She grimaced each time one hit the ground. But then they got to their feet, ruefully shaking their heads, and slapping their jeans with their hats. *Yikes. Why would anybody want to do that? I sure wouldn't.*

"My great-grandma did this," Sam said.

She stared at her friend, her mouth falling open. "What? A woman?"

"Really?" Brad, who was filming the event, swung the camera back to Sam. "Tell me about her."

"Well, Grandma Nettie mostly rode steers—in those days they weren't the little yearlings the kids ride now. They were big, rangy, long-horned ones brought in off the prairie. Some were even full-grown older bulls that had been castrated."

Electra gasped. *Wow. She must've been one tough woman.*

"Did she win any competitions?" Brad prompted.

Sam nodded. "Yeah, she once beat Marie Gibson who was a world champion bronc rider."

"Pretty impressive." Brad asked more questions. Finally, he lowered the camera. "That's great, Sam, thanks. Well, I think I'll go talk to the winners and the not-so-lucky." He winked. "Catch up with you later, and we'll do the rest of your interview."

"You did really good, Sam." Electra grinned at her. "That wasn't so hard after all, was it?"

The cowgirl blushed. "No, not too bad."

After the last bull had been ridden—or cowboy bested—the winners of all the events rode a victory lap around the arena. The band followed, playing "God Bless America," and the rodeo royalty in bright blue, red, and spangled costumes once again displayed the flags. When the applause died away, Clyde took up the bullhorn. "Ladies and gentlemen, thank you all for coming. Now please join us for the barbecue. I hope you enjoy yourselves."

Most of the spectators drifted over to the tables by the fire pit, where men and women cut and served melt-off-the-bone beef and helped themselves to the bounty of food. Electra and Sam loaded plates and searched for a place to sit. Spying Teresa at a picnic table, they joined her.

"This is the most fun I've had in years." The real estate agent's face beamed. "One of the reasons I came back to this area. These old-fashioned neighborhood rodeos were part of my childhood."

Sam nodded. "Me too. I think they're lots more fun than the big fancy productions in the cities. Did you enjoy it, Electra?"

Giddiness raced through her. "Yeah, it was awesome and fun and wild and dirty and those guys getting bucked off—ohmygosh and your grandma did that? I can't believe it." She blew out a breath and shook her head.

"Yup, she was a brave woman."

"Ohmygosh, she must have been." *I would never want to do it. But what a cool thing for Sam to have a great-grandma like that.* She cut into the meat and took a bite. *Yum.*

The two women chatted for a while, then pushed their paper plates away. "Seconds?" Sam asked Teresa.

Her friend patted her stomach. "No way."

"Surely you saved room for homemade ice cream." Brad came up behind them and plopped bowls of the soft creamy dessert in front of them.

Teresa winked. "Of course, we did." She scooted down the bench to let him sit beside Sam.

Sam took a bite. "Mmm. This is way better than Ben and Jerry's."

"That's cuz me and Sapphire were turning the handle for this batch." Electra pointed to her young friend who bounded up to sit across from them. "It was so cool! Who knew…? I mean, making your *own* ice cream?"

Sam raised her brow. "So *that's* what makes it so special— you guys made it."

Her compliment rushed through Electra like warm summer rain, and she couldn't keep a smile off her face.

After they finished eating, Brad asked to interview the cowgirl some more.

"Let's go look around," Electra suggested to Sapphire and Wendy, so they wandered around to watch men play horseshoes and the ladies clean up the tables.

What a fun day. She'd never experienced an event like this or seen how all the neighbors came together to put it on. This cowboy living wasn't so bad after all. Maybe even better than the city. She allowed herself a secret grin.

In the driveway leading to the house, a group of musicians gathered with fiddles, guitars, and a banjo and launched into the first chords of "Tennessee Waltz."

Out of the corner of her eye, Electra caught Brad take Sam's hand and lead her to the improvised "dance floor"— gravel the men had raked and smoothed earlier.

She moved closer to observe them spin around the area. Light from the lanterns illuminated the two as they gazed into each other's eyes. *Wow. They dance really good together.*

At the end, he twirled her around, then bent her backward with a flourish. "Thank you, *Madame*." He bowed and kissed the back of her hand.

Sam giggled. "That was fun. Thank *you*."

Electra huffed. *Mush. Yuk.* She spun on her heel, her back to the couple. Did Mom and Dad ever dance and look at each other like that? She couldn't remember a time when they weren't arguing about something, even before…the accident. She was unable to swallow the lump that rose in her throat.

She wandered off to find a stump to sit on and watch fireworks light up the sky. *Jimmy would've loved this.* How could she even think about enjoying herself when…? A longing filled her core until it became too painful to bear. She tightened her fists, digging her nails into her palms.

CHAPTER TWELVE

The next evening, after cleaning up the remains of the festivities, Sam and Electra and Clyde and Irene piled into their vehicles and drove to the Jersey Lilly to watch the documentary Brad had filmed for the Big Open. Horace, already seated at a big round table, waved them over. They ordered food and drinks. Gradually, a few more ranchers without TV at home gathered as the time approached.

Electra fisted her hands when Jack Murdock walked in and sat at their table. "Hello, Samantha, Electra."

Sam gave him a curt nod. "Hi, Jack."

What the heck is he doing here? Electra frowned. Probably trying to put more pressure on her friend to give up her lease. Sam had told her what he tried to do. *Not gonna happen, Jack... I hope.*

Brad breezed in a few minutes before 7:00 and pulled out a chair next to Sam. "Hey. Sorry I'm a little late." He signaled Billy Cole for a beer. The proprietor nodded and picked up the TV remote to bring up the audio before he brought more drinks to their table.

Chattering ceased and the sounds of silverware on plates quieted as the narrator introduced the documentary. "We're here in Montana, Big Sky Country, where the wide-open spaces beckon, fresh breezes blow, rich grasses grow, and the deer and the antelope literally play..."

The narrator continued speaking the praises of "beautiful eastern Montana" and how few people inhabited the area. "Wouldn't you love to drive through a wildlife park and see buffalo as they used to roam…?" On the screen, a bison herd dotted the rolling hills. "…or even exotic animals like elephants or tigers…" Photos of these wild animals had been super-imposed into Montana scenes.

Ohmygosh, like a big zoo. Electra pursed her lips. That didn't look right. Not like Montana.

Sam's mouth gaped. "Did you do that?" she hissed at Brad.

He focused on his beer. "Well…" He shook his head as more photos and more rhetoric filled the TV screen.

The ranchers mumbled and squirmed in their chairs. "Boo!" someone yelled.

"Turn the dadgum thing off." Horace stood and gestured to Billy who hit the power button.

As one, the group faced Murdock. He held up his palms. "Gentlemen. Ladies. Let's try to have an open mind here."

Snorts and laughter greeted his comment. Electra heard words her mom definitely wouldn't approve of.

"I know you love your land. But, in reality, you are barely subsisting. Wouldn't you like to live more comfortably, have a little financial cushion to ease your golden years?"

Clyde stood and slammed his palms flat on the table. "What do you know about our lives and what we want? What right do you, or this big-city Roberts guy have, to tell us what we need or want?"

"Yeah." Horace stood beside him. "This is our land, our lives, our decision to make, and we don't appreciate this high-falutin' pipe dream. 'Big Open,' my hind leg."

The group guffawed, but sobered quickly, adding their opinions until Murdock finally stood. "Well, folks, sorry you feel that way. I was just trying to help make life a little better in this part of the state." He gave them what Electra thought was a phony smile. "Think about it a while. If any of you are interested, let me know." He tossed a handful of business cards on the table and pivoted to leave.

Near the door, he paused. "Mr. Roberts will be in town a week from today, and he'd like to set up a meeting. Maybe he can ease your fears, explain things a little better." He hurried out the door as shouts followed the slam. "No, don't come back. We don't want your rhetoric."

Everyone talked at once. "Low-down, lyin' scum." What right do they have?" "This is OUR Montana."

Sam swung toward Brad whose face was crimson. "What did you do? Why?"

He put a hand out, palm up. "No. Wait. I didn't do the final edits on this piece. I took the footage for the area—"

"And the tigers and elephants?"

"The director ordered me to do that. I'm at their mercy. If I want to get paid—"

Sam snorted. "Paid, huh? Blood money."

Electra shot Brad a glare. *Why* would *he do that if he didn't believe it? This doesn't make sense.*

"Is that all this country means to you, just a paycheck? 'Just doin' my job,'" Sam mimicked. "I really thought better of you." She grabbed Electra's arm. "Let's go."

Oh-oh. Trouble in paradise. And just last night they were all lovely-dovey. Her heart ached for her friend. She knew how much the cowgirl loved the land. *And we thought Brad was going to help. Men! Can you trust any of them?* Turned out she and her mom couldn't even trust her dad. So why would she or Sam trust a stranger? Brad said one thing and did another.

The door slammed behind them, and Sam stomped to the pickup, muttering, "Turncoat. Traitor. I can't believe..."

She sat in the passenger seat, staring at her friend, wide-eyed. "Did Brad really make that film?"

The cowgirl stomped on the accelerator, and the pickup fishtailed on the dirt road. "Yeah. He did. He's as bad as Jack Murdock and that New York scum Roberts."

Sam's cell phone rang as she headed out of town. She glanced at the screen and spat out, "Brad." She threw the phone on the floor where it bounced and vibrated and continued to ring.

At home, Electra hovered just out of sight and gasped as Sam took a bottle from a high cupboard above the refrigerator. The label read Vodka. Her friend stomped to the porch and sat with a thump, tipping the bottle to her lips. Then she poured more into a glass and sat, her upper body hunched over the drink.

Ohmygosh! What is happening? This wasn't like Sam. This was like her dad used to act. *That wasn't good.* Her breath locked in her chest, and cold sweat shivered over her body. What could she do? Nothing. Nothing she did or said to Dad ever made a difference, just made him madder.

After several long minutes of agonizing—should she go out there, or should she leave Sam alone?—she stiff-walked to the door and stuck her head out, licking her lips. "I'm going to bed, Sam. G'night."

The cowgirl hurriedly stashed the bottle out of sight alongside her leg. "Okay. Yeah. I'm gonna go soon too." She gave a weak smile. "Good night."

In bed, Electra rolled from one side to the other, flinching at the night noises. Her stomach tightened rock-hard. *Mom put up with a lot from Dad.* Memories flickered of shouted arguments, slammed doors, the car roaring away, Mom sobbing in her bedroom. Would Sam end up a drunk like Dad and leave her too?

She picked at the scabs on her arms. Physical pain obliterated the heart-hurt. Finally, she heard the door close downstairs and Sam trudging to her room.

Then she slept.

***

The next morning, Electra's head was fuzzy. Sam greeted her with a watery smile. The cowgirl's minimal conversation was light and breezy but forced. At Clyde's, she went about the chores like a robot, muting her phone when Brad apparently called and deleted her voicemails without listening.

Electra woodenly followed, doing what was required. After receiving a curt "Nothing!" from Sam to his enquiry of what was wrong, Clyde gave them both a wide berth.

Horace stopped by and the men grumbled and cursed about the meeting and documentary. "Has anybody sold to this Roberts?" Clyde asked.

Horace shook his head. "Nobody around here. Well, one couple closer to Forsyth did, I guess. The husband had a stroke, and the wife couldn't handle the work."

"You'd think they'd get the message. We don't want no part of their fool scheme." Clyde spat a stream of tobacco, raising a tiny dust cloud.

***

The next Monday, toward the end of the day, Clyde approached Sam and Electra. "Why don't you knock off early and head home."

"Well, I planned to go to that meeting. Might as well go from here."

Clyde shook his head. "I think you should stay away tonight." He narrowed his eyes with a steely gaze.

Electra snapped her eyes wide. *What's this all about?*

Sam stepped back. "Uh… well… I…"

"Go home," Clyde repeated.

"C'mon, Electra." She stalked to her truck, and they headed down the road.

Electra clickeed her seatbelt and frowned. "Why doesn't he want us to go tonight?"

"I'm not really sure. That was weird." Sam chewed on her lower lip and tapped the steering wheel in a nervous finger dance.

When Sam drove into Ingomar, Electra's pulse raced. *Clyde's gonna be mad.*

She parked out of sight behind the post office but within sight of the entrance to the Jersey Lilly. "You stay inside." Sam stalked to the front of the truck.

Flutters erupted in Electra's chest. *What is she doing?* She got out, staying behind the open door.

They'd been there a few minutes when Clyde's truck parked in front of the bar. Horace's pickup pulled in beside him. The men stood talking as several more vehicles joined them. Clyde studied his watch and then gazed up the dirt road that led from the highway into Ingomar. A plume of dust rose in the gray, dusky distance.

As if choreographed, the men reached inside their trucks and retrieved rifles and shotguns.

Electra gasped. *Ohmygosh, what is happening?* It was like a scene from an old TV western that Jimmy used to watch. Her pulse throbbed in her neck. She bit at a hangnail.

About a dozen men lined up on the boardwalk in front of the Jersey Lilly. Billy came out the door, also toting a long gun.

A sleek black SUV, now covered in dust, snaked its way down Main Street toward the saloon, and slowed even more as the driver apparently caught sight of the line of men. The vehicle stopped, and after a long minute, Murdock and Roberts eased out.

Roberts held his arms out, palms up. "Gentlemen. Can we talk?"

The sound of a dozen rifles cocking snapped him to a halt.

Electra jumped at the sound and took in a gulp of air. *Ohmygosh, are they going to shoot him?*

"You ain't welcome here." Horace's voice was a ribbon of steel.

"C'mon, folks." Roberts took one tentative step forward. "This isn't the wild West. We're a civilized society now. Please hear me out."

The barrels raised, all pointed directly at him.

Sam joined Electra, sheltered behind the pickup door.

Ice raced through her veins. Holding back a scream, she stood, fascinated by the scene, wanting to hide, yet frozen in place.

"You heard the man," Clyde said. "We're done talkin'. Get out."

Roberts' Adams apple bobbed, and his mouth opened and closed like a fish out of water. "All right. All right. Easy." He backed toward his car, hands raised. "I'm leaving now."

"And don't come back!" someone else hollered.

Roberts and Murdock jumped in and slammed their doors. Dirt and gravel flew as the vehicle spun and swerved away.

Whew. That was close. "What just happened?" With a giant exhale, Electra squinted at her friend. "That was just like that TV show, *The Wild, Wild West*."

Sam's pale face slowly swiveled toward her, her mouth also gaping. Then they both grinned at the same time. It *was* the wild West!

***

The next day, while working, Electra heard a vehicle crunching up the driveway and peeked out of the Bruckners' barn. A large, green 4x4 pulled in and parked at the corral where Clyde worked. Sam moved to the door beside her. "Uh-oh."

Sheriff McCollum got out of the truck, and Clyde met him at the gate. "Howdy, Sheriff. What can I do ya for?"

The tall, muscular law officer put out his hand to shake. "Nice day."

"Yup." Clyde nodded.

Electra stayed in the shadow of the barn door, her palms suddenly sweaty.

Sam wiped her hands on her jeans and leaned around the corner.

"Well..." The sheriff cleared his throat.

He sure does take his sweet time spitting it out. Electra shook her head. *Just say it already.*

"I had a visit from a Scott Roberts and Jack Murdock this mornin'." McCollum leaned against the corral fence.

An alarm rang in her brain. *Oh no! I hope Clyde isn't in trouble.*

The rancher switched his chaw from one cheek to the other. "Oh, yeah?"

"They said somethin' about an 'armed stand-off' at the Jersey Lilly last night." His mouth twitched at one corner.

"They did, huh?" Clyde spat a stream of tobacco into the dust.

"Yup."

Was he going to arrest Clyde? Electra's stomach twisted into knots.

Sam's fingers scrabbled at the wood door frame.

"Well... I guess that's true. We'd dis-invited Mr. Murdock and Mr. Roberts with their 'Big Open' scheme and told 'em we weren't sellin'. But they showed up anyway."

"Figured as much." McCollum kicked at a dirt clod. "Told 'em I'd come talk to you, but they best fergit about that whole thing anyway. Nobody in the country is interested in lions and tigers." He grinned and gazed around the corral. After a long pause, "Hear you had a purty good turnout for your Fourth celebration."

Clyde pushed his hat back. "Yup. Real good this year."

"Well, gotta be goin'. Take care, now." The sheriff touched his hat and got in his truck.

Electra realized her mouth hung open once again. *Ohmygosh, another close call. What IS this place? Am I in a time warp?*

She followed as Sam marched out of the barn.

"Wow." The cowgirl's voice echoed Electra's amazement.

Clyde smirked. "Yeah. Guess he agrees with us."

Mrs. Bruckner came running from the house. "Oh, my stars, I was so afraid he was going to be hauling you away." Her face was pale. "What did he say?"

"Nothin'." Clyde shrugged. "Roberts and Murdock complained, but he told 'em where ta stick it, I guess."

His wife shook her head. "You guys and your 'wild West' antics." She winked at Sam. "It'll be the death of me yet."

Sam nodded. "I know. We saw the whole thing."

Clyde jerked his head back. "You did? That was a foolhardy thing to do. It coulda gotten ugly. I told you to stay home."

"I couldn't. I needed to know what was going to happen. My ranch and my future are at stake too." She held her palms out. "Don't worry. We were out of the line of fire, behind the post office."

The rancher huffed a sigh, his face stern, but then it crinkled. "All's well that ends well, I reckon. Dinner ready?"

Both chuckling, Electra and Sam followed him inside.

CHAPTER THIRTEEN

After they got home that evening, Electra gestured at the wall phone. "Is it okay if I call Mom?"

"Sure..." Sam hesitated a moment. "Maybe...don't tell her what happened with the guys and their guns? It might scare her."

Electra shrugged. "Yeah. Okay. New York city has stuff like that all the time though. Well, maybe not *exactly* like that." She grinned. "I still think we got in a time machine and went back to John Wayne days."

Her friend giggled. "Yes, it sure did look that way, didn't it? Got the message across though."

"Yeah! I'm glad we were there to see it. Even though I was really scared...were you scared?"

"Oh yes, I certainly was. And more afraid of your mom if something happened to you on my watch." She shuddered.

Electra put an arm around her friend. "Well, it didn't. So there."

Sam squeezed back. "Tell your mom hi. I'm going out to check on Sugar."

"Hey, baby girl." Mom's voice rose when she answered the phone. "How're you doing? Still having fun on the ranch?"

"Oh yeah, lots and lots of fun, working with the group home kids and the rodeo and Sam's friend Brad made a documentary about the "Big Open' and now Sam's mad at him.''

Her mom chuckled. "Well, sounds like you're not getting bored, that's for sure." Her voice lowered. "Say, I'm going to take some time off work and come out there in August. I want to get recharged before we head back home."

We. Home. Her chest tightened. The time was coming. Summer was almost over, and she'd have to go back to school…in New York.

"You still there, honey?"

Her breath hitched in a half-sob. "Yeah."

"You knew you'd have to come home again, right?"

"Yeah." Her voice came out in a little-girl squeak.

"Sweetheart, I know you love it there. But the deal was, just for the summer. You have to go to school. Besides, I miss you."

She dug her fingernails into her upper arms. "But it's all gone so fast. It's too soon."

"I know. But you have a few weeks left. So just enjoy it and store up all those fun memories you can share with me and your friends."

My friends. Will they still like me? Somehow, deep inside, she knew she'd changed. *I like different things now.* Would they notice? Would they still accept her? Dread scratched at her chest cavity.

"I love you. Okay, sweetheart?"

"O-kay, Mom. Talk to you soon. Love you too."

She replaced the receiver slowly, as if in a trance, and trudged to the door, the end of the summer a boulder on her back.

The air had cooled, and the sun barely peeked over the undulating horizon, spreading its orange and gold fingers of light. She climbed to the top rail of the corral and waited for Sam to ride in.

The cowgirl dismounted. "How's your mom?"

Electra shrugged. "Good." She forced a bright tone. "She's coming here the second week of August, so she can ride and visit with everybody again."

Sam smiled. "That's great. I'll be glad to see her."

"But then I have to go back with her." Her shoulders slumped. "She says we have to go shopping and get ready for school."

Sam removed Sugar's bridle and let her trot out into the enclosure near the barn. "Yes, I suppose you will need some new clothes."

Tears trickled down Electra's cheeks. "But I don't wanna go back to New York. I wanna stay here," she wailed.

Sam reached out a hand, and she jumped down from the fence. Burying her face in Sam's chest, she sobbed.

Her friend patted her back. "I know. I'm going to miss you too. You're an important part of my life now. We'll keep in touch."

When her sobs were spent, she withdrew from the embrace. Sam peered into her eyes. "We knew this day would come. It's been a great summer, and you've done such a good job, helping me here and at Clyde's. We can always look forward to next summer, if your mom says it's okay to come back then."

Electra nodded and sniffled. "She better."

"I'm sure she will, when she sees how much you've grown up." The cowgirl put her arm around her shoulders. "C'mon, let's go up to the house and have some supper. That always helps."

"Okay, sure." Then she remembered. "Oh yeah, Brad called."

Sam stiffened.

"He said he would really like to talk to you and apologize for the misunderstanding in person."

Her friend stopped and stared at her. "You talked to him?"

"Sure. I thought it was Mom calling back." She held Sam's gaze. "Y'know, I thought he was a poopyhead when I first met him, but he's really not a bad guy. I don't think he meant to hurt you with that documentary. I think he really likes you."

Sam blinked. "Oh, honey. Thank you for saying that. But I'm still really mad at him, and he's going to have some 'splainin' to do, when—*if* I decide to ever see him again." She cuffed Electra's shoulder. "Quit meddling in my love life, okay? Let's go eat."

***

Over the next few days, whenever Brad called, Sam still ignored the messages. The trial loomed and seemed to occupy every waking moment for the cowgirl. Electra stood back and observed her friend frantic with nerves. She chewed the inside of her cheek. *I'd be nervous too. Wish I could help.*

Sam practiced a speech, revised it, then scrapped it altogether. Electra stepped carefully around her friend, as if she walked on eggshells. Sam even lashed out at good ol'-easy-going Clyde when he spoke to her. *Yikes! That's not like Sam.*

The cowgirl paced, she mucked out stalls, she brushed horses. "Maybe I should just call it off," she blurted one day. "Maybe getting my $500 back is not worth all this fear and anxiety."

"Oh no, please don't give up." A stab of fear sent cold shivers through Electra. "You *have* to get Apache back…for me. You gotta do it for me." She couldn't keep the whine out of her voice. "Remember your grandma Nettie. What would she do?"

The reminder was enough to bring a lopsided grin to Sam's face. "You're absolutely right. I can almost hear her voice: *Follow your dream.* And I do want to get Apache back for you."

"All right!" She high-fived her friend. "Way to go."

The evening before the 21st, Sam sat with a book, but hardly flipped a page. She stood and went to the kitchen, gazing up at that high cupboard above the refrigerator.

No. No-no. Don't do that. Electra's legs twitched, poised to jump up from the sofa and run in there. She would throw herself in front of her friend to stop her. When Sam shook her head and ambled back into the living room, she sagged against the cushions, relief flooding her body.

"Okay, enough of this. I'm going to bed. Tomorrow will be here before we know it."

She grabbed Sam's hand. "Don't worry. It will be all right. I'll say a prayer for you tonight." A memory from the past welled up inside. Her family had once gone to church every Sunday when she was a little girl. When had they stopped? *Well, maybe prayer will work for Sam, even though it didn't bring Jimmy back.*

"Thank you, my dear. I'll need it."

She could barely sleep that night, pins and needles prickling her skin, and butterflies fighting in her tummy. She could only imagine Sam, downstairs, tossing and turning, and how she must be feeling.

***

Teresa drove up in her SUV at 7:30 a.m. Electra got in the back seat. Piling in front, Sam grumbled, "Oh, my nerves. I'm shot." She peered at her friend. "You look all chipper and cheery this morning."

Teresa winked. "I think maybe I got a little more sleep than you did."

"Does it show that bad?" Sam pulled down the visor with the mirror and groaned at the reflection of blotchy cheeks and dark circles under her eyes.

Electra blinked her own gritty eyes. Despite mascara and eyeliner, they had stared back at her from the mirror this morning red rimmed. She clenched her hands, which in spite of the promise of a 90-degree day, were cold and clammy. *I sure hope this goes okay. We have to get Apache back.*

After about an hour, they arrived and parked in front of the two-story, gray courthouse. "Well, here we are." Teresa reached over and patted her friend's knee. "You'll do fine. We're here with you." She threw a wink over her shoulder at Electra.

With a grim, determined set to her face, Sam gathered her files, got out of the car, and walked up the steps.

Electra followed, her legs heavy. The stairs seemed much steeper than the last time they were here.

Inside the lobby, the cowgirl stopped short as Brad strode toward them.

"Good morning, ladies." His dark brown eyes crinkled at the corners with his smile.

What's he doing here? Is he going to support Sam or is he going to cause trouble? Electra narrowed her eyes at him.

Sam frowned and echoed her thoughts. "What are you doing here?"

"I came to support you. Listen, I'm really sorry—"

"I can't talk about that right now, Brad. I'm headed into court, and I have more important things on my mind." Sam brushed past him to go down the stairs.

Electra hung back. His presence seemed to rattle her friend more than a little.

"Okay, but I think you might want to see these." His voice rose to attract her attention.

Sam stopped in mid-stride and let out a loud exhale. Finally, she about-faced. "What is it?" He handed her a manila envelope. Peering at him from beneath lowered eyelids, she took out several photos.

Peeking over Sam's shoulder, Electra's breath caught. *Apache.*

"I stopped by the pasture yesterday. Thought these pictures might help your case."

The photos showed the horse standing next to a half-filled water tank with no evidence of feed in the same bare pasture where they'd found him. His head hung low, and his ribs once again showed through his dusty coat. Sam swallowed audibly.

Electra wailed, "Oh no." The hard lump in her chest softened. *Brad really is trying to help.*

"Thank you." Sam gave him a quavery smile. "I appreciate this." She put the pictures in her folder.

Electra followed her friend down the gray-carpeted stairs. Stopping at the clerk's window, Sam gave her name and who was with her.

The woman gestured. "C'mon, I'll show you to the courtroom."

In the hallway, several men stood by the court's door. "Smythe," Teresa whispered, "and the nephew. I don't know the other guy."

The clerk stopped in front of the group. "Mr. Smythe, Todd, you checked in with me, but who is your friend here?"

"Oh, this is my attorney, Justin Bragg."

She shook her head. "I'm sorry, sir, but no attorneys are allowed in small claims court. You'll have to wait outside."

"But…" Smythe sputtered.

"Judge Pepperman will not allow it." She gestured toward the stairs.

Bragg shrugged. "Okay. Worth a try, Richard." He shook his client's hand. "Good luck."

The clerk unlocked the door, and they filed in. Sam and the Smythes took seats at folding tables in front on opposite sides. Teresa, Electra, and Brad sat in chairs behind her. Sam's hands shook as she opened her file, laid everything out, and sat staring at the photos and papers.

Okay, she needs something extra here. Electra offered up a quick prayer. *Dear God, please help her not be so nervous.* She leaned forward and patted her friend's shoulder, rewarded with a tiny smile.

The door opened behind her, chairs creaked, and low male voices conversed. Electra didn't look to see who it was but chewed at her ragged fingernails. Sam sat so still in her chair she looked like an ice sculpture. Electra's leg muscles twitched, and her mouth felt like the dry prairie. She could only imagine what Sam must be experiencing.

After what seemed like an hour, a man entered from a door near the front, dressed in a dark suit and tie. He stopped behind a tall, light-oak desk. Behind him, an American flag adorned the corner. He brushed a hand through salt-and-pepper hair and acknowledged the group. "Good morning. I'm Judge Pepperman." He put on half-glasses, picked up a piece of paper, and read off a number. "This is small claims court, and this is Moser vs Smythe." He glanced up. "Is that correct?"

Sam nodded. Smythe rumbled, "Yes, sir."

The judge sat in his black leather chair. "All right then. We will proceed. I'll be recording this session." He set a small handheld recorder on his desk. "The plaintiff—that's you, Ms. Moser, will present your case first. I ask you, Mr. Smythe, to remain silent until she is finished, and then we will hear your presentation. No attorneys are permitted." He rested his gaze on Sam. "Ready, Ms. Moser?"

"Yes." Her voice came out with a squeak. She cleared her throat and rose.

Teresa whispered, "You'll be fine." A low murmur echoed from Brad.

Yes, you will. You are a strong cowgirl, just like your great-grandma Nettie. Electra willed positive thoughts toward her friend.

Sam swallowed. "Thank you, your honor." Then she stopped, as if frozen.

The judge gave her a kindly smile. "It's okay. I don't bite. Go ahead when you're ready."

Electra's chest tightened. *He looks like a nice man. Will he believe Sam?*

Her friend took a breath and let it out audibly.

You can do this. Electra crossed her fingers.

"I'm Samantha Moser. I was made aware of a starving horse by Teresa Knudson," she pointed to her friend, "who knew I had a rescued mare. She thought maybe I could help this poor animal." Her voice grew stronger as she appeared to warm to the story. She chronicled the events: seeing the horse nearly dead, talking to the animal warden with no results.

Heat rose inside Electra as she remembered their confrontation. *He was no help at all.*

Sam told of bringing feed and a tub for water, and then meeting Todd Smythe, the nephew, the offer to buy the horse, and the subsequent "sale." She gave the judge the photos Teresa had taken, the copy of the hand-written bill-of-sale, and the pictures after she had taken care of the horse for several weeks, plus a copy of the vet bill.

Then Sam gestured toward her. "This young lady came to work with me this summer, very unhappy and troubled over the loss of a brother and her father." She showed the judge a picture.

My old Goth-girl look. Electra snorted a half-laugh.

"She was so moved by the plight of this horse I call Apache, and he immediately responded to her in such a…a marvelous way." Sam paused, her mouth working side to side. "Your honor, I have witnessed a couple of miracles with kids and horses recently that I never would have dreamed." Her voice caught, she paused, and focused on the judge. "Your honor. This claim is to get my five hundred dollars back, but I truly believe, I feel it—" she put a hand over her heart—"if I could get Apache back, that would be my wish come true. This horse…and this girl deserve happiness."

Electra's heart puddled, and her lip quivered.

Sam laid Brad's photos on the judge's desk. "These were taken yesterday by Mr. Ashton there. As you can see, the horse is still not being well cared for." She went back to her chair and sat.

Judge Pepperman leaned forward and studied the photos for several eternal moments, creases deepening in his forehead.

Then he nodded at Smythe. "Mr. Smythe, your turn. I believe you are the owner of the horse and guardian of your nephew Todd, who is under age eighteen, is that correct?"

Fighting an urge to throw up, Electra steeled herself. *What lies is this jerk going to tell?* Teresa took her hand.

Smythe stood. "Yes, your honor. That is correct. This was my late wife's horse, so I didn't want to sell him, but I was out of the country on business for an extended period. My nephew was in charge of caring for Sebastian—who Ms. Moser calls 'Apache'—but he did not have power of attorney to sell the horse. So as far as I was concerned, the sale was null and void, and I enlisted the assistance of the Rosebud County Sheriff and Warden Madison to retrieve my property, which I considered stolen."

Electra clenched her fists and bit her lip to keep from crying out a protest. *Sam paid that little punk.* She glanced at the men at the back of the room and did a double take to see Sheriff O'Connor, the Custer County Sheriff, and the animal warden. *That's right.* She remembered Sheriff O'Connor told Sam he would see if Madison would be a witness. But what would he say? *He sure didn't seem to care that Apache was almost dead.*

Sam's fists were clenched on top of her papers, her shoulders appeared as rigid as stone.

Judge Pepperman scrutinized Smythe over his readers. "But you received a check and cashed it?"

"No, *I* didn't. I never saw a check." His eyes shifted momentarily toward his nephew.

"Did you cash the check, Todd?" the judge asked.

The teenager shifted in his chair and stared down at the floor.

"Answer the judge, Todd." His uncle prodded his shoulder.

"Um…no." He shook his head.

What? That little liar. Electra nearly jumped out of her seat. Teresa laid a restraining hand on her arm.

Sam put her hands on the table to rise. The judge swiveled his head toward her. "Ms. Moser, do you have a bank statement that shows the check went through?"

Sam hesitated. "Yes, your honor. I know I saw it on my statement." She riffled through her file folder. "Oh, wait." She opened her purse and dug out her wallet. "Here's the canceled check, your honor."

Electra drew in a relieved breath. Teresa grinned, and Brad gave a thumbs up.

Pepperman took the document and flipped it over to squint at the back. Then he leveled his gaze at Todd. "Looks like your signature right here, young man."

The boy's face reddened, and he squirmed again.

The judge continued to stare at the teen for several moments. Then he studied the photos and papers again. Then scanning the back of the room, he finally spoke. "Mr. Madison."

The animal warden stood. "Yes, your honor."

"I see you are listed as a witness. Ms. Moser called you about the condition of this horse, is that correct?"

"Yes, your honor."

"And you went to the pasture and saw him in this emaciated state?" The judge held up the photo of Apache Teresa had taken at the beginning.

The warden shuffled his feet. "Yes, your honor."

"And you did nothing?"

Ha ha, you dweeb. It's coming back to haunt you. Electra bounced her knee.

Madison's face flushed in red blotchy patches. "Uh…well, no, your honor. At the time I was there, the horse had water and feed, so I deducted that it was being cared for."

"That's because I bought the water tub and the feed!" Sam blurted out, her neck and face scarlet.

The judge held up a hand. "And did you check with the owner or go back at a later date to see if the horse was being cared for?"

Madison studied his fingernails. "Um, no, your honor. I came to Ms. Moser's with Sheriff O'Connor to return the horse to Mr. Smythe, and he appeared to be healthy at that time. Mr. Smythe was back home by then, so I assumed the care would continue."

Sam huffed a breath.

Electra closed her eyes. Heat seared through her body and her insides shook. *Stupid blockhead!*

"Thank you, Mr. Madison. You may be seated." The judge shuffled the papers and photos and pursed his lips as he appeared to study each one again.

The cowgirl rubbed her hands. Electra bit vigorously on a thumbnail. Did they dare hope he would be on Sam's side? Teresa raised her eyebrows and nodded. The courtroom was silent except for the papers and an occasional throat-clearing or foot-shuffling. The wall clock ticked in slow motion.

At last, the judge gathered up the paperwork, tapped it on the desk, and removed his glasses. He stood and walked around to stand in front of the Smythes. "Todd, do you know that endorsing that check and selling property that doesn't belong to you is a crime? Something that could send you to jail for up to five years?"

The boy's face went as pale as if he'd borrowed Electra's Goth makeup.

"Mr. Smythe, you are the boy's guardian. Do you want to press charges against your nephew?"

Electra wrinkled her nose. *Yeah. Do it! Send the little brat to jail.*

The man's face was equally pale. "No, your honor, I do not."

Darn. Too bad.

"All right. I will let you handle that on your own." The judge pointed a finger at Todd. "Listen, kid, you just got off easy. Anyone else would've thrown the book at you. I hope you've learned your lesson."

Then he narrowed his eyes at Smythe. "As for you... In my opinion, this horse looked to be nearly dead when Ms. Moser attempted to rescue him. The photos show a marked improvement by the time you demanded his return, and now..." Pepperman reached back and picked up yesterday's photo, "it appears he is nearly as bad as he was in the initial photos."

"Well, Sebastian is an older horse and—"

Electra sat bolt upright. "No! He's not Sebastian, he's Apache! And it doesn't matter if he's old or not."

Sam gasped and gave her a withering glare.

The judge put a palm up toward her, shook his head at Smythe, and then spoke to Sam. "This court and this case are for monetary awards only."

Electra's heart plummeted, and she stifled a cry. It was too much to hope they'd get Apache back.

"I'm ordering you, Mr. Smythe, to repay Ms. Moser the five hundred dollars plus reimbursement for her vet bills."

Her lip quivered. *At least she'll get her money back. But not my Apache.* Her thoughts spun. For the first time in her life, she'd found something to love more than herself, more than the memory of her brother. She'd had something to live for, a purpose. Numbness blanketed her and muffled the sounds of the courtroom.

Sam leaned back and took Electra's hand in hers. Tears trickled down her cheeks, matching the ones running toward her own chin.

"However, due to the circumstances and appearance of this horse, I am calling this a case of animal neglect and abuse, and in lieu of allowing the sheriff to file charges, I am recommending you also return the horse to Ms. Moser."

Electra's chest was tight, her heart like a stone. She heard the judge's voice, but the words barely registered. She held Sam's sad gaze.

Teresa's "Yes!" startled them both. Brad's face broke into a huge grin.

What is happening? Electra blinked. *What did he say?*

Sam frowned and twisted back to the front.

"Can I expect compliance from you, Mr. Smythe?"

The man's face darkened. "Yes, your honor. I will write out a check right now, and Ms. Moser may come and pick up the horse whenever she wishes."

Sam swiveled back to her friends, her mouth open.

Pick up the horse? Electra's hand flew to her chest. "Sam? Is it… Are we…?"

The cowgirl nodded, the corners of her mouth rising.

The words finally registered on her brain. *We're getting Apache back.* She jumped up and whooped. Teresa put a restraining hand on her arm. The courtroom buzzed with reactions as everyone seemed to speak at once.

Judge Pepperman banged his gavel. The sharp report quieted the audience. "All right. Mr. Smythe, come forward and write out your check and make arrangements with Ms. Moser to retrieve the horse. This court is adjourned."

Teresa leaped from her chair and grabbed Sam in a bear hug. "I knew it! I knew you could do it. Congratulations."

Electra squealed. "We're getting Apache back. We're getting Apache back." She danced around the chairs, twirling, and whooping.

Sam moved to the judge's desk, where Smythe handed Pepperman a check. The judge studied it and then gave it to her. "Okay, young lady." He squinted at Smythe. "And the ownership papers?"

"I'll put 'em in the mail." His answer was curt.

The judge shook his head. "You'll need to sign papers right now to transfer ownership to Ms. Moser. You can do that with my clerk at the window down the hall."

"All right." He bit the words through thinned lips.

"Thank you, Judge. Thank you, Mr. Smythe." Sam spoke remarkably calmly. "This afternoon all right to pick him up?"

Electra squealed again. "We're getting him today? Really? Yes!" She high-fived her friend and skipped around the room, fighting her urge to rush forward and flaunt their victory in his reddened face.

"Whenever," Smythe grunted and stalked out of the courtroom.

Sam waved the check at her group. "We did it."

Brad offered his hand. "Congratulations."

She took his in both of hers. "Thank you, Brad. I think your photos tipped the verdict. Thank you so much."

Electra's anger at him melted. *He really* did *help us.*

"Glad to be of service, ma'am." He gave her a little-boy grin. "May I buy you ladies lunch to celebrate?"

Sam's face wreathed in a huge smile. "Oh, thanks, but I need to get home, get a trailer, and come back for Apache right away."

As they exited the room, Electra caught sight of the Custer County sheriff, his face about an inch from Warden Madison's crimson one. "I've half a mind to fire you right now."

"B-b-bu—" The warden's lower lip quivered like a scolded child. His face reddened, and veins bulged in his neck.

The sheriff's finger jabbed Madison's chest. "I don't *ever* want to hear anything like this again. Do you understand me?"

The warden's head bobbed up and down in rapid fire motion.

"I'll be personally supervising your calls and reports from now on." The sheriff moved back. "Now get to work."

Electra giggled, and she and Sam exchanged a grin. *Serves him right.*

Sheriff O'Connor came up to them. "Congratulations, Sam. Glad this worked out for you."

"Thank you for all your help, Sheriff. I appreciate it."

He pushed his hat back, touched the brim with two fingers, and walked down the hall.

CHAPTER FOURTEEN

On the drive home, the urge to run, jump, and scream had Electra dancing on the back seat. Sam whooped and sang at the top of her lungs, Teresa harmonizing and giggling as she drove. Electricity sparked from one to the other.

"I can't believe it!" Electra repeated over and over. She couldn't stop grinning and pumping her fists into the air.

"I can't either. Oh, Teresa, I was so nervous." The cowgirl swiveled her head toward her friend. "I thought I was going to melt into a big steaming puddle in the middle of the courtroom." From her seat behind Teresa, Electra caught a glimpse of Sam's cheeks shining with tears, her eyes wide and glowing.

"I knew you were, but you spoke very well, and I could see that your story touched the judge, especially about Electra's transformation." Teresa met her gaze in the rearview mirror. Then back to Sam. "I'm so proud of you. You've done a good thing here."

Sam blinked rapidly. "Thanks. And thank you for being here with me. That means so much. You're a good friend."

"You're welcome. But you gotta give Brad some credit too. He's been a big supporter of yours, and those photos…"

The cowgirl bent her head and appeared to study the floorboard. "I know. He didn't *have* to do that, especially since I've been ignoring his calls lately. I dunno, I was just so mad at him for doing that stupid documentary for the Big Open people."

Teresa shrugged. "I can understand why you were, but he was merely doing his job, one that he'd been contracted for before you even met him."

"Yeah. I guess you're right." She gave her friend a lopsided smile, then to Electra, "So, what do you think we should do first thing after we get Apache?"

"Give him a big hug!" She bounced again, but then she sobered. "Should we take him to the vet, make sure he's really okay?"

Sam nodded. "Y'know, that's a good idea. We should get him checked out."

At home, Teresa stayed long enough to help hook up the borrowed horse trailer. "Good luck. Let me know how things go." She got into her SUV, waved, and drove off.

"Okay, let's go get Apache." Sam jumped into the pickup, and Electra bounded onto the passenger seat.

"Yeah. Let's go!" She fidgeted as Sam pulled away from the house. "Can you drive faster?"

Sam chuckled. "Not with this trailer and not on these dirt roads. We'll make up some time when we get to the highway, but we don't want to get into an accident before we even get him."

Electra punched on the radio, and they soon wailed to an oldies' country station.

Sam grinned at her. "You've changed. You wouldn't have been caught dead listening to country music when you first got here, much less the oldies."

"Well…they're not so bad." She smirked. "They've got a good beat, and I like the stories they tell."

Her stomach tightened when Sam steered the truck up the dirt road toward the pasture. Remembering the goon who'd greeted them last time they'd come to see the horse had her on the edge of her seat. She wouldn't be shocked if Smythe had changed his mind and wouldn't let them take Apache. A glance at her friend revealed a tight face. *She must be thinking the same thing.*

The windmill came into sight, blades spinning in the hot wind. Dust swirled from the pasture across the road. She held her breath when she didn't see the horse. "Where's Apache?" She leaned forward and peered through the dirty windshield, a lump forming in her throat. *Did they take him away?*

Sam drove over a little rise.

"There he is," Electra cried out with relief, and Sam exhaled.

The horse stood near the water tank, head down, just like the photos Brad had taken. Sam pulled up to the gate.

Almost before the truck stopped, Electra was out of the door and strode toward the horse. She crawled through the barbed wire fence and made little mewling sounds as she slowed and approached, hand outstretched.

Apache raised his head and blinked huge, liquid brown eyes as if he couldn't believe what he saw. Her heart melted like butter in sunshine. She held her hand out so he could smell her. The gelding blew softly, bobbed his head, and then whickered. With a big smile, she smoothed her palm over his nose and up his face to his ears. "Hello, boy. It's okay. I'm here now." She threw her arms around his neck and buried her face in his dirty, matted mane. Her tears wet his neck, and the dust from his hair muddied her face. *We did it. We got him back.* At this moment, nothing else mattered.

They had rescued Apache once again.

***

After a couple of minutes, Sam came up behind her. Electra sniffled. "I'm so glad to see him." She swiped her sleeve across her nose.

"Me too." Sam ran her hands over his neck and down his legs. "Easy, boy, easy." She spoke in a low, soothing voice. "Well, other than being very thin, I don't think he's in too bad shape. No bumps or sores." Glancing at the empty feed trough and the few inches of scummy water in the tank, she clenched her jaw. "I forgot the ramp for the trailer, so I'm going to pull into that coulee there, and we can get him loaded."

Electra nodded. "Okay. I'll stay here with him till you're ready."

Sam drove to the wash, backed down into it, and got out, shaking her head. She backed again, got out, drove forward, backed again, trying to get the trailer to line up just right.

Aw, poor Sam. She's having trouble. Just as she was considering going to help her, a pickup pulled up. Brad! *Oh good.*

Sam waved out the window, spun the wheel, and backed up with him directing.

"Good," he yelled.

She jumped out. "Whew. Thanks. I was about ready to *ride* him home."

Brad chuckled at her joke.

"C'mon, boy, you're coming home now." Electra led Apache to the trailer. Her heart squeezed. *The poor guy. He looks so bad again.* "Don't worry, we're going to help you get better." She gave his face a soft caress.

The three loaded him without any trouble. He bobbed his head, his eyes brighter, and entered the trailer eagerly. Immediately he moved to the front where Sam had hung a bucket of oats on a stanchion.

Brad's warm brown eyes shone as his face crinkled into a

smile. "Horse rescuer extraordinaire. I'm so proud to know you."

Sam's face pinked. "Thanks. You had a hand in this too—it wasn't all me."

He scuffed his boot in the dirt. "Naw. I didn't do anything."

"No, really. I couldn't have done it without you and your trusty camera."

"Yeah, thanks, Brad. You really *did* help us." Electra had to give him credit. *He's not all bad—he just made a mistake with that documentary.* But…Teresa was right. He'd started that before he even knew her and Sam.

The cowgirl wiped her palms on her jeans. "Well, I gotta get going. We're going to get Apache checked out before we take him home, so…"

"Okay, that's good. Um… I guess I'll see you around then." Brad touched two fingers to his hat brim.

"Yeah." Sam nodded. "See ya."

"Bye, Brad."

They got into the truck, and Sam drove cautiously down the dusty road toward town.

Electra twisted to peek through the back window at the horse in the trailer. "Oh, Sam, I can't believe it. We got Apache back!" Her face tingled, and she felt like she'd moved from a dark shadow into a patch of sunlight.

Sam's face shone. "I can hardly believe it myself. This poor guy needs a good home, good food, and somebody to love him."

"Yeah." Happiness radiated through Electra's chest like musical notes. She settled back in her seat. "Y'know…what Brad said… You *are* a horse rescuer. And…" she swallowed, "you're my hero."

Sam cleared her throat. "Oh…oh, Electra…th-that's the nicest thing anybody has ever said to me." She blinked rapidly. "I'm so glad you were here to help me. You're a hero too—Apache's hero."

Her heart gave a leap. *Me? A hero? Ohmygosh.* Nobody had ever told her anything like that—not Dad, not Mom, not even Jimmy. *I wish he was here to see this.*

Now they were both sniffling. Electra rummaged in the glove box for a packet of tissue, took one, and gave one to Sam. She giggled then, and a happy bubble floated from her heart to her throat. Sam whooped, Electra joined in and increased the volume on the radio until the music reverberated through the cab with their laughter.

***

The vet unloaded Apache, ran his hands over the bay's body, checked his teeth, took his temperature, and drew blood.

Electra peered over his shoulder at every move. *Oh, I hope he's okay. If that Smythe guy hurt him, I'm gonna...* She pushed out a breath and clenched her fists.

The vet spoke. "He's very underweight and weak, but actually not quite as bad as last time you brought him in."

"Thanks, Doc." Sam wrote him a check, and they loaded the horse.

At home, Sugar greeted them with a rumbling nicker and pranced around the corral as they unloaded Apache. The mare ran up to the gelding, and they touched noses. Then she arched her neck and raced around the paddock again. Apache bobbed his head and whinnied, following along the fence a little ways after her before stopping, apparently to rest.

Electra giggled. "They're glad to see each other."

"Yeah, I think they are."

She helped Sam give Apache his feed and the vitamins Sam bought from the vet, get him settled into a stall, and then fed Sugar. Electra grabbed a brush and currycomb to groom the bay. Dust and matted hair floated to the ground, and she could see his reddish-brown coat once again.

"Good job, Electra. Well, I'm going up to the house now."

"Okay. Uh…Sam?"

"Yes?"

"Can I sleep out here tonight?"

"In the barn?"

Electra nodded.

"Um…well…" Sam shrugged. "I guess so. If you want. It's dirty, maybe mice and bugs. Not going to be very comfortable."

"That's okay. I don't care. I'll bring my sleeping bag down and make a bed of hay, and we'll be fine." She couldn't bear to be away from him for one more minute.

Sam smiled. "All right then. You want to come up for supper?"

"Yeah, ah, okay, but can I just dish up and bring it back here?"

The cowgirl chuckled. "Sure. How about I bring a plate for both of us, and we'll have a picnic here with Apache and Sugar."

***

Over the next several days, Electra opted to stay home while Sam went to work at Clyde's. She didn't want to take her attention off Apache for even a few hours. *He needs me.* For the first time, she had a living being who relied on her, she could care for, and lavish her attention on.

The horse lifted his head, whickered, and came to the fence whenever he saw her. It cheered her soul, and a quiet contentment spread through her. She had never known such unconditional love and trust.

As she brushed him and stroked his velvet face, her grief and anger and discontent fell away, and a palpable current of strength flowed between them. Every day she saw improvement—brightness in his eyes, holding his head higher, a stronger whinny. She buried her face in his mane and breathed in the musty scent of horse, a healing aroma better than any expensive perfume the shops in New York carried.

She could picture her own healing unfolding like flower petals as Apache healed.

***

Finally comfortable to leave Apache for the night, Electra ambled in from the barn one evening about a week later. Sam sat on the porch swing reading in the lowering, velvet shadows of dusk. "How's he doing tonight?" she asked.

"Ohmygosh, he is doing so much better, I just can't believe it. I think I can sleep in the house tonight and not be awake all night worrying about him."

"That's wonderful. I can definitely see a difference, especially in his eyes. You're working miracles with him."

A pleasant fluttering in her tummy responded to the compliment. "Thanks."

The phone shrilled into the peacefulness. Sam jumped up, hurried into the kitchen, and picked up. "Yes? Oh hi, Brad."

Electra giggled. *Wonder if he's on her good side today.* As she headed into the bathroom to wash up, she heard her friend say, "Electra's taking good care of him, and he's getting stronger every day. His coat is smoothing out, and his eyes are clear. I think he's happy."

She smiled, her face toasty. *Yes, he does seem happier.*

When she came back, Sam stood silent in the kitchen, her hand still on the receiver after she'd hung up.

"What's the matter?" Electra peered from the doorway.

"The TV station is showing the documentary about us tomorrow evening. I'm not so sure I really want to see it."

"Why not? You rocked the interview. B'sides, I want to see it—me and Sapphire and the kids from the group home are in it. It'll be fun." A new rush of excitement had her up on the balls of her feet. "You're not really going to skip it, are you? Please? Please?"

Sam rolled her eyes. "No. We'll go. Brad is buying us dinner. And I do want to see the part with Ellie and Trixie and at Clyde's and all." She reached into the cupboard for a bag of chips. "I hope he didn't mess with it like he did with the Big Open documentary."

"He wouldn't." Confident, Electra reassured her. "Sam…?"

"Yeah?"

"You got your five hundred dollars back from Mr. Smythe, didn't you?"

"Yes."

"And Miss Ellie said she would sell Trixie for five hundred dollars, didn't she?"

Sam nodded. "She did."

"So…are we—you—going to buy Trixie?" She attempted a hopeful tone, even though nerves jittered and left her short of breath.

"Well, I've been thinking about that a little. I sure would like to. And it is the exact amount I need." She paused.

"And…?"

"But now we have another horse to feed and with his medicine and supplements and all, it's going to cost a lot more to do that." Sam avoided her gaze and stared down at her boots. "That five hundred is all the cushion I have—for any emergency expenses."

Electra couldn't help frowning. Her concern for Trixi grew and threatened to choke off her voice. "But what will happen to Trixi? Miss Ellie said she can't keep her and she really likes us and she want us to have her and now we have the money and…"

"I know, honey. Let's watch the show tomorrow and see what happens. Maybe somebody out there will want to give her a good home."

"Okay." Electra jutted out her lower lip. She sniffled and shoved her hand into the chip bag. "But I can't see you just giving up like that." She crunched on the chips with a vengeance, worrying more about Trixi's future than hurting her friend's feelings.

CHAPTER FIFTEEN

Horace, Clyde and his wife, and Brad were already at the Jersey Lilly when Sam pulled up. Brad met her at the entrance, opening the door with a flourish. "Evenin', ladies. You're both lookin' mighty spiffy tonight."

Electra executed a mock curtsey. "Thank you, Sir Brad."

He was dressed in black jeans and a crisp royal-blue shirt with an agate bolo tie. A wayward dark curl fell onto his forehead as he bowed.

Sam flashed him a raised-brow look. "You're not so bad yourself."

"Your table awaits, m'lady." He took her elbow, escorted her into the dining area, and pulled out her chair, then did the same for Electra.

Wow, he's sure putting on the gallant act. She couldn't help but grin. Maybe he'd win Sam's heart after all.

"Coke for the young lass?"

Electra nodded.

"And for you, Madame, would you allow me to buy a bottle of Billy's best wine?"

"As long as it's not 'Two-Buck Chuck,' sure." Sam giggled.

Brad stared up at the ceiling and shook his head. "You doubt me?" He strode to the bar and came back with a bottle and Electra's soft drink. He poured Sam and himself a glass then held his up toward the Bruckners and Horace. "Here's to our 'Horse Rescuer.'" He brought his gaze back to Sam with an intense expression. "May you rescue many more."

"Hear, hear!" Horace boomed and raised his beer mug high. Electra giggled, Irene Bruckner applauded, and Clyde gave Sam a wink and a nod. The cowgirl's neck bloomed rosy, spreading to her cheeks, and she averted her attention to her wine glass.

Electra smirked, enjoying her friend's shy embarrassment. *She deserves the praise, even though she's too modest.*

Billy brought out chicken-fried steaks for Sam and Brad and a big, juicy cheeseburger for Electra. They all tucked into their food like starving ranch hands while Billy found the right channel on TV and adjusted the volume.

The program began with a shot of a horse herd—bays, blacks, roans, and palominos—muscles rippling under sleek coats, and their manes and tails flying in the wind as they raced across a green prairie.

"Modern horses have been near and dear to our American hearts since the Spanish Conquistadores reintroduced them to the continent in the sixteenth century." Brad's voice narrated as the camera panned the beautiful, strong animals and the rolling hills against a clear, ultramarine sky.

Ooooh, cool. Electra glanced at Sam.

Her friend raised her eyebrows toward Brad. "Wow." He winked.

Electra squirmed with an inner giggle. *They like each other.*

"Horses have been used for transportation, working fields, rounding up cattle, and for entertainment in rodeos."

As he spoke, the documentary showed clips of horses in various occupations.

"Many today are beloved pets and part of the family." A smiling group gathered around a sleek black mare, brushing, petting, and hugging her.

Then the scene changed to a still photo of Apache, his head hanging, ribs showing through his dirty coat. Electra gasped. *Ohmygosh, he really did look awful.*

"And yet," the narration continued, "there are those who abuse or neglect these animals who have given us so much. This is Apache, a horse discovered almost dead recently near Miles City, Montana."

Sam sat up straight when the next scene showed her riding down the hill toward the camera. "This young woman, Samantha Moser, came to the rescue." Her face flushed again, and she shook her head.

Electra grabbed Sam's arm and held on tight while Brad went on to tell the story with its happy ending, blinking back tears and biting down hard on her lip. She saw Sam's eyes glisten too.

"Now, we have another horse who needs to be rescued. Many of us are familiar with the illustrious career of Miss Ellie Hunt and her famous trick-horses. All her horses have been named Trixi, in honor of another famous trick rider, Trixi McCormick. This is the last one she's trained and exhibited for the past twenty years." Brad continued the story with Ellie's background, photos from her performances, and then showed Trixi as she lay down and let Electra mount.

The audience in the Jersey Lilly applauded, and it was Electra's face that warmed.

Brad continued interviewing the tiny but feisty older woman leaning on her walker.

"Now, I can't live on my own anymore, and I'll be moving into an assisted living facility." Ellie peered directly into the camera with a tear glistening in the corner of one eye. "I can't take my dear Trixi with me, and I want her to go to a good home, with someone special who will love her as much as I do." She faced Sam on-camera. "Someone like this lovely young woman."

"Yeah." Electra nodded vigorously. *Please, Sam, please!*

Brad went on to talk about some of the experiences from the group home kids at Clyde's, including snippets of the interviews with Electra, Robin, Sapphire, and how they'd been impacted by interacting with horses.

Electra bounced in her chair. "Look," she whispered to Sam. "That's me. Cool."

Her friend gave her a proud smile. Clyde flashed them a thumbs up, Mrs. Bruckner gave a smiling nod, and Horace beamed with a proud grandpa twinkle in his eyes.

Her attention reverted to the TV as Brad the narrator came on screen. "So, you can see what miraculous things can happen when horses—and kids—are rescued. But funds are short. Miss Ellie and Miss Moser need another miracle to save Trixi." The segment focused on a picture of Ellie and Sam talking, with Trixi in the background, reaching her head expectantly over the fence toward them. "Cowgirls Don't Cry" played as the photo faded and the credits rolled.

The Jersey Lilly group applauded and whistled. Everyone abandoned their tables and hurried over to congratulate Brad and hug Sam and Electra. "You were wonderful," Irene Bruckner gushed.

"Way to go, little gal!" Horace clapped Sam on the back and then hugged Electra whose face heated again.

"Good job." Clyde clasped Sam's hand. "I'm proud of you."

"Thank you. I really didn't do anything. This is all Brad."

Sam turned to him. "That was awesome. You… I…" Her voice choked, and she faced away.

Electra swallowed a lump. *Aww. Yeah, thanks, Brad.*

Irene encircled her friend with a warm hug. "It's okay," she murmured. "It's okay."

Sam leaned into the motherly embrace for a long moment, then she drew back, blinking rapidly. "Thanks." She faced Brad again. "Thank you again for all your help. I just hope… this will help find Trixi a good home."

No! The words hit her like a kick to the stomach. "B-b-but," Electra sputtered. Her voice rose as she continued. "Miss Ellie said she wants *us* to have her, and, and now you have that five hundred from Mr. Smythe and we could buy her and bring her here and she'd be so good for those kids from the group home and other kids and I want to learn to trick ride and…" Her words faded as she ran out of breath. "Please." Her eyes stung, and her lips quivered.

"I know, sweetie. I agree with you, and I'm really torn. There will be lots more expenses on top of the purchase of another horse. I'm not sure what I should do." Sam addressed the group. "I need to go home and think about this, sleep on it. Thanks again, everybody, for all your support. I do appreciate each one of you."

Electra's insides warred between dejection and hope. Would Sam make the "right" decision to buy Trixi? She followed her friend out the door, her breath locked in her chest. If only she had some way to make some money to help Sam get Trixi.

***

Clyde had told them to take the day off, so for breakfast Sam made pancakes—"flapjacks" as Grandpa Neil and Great Grandpa Jake called them, she explained.

"That's a good name. I like it." Electra grinned as she poured a stream of chokecherry syrup over hers.

"After we clean up, let's go for a little ride," her friend suggested.

"Can we?" Her heart jumped with anticipation. "Yeah! Let's!"

"We'll just go out a little ways and see how Apache manages," Sam said. "I don't want to fatigue him or hurt him."

She shook her head vehemently. "No way."

After saddling up, they rode the horses at a walk to the nearest pasture to check on the grass and water for Murdock's cows, which were part of the lease agreement with Murdock. Apache held his head high and flicked his ears back and forth as they talked. Electra felt his muscles ripple strong beneath her. She took in the fresh air, and her shoulders relaxed in the balmy sun. The weight of the world seemed to float away when she was outside, with a horse. This was the best way ever to celebrate getting her Apache back.

She chuckle-snorted. *Boy, have I changed—thinking, living, breathing horses. I wouldn't have been caught dead by my friends on a horse in New York.* Even though her mom had taken her on a few rides at a nearby stable, she simply hadn't warmed to the huge animals…not like she had with Apache. He was different. He needed her. He loved her—no matter what. *And I love him.*

"He's doing really well," Sam observed. "He's come a long way in a short time—thanks to you."

A laugh bubbled up from Electra's chest. "Thanks. I'm so glad to have him back."

After a few minutes, the cowgirl spoke. "I've made a decision."

"Oh yeah?" She held her breath, hoping to hear what she wanted.

"When we get back, I'm going to call Miss Ellie and tell

her I'll buy the horse."

"Yes!" Electra squealed, and Apache flinched. "Oh sorry, boy." She patted his neck and sat up in a more sedate manner. "What about the money? You won't have anything extra if… like if Apache or Sugar got sick or something."

Sam nodded. "I know. But I didn't have that money before the court ruled in my favor. So, it's kind of like a bonus now. And it's the exact amount I need to buy Trixi. I almost feel like it's a message, a gift…" she lifted her face to the sky with its wisps of angel hair clouds, "maybe from above."

"Cool." Electra studied the horizon. "I remember Mom saying one time that if you step out in faith, God will provide." It had been a while since Mom talked about God or that they'd even gone to church. She'd been convinced God had forgotten about her and Mom after Jimmy died and Dad left. Not much faith was left over with all the pain…until she'd come out here to Montana and witnessed the splendor of creation and seen the miracles horses could do. She'd found herself sending up little prayers every now and then. And it seemed to have worked in helping them get Apache back. Maybe God hadn't forgotten her after all.

"Wow." Sam's voice broke into her thoughts. "That sounds pretty wise. Let's hope it's true."

"Yeah."

After checking and counting the white-faced Herefords and their growing calves, the two reined the horses toward home.

Even though Electra tried to ride quietly, an aura of nervous energy thrummed inside. "Oh, Sam, I can't wait. I'm so excited. We're gonna get Trixi!"

Sam grinned. "I'll call Miss Ellie as soon as we get home."

She clapped her hands. "Ohmygosh I'm so excited. So *excited.*"

At the barn, they unsaddled and brushed the horses and then headed up to the house. Sam punched in the number and put the phone on speaker. Miss Ellie answered after the first ring. "Oh, Samantha, I'm so glad you called. I was hoping… I don't have your phone number."

"I've been doing a lot of thinking, and I've decided I want to buy Trixi." Sam explained her feelings about the "gift" and that she thought the horse was meant for her and Electra.

"What I wanted to tell you is my phone has been ringing off the hook this morning after that wonderful show," the older woman gushed. "I've had a number of offers for my horse…"

Sam's eyes went wide.

Electra gulped. Oh no. Had someone else come up with more money? She could barely breathe.

"But, my dear, none of them have come close to the feeling I have about you. I want *you* to have my Trixi."

"Oh!" Sam flashed Electra a thumbs-up. "Thank you."

Ohmygosh, yes! She squealed then clapped a hand over her mouth.

"I'm so happy. I knew the moment I met you that you were the right person." Ellie paused. "You won't regret it."

"I think you're right." Sam smiled.

Ellie chuckled. "So, Trixi is yours. With the caveat that I get to come visit her now and then."

Electra ran around the kitchen, whooping now.

Sam and Ellie both laughed. "I think your young friend is excited," Ellie said. "I am too."

"Me three!" Sam slapped her thigh. "And yes, you can come visit as often as you want. We'll even come to Billings to pick you up sometimes, if you'd like."

"That sounds just wonderful, my dear." The woman's voice hitched a little. "I can make my move now with a great deal of peace."

"I have to work the next couple days, but we'll come in Saturday to pick her up." Sam said her goodbyes and disconnected.

For a long moment, Electra, spent from celebrating, quivered in the doorway and stared at Sam. Then the cowgirl gave a whoop too and rushed to wrap her in a giant bear hug. Together they jumped up and down like two ten-year-old schoolgirls.

"I can't believe it! I can't believe it!" Electra's excitement built like flood waters in a creek. "I gotta call Mom. Is that okay?"

"Of course. You do that, and I'll make us some lunch."

CHAPTER SIXTEEN

Electra glanced up from drying dishes when she heard a vehicle outside. A white sedan pulled up the incline to the house.

Sam frowned, her hands poised above the soapy water as a man got out of the driver's side and walked around to the trunk. He took out a wheelchair and then opened the passenger door to help a woman out.

Puzzled, Electra leaned closer to the window. *Who the heck is that?*

Sam's mouth dropped open. "Kenny!" She grabbed the towel and wiped her hands as she headed to the door.

Huh? Who's Kenny? Electra followed as far as the opening.

Her friend's face was as pale as a sheet, and she gulped in short pants of air. She stood on the porch, simply staring at the pair below the steps.

"You look like you've seen a ghost," the woman said.

"Jace." Sam's voice was shaky. "Kenny. What are you doing here?"

The man grinned, his white teeth flashing through his tan. "You wouldn't return our calls, so we thought we'd come up for a visit and surprise you."

"Oh." Sam stood still. "Well…um… It's a…surprise all right."

"Can we come in?" Jace brushed back her shoulder-length jet-black hair.

"Um, yeah. Sorry. Yes, do come in."

Electra stared through the screen door. *Who are these people? Sam seems really upset.* Alarm bells jangled in her brain.

Kenny circled the wheelchair backwards and pulled it up the steps.

"Can we just sit out here on the porch?" Jace smiled at Sam. "It's such a beautiful afternoon, and Kenny told me all about how you guys restored this porch and the house."

As if in a daze, Sam nodded in slow motion. "Of course."

Electra opened the screen and joined Sam. "Hi. I'm Electra." She held out her hand to Jace and then Kenny. "Would you like some iced tea?"

"Oh. Yes. I'm sorry." Sam shook her head like a wet dog. "This is my friend Electra who is helping me out this summer. Iced tea sounds great, honey. Could you bring us all some?"

She went back into the house, returning in a few minutes with a tray of glasses and a plate of chocolate chip cookies. Curiosity wormed at her. *I sure want to know who these people are and why Sam is so upset to see them.*

Jace helped herself and bit into one. "Mmm. Home-made. Did you bake these?"

"Sam and I did." Electra sat on the porch swing next to her friend, scanning from Jace to Kenny and back again. "Do you guys like horses? We have two now. Sam already had Sugar, and we just rescued Apache. He was almost dead from starving and we had to go to court but now we have him and next we're going to Billings to buy Trixi, an awesome trick horse, she was going to maybe go to auction if we couldn't rescue her because her owner is going to a nursing home and—"

"Whoa." Jace held up her hand with a titter while Kenny guffawed from his perch on the porch railing. "Sounds like you two are quite the horse women. I always knew you loved horses, Sam. Take after your great grandma, huh?"

The cowgirl nodded. "I guess so. Yes. I can't stand to see any animal suffering."

Jace smiled. "Remember the time when we were kids, we went to this riding class, and you saw a baby bird on the ground? We just had to stop the whole group while you located its nest up in a tree, picked up the little creature with your gloves on so it wouldn't have your scent, and climbed up there to put it back."

A blush rose up Sam's neck. "I do remember that. The instructor was so 'by the book' and insisted we had to get back before a certain time, and I was holding up the lesson."

"Wow. That's so cool, Sam. You really are a rescuer." Admiration grew in Electra's mind.

Sam shook her head. "Well… I don't know about that. I do what I think needs to be done."

Jace gazed around the yard at the cottonwood trees rustling in the breeze, the corrals, and the red and white barn. "This is such a nice place. It's so peaceful." She leaned back in her wheelchair. I can understand why you don't want to leave."

Kenny snorted. "Well, you ain't seen the winters. Snow up to your neck and cold enough to freeze the brass ba—" he threw a quick glance at Electra—"er, doorknobs off a monkey. I darn near died out here…in the middle of nowhere." He gave Sam a piercing eye.

That sounds like an adventure story I'd like to hear. Electra swiveled her head from one to the other. *He doesn't seem like he'd fit in here, in Montana. He's not a cowboy, that's for sure.*

"Well—" Sam opened her mouth and stopped mid-word when a white pickup drove up the incline.

Brad.

Hmm. This is getting interesting. Electra frowned, a dark cloud of foreboding settling around her. Somehow, she couldn't imagine Brad and this Kenny guy being best buds.

Sam rose and walked to the edge of the porch as he got out of the vehicle and bounded up the stairs toward her.

"Hi, Sam." He gave her a quick peck on the cheek, then peered at the group staring at him.

"Hi, Brad." Electra called out. When Sam made no introductions, she continued, "These are Sam's friends from Phoenix, Jace and—"

"Kenny." He stood from the railing and stuck his hand out. "Sam's fiancé."

Brad's mouth dropped.

So did Electra's. *Her* fiancé? *She's never said anything about a Kenny or a fiancé.*

"No. I…" Sam stood frozen, her mouth opening and closing, no sounds coming out.

Brad's face went blank. "Oh. Well, I'm sorry to interrupt. Just had some news about the documentary. I'll talk to you later." He pivoted abruptly on his boot heel, strode to his pickup, and drove away, gears grinding and dust spraying behind the tires.

Electra's heart thundered like a racehorse. *Ohmygosh, this is bad, really bad.*

Sam took several strides off the porch, reaching after him. But he was gone.

Then she faced Kenny.

"That…was uncalled for. An out and out lie. You are NOT my fiancé." Her voice was icy. "You. *You* are the one who left me." She stomped up the stairs and took a wide stance in front of him. "*You* are the one who can't understand my connection with this ranch. *You* are the one who couldn't hack it here. You!" Her body shook visibly as though from an earthquake tremor.

He held out his hands, palms up. "Hey. I tried to compromise with you. Made all kinds of suggestions—come back to Phoenix and save up more money, spend winters there and summers here—"

Sam jabbed her finger into his chest. "You never intended to come back here. And I don't want you here now." Her voice rose with every syllable. "Get out! Get *out* off my property. I don't *ever* want to see you again."

Fear iced Electra's veins. *Whoa. She is really ticked off.*

Kenny took a step back. "Now, now, let's just talk a little—"

"No! I'm done talking. I've started my life here, by myself, thank you very much. Now get out of here. Go!" Sam screamed, her face flaming.

Ohmygosh! Who is this guy, and what did he do to Sam? She jammed trembling hands into her armpits. *He hurt my friend.* Leg muscles quivering, she fought the urge to go after him and pound on him, to scream at him too. Her feet twitched and nearly began to move on their own. *I really hate that jerk.*

He bounded down the steps and then looked at Jace.

She waved him off. "You go. I'll be fine."

Still shaking his head and muttering, he stomped to the car and roared off.

Electra could only stare as tears rolled down Sam's cheeks. Her friend stood rooted to the spot. Fear iced through her blood. She'd never seen the cowgirl so enraged.

"Sam? Sam?" Jace leaned forward in her chair, a worried expression on her face.

As gently as she could, Electra touched her friend's arm. "Are you okay?"

In slow motion, Sam swiveled her eyes to the side as if in a faraway daze. She allowed Electra to lead her to the porch swing and took the offered glass of iced tea with shaking fingers. Her breaths came rapidly, punctuated with tiny sobs.

Ohmygosh. What is happening? What can I do? Electra's throat constricted. She sat in the swing beside her friend and put an arm around her shoulders. Jace rolled her chair nearer and took her hands. Finally, Sam's breathing slowed, and her body stopped jittering.

She inhaled and let out a long sigh. Lifting her eyes from her lap, her mouth quivered. "I…guess I lost it."

Electra grinned. "Yeah, you kinda did. You were awesome."

"I think that needed doing." Jace squeezed her hands.

"Maybe…I guess." Sam shook her head. "But that's not me. I don't lose my cool—usually." Then she gasped. "Brad. He's gone. I let him go. I didn't stop him. I froze." Another tear followed the tracks on her cheek. "Oh my, what have I done?" She buried her face in her hands and sobbed again. Electra and Jace patted her and murmured soothing sounds.

Poor Sam. Electra's eyelids stung. She wanted to cry with her. *How can I help her?*

Finally, her friend leaned back in the swing. "I think I'm okay now. I'm… I'm sorry, you guys."

"No need to be sorry," Jace said.

Electra shook her head. "No, you don't." Deep inside, she understood the cowgirl's anger. After her dad left and she watched her mom's heart break, she'd wanted to find her dad and scream and yell at him. *Why do men do that to us?*

"What was Kenny thinking anyway? I never realized he was so manipulative. What a jerk! He's the one who left me, but he won't let go. He wanted things to go his way, not *ours.*" Sam took a long swig of tea.

"It does seem that way." Jace paused. "But he did get me here."

Sam swung her gaze toward her. "Yeah. What *are* you doing here? We haven't spoken in years."

Even more puzzling. Electra's mind whirled. *Wonder why not. And why is she here now?*

Lowering her head, Jace's dark hair fell forward. "I know. It's my fault. I'm sure you blamed yourself…for our fight, and what happened…" She gestured at her legs. "And for a while I did too. Anything to not have to own up to my own stupidity."

"I should've tried harder. Wrestled the keys away from you. Knocked you down. Something!" Sam shook her head vehemently. "But I didn't. I just let you go."

Electra peered at Jace, hunched in her wheelchair. "You were in a bad car accident?"

Jace nodded.

"My brother was killed in an accident. My dad blamed himself, and he went away." Electra bit her trembling lip.

"I'm so sorry." Jace sighed. Her navy-blue eyes clouded. "For years, I've been bitter, blaming everything and everybody. I pushed everyone away, just wallowed in self-pity. And I continued to drink…to numb the pain, the loss."

She gave a mirthless laugh. "But of course, that made everything worse. I lost everybody who tried to help. My own family gave up on me."

Sam grimaced. "And I left you too."

"About a year ago, I really hit bottom. I was living—well, existing—in an abandoned house, a foreclosure owned by the bank. Nobody ever came by, so a bunch of us just flopped there. Most everybody was on drugs. I did a little, but mostly booze—all I could afford."

"Oh my gosh, Jace. I had no idea." Anguish crumpled Sam's face.

"Nobody did." Her friend lifted one side of her mouth in a wry smile. "I got so sick. Malnourished, no heat, got pneumonia. I was fortunate that one of my roommates was finally sober enough one day to get me to the hospital."

Electra sat still, her eyes and mouth open in shock. She pressed a hand to her chest. *Would Dad end up like that? No, he wouldn't. He's a grownup with a job and…* No, she couldn't let herself go there.

"For the second time in my life I saw the white light and felt such a peace beckoning me. I almost followed." Jace shrugged. "But something called me back, and when I woke up, I realized I'd been given two second chances, and I'd better not blow this one."

Sam took her friend's hand.

"The chaplain came by every day. At first, I resisted the idea that I had a problem. One day he brought a 'friend' to visit. I was ticked when I found out she was in AA. But they both kept coming, and I had a lot of time to think about my situation. I've been going to meetings ever since." Her face lit up. "And I just got my one-year sobriety chip a week ago."

"That's wonderful." Sam gave her a hug. "I'm so happy for you." She huffed a little laugh. "And I was just about to offer to get us something stronger than tea, after all this."

Jace laughed. "Nope. Thanks, but that did not solve my problems. I can look back and see that I never wanted to take responsibility for my own actions. Taking another drink was my way of escaping."

Sam inhaled sharply and glanced toward the kitchen.

Electra tipped her head. The vodka bottle. *Jace is right.* It didn't help Dad. And it wouldn't help Sam either.

"Trouble had a way of always finding me, no matter how hard I tried to get away." Jace took a sip of her iced tea. "Anyway, you've heard of the twelve-step program, right?"

Sam nodded.

"One of the steps is to make amends to the people you've harmed with your addiction."

Sam blinked and cocked an eyebrow.

Electra listened intently. *Twelve step? Amends?* This was a lot to take in, but she was fascinated by their conversation.

"You were my best friend. I pushed you away. You were hurt by my actions and my accident. I haven't been able to find a way to get here before now, but I wanted to apologize in person to make things right." She brushed a strand of dark hair out of her eyes. "I hope you'll forgive me."

Sam stifled a gasp with a hand over her mouth. Silence hung over the women. "I..." Her voice squeaked. "Forgive *you?* I don't think *you* need forgiveness. I—"

"Yes, I do." Jace's eyes glistened. "I can't move on and heal—mentally or spiritually—until I own what I did and receive atonement."

Listening to the two friends, confusion and hope rose and fell in the aching void of Electra's heart. *Forgiveness. Atonement.* What could that be about in her life?

Sam leaned forward and took Jace's hands. "Of course, I forgive you. But...I am to blame for our relationship dying too." Her eyes filled with tears. "Will you forgive me?"

Her friend nodded. "Yes. I forgive you."

They embraced for a long moment.

Ohmygosh. Could it be that simple? Tears tickled her cheeks, but Electra smiled. "That is so cool. I'm so glad." She inhaled loudly. "I wonder if Mom knows how to contact Dad. Maybe if he... Do you think I...?" Her heart expanded with hope. She stood. "I'm going to go call Mom. If that's okay."

Sam stroked her arm. "Yes. Call your mom."

***

A silence followed after Electra told her mother about Jace and Sam. When she spoke, her voice was husky. "Oh, honey, that's lovely for them. Yes, I know about AA and their twelve-step program. It's a good one, very healing for many people."

"Do you think Dad would…?"

"It has to be the person's idea. They have to *want* to change. There's nothing anyone can do to force it."

***

The women sat on the porch the rest of the afternoon, sipping iced tea from tall glasses Electra kept refilled and catching up on their lives as the sun dipped toward the far butte and painted it with molten gold. Even though she found their conversation fascinating and heart-tugging, she broke in. "I'm getting hungry. What if I fix some hotdogs?"

Sam leaned back in the swing and laughed. "I've completely lost track of time. Let's go inside and have some supper. Yes, please get the hotdogs started, and I'll make a potato salad from the leftover spuds." She opened the screen door for Jace to wheel through.

"Say, did you talk to your mom?" Sam followed her inside.

"Yeah. But she said she didn't know how to get ahold of Dad." She gave Jace a tiny smile. "But maybe if he gets to a certain point, like you did, he'll call us."

"Yes." Jace smiled back. "I think he will."

A hummingbird pulse fluttered in her throat. *Oh, I hope so. Please let him be okay.*

After supper and visiting until late, Sam changed the sheets on her bed downstairs for Jace and spread out a cushion and sleeping bag in the second bedroom upstairs for herself.

Electra frowned. "You take my bed. I can sleep better than you on the floor."

Sam gave her a hug. "You're so sweet. I'll be okay. You don't need to do that."

"No. I want to. It'll be like camping." Electra stripped the sheets off her bed for Sam. "I like camping."

CHAPTER SEVENTEEN

The next morning, Electra lurked just around the doorway as Sam made a phone call. After a long minute, she heard her friend take a ragged breath. "Brad, it's Sam. I need to talk to you. Things are not what they seem." A pause. "I'm sorry. Please. Call me."

Electra sent up a quick prayer. *Please, God, help them get together.* Prayer *had* worked for Apache, maybe it would again.

With reassurances from Jace that she'd be all right by herself, Sam and Electra headed off to work at Clyde's.

Arriving home again that evening, Sam's head immediately swung toward the answering machine. No blinking light.

Oh dear. What is that Brad doing? Did he really believe that jerk?

The cowgirl hugged Jace. "Did anyone call today?"

"Nope. Not even a telemarketer." Her friend gave Sam a curious glance. "No word from Brad?"

Sam shook her head and busied herself fixing tomato soup and grilled cheese sandwiches.

The rest of the week followed suit. No phone call from Brad. Electra's heart ached for her friend. *C'mon, Brad, please call! You gotta know the truth.*

At the end of the week, they stopped at Horace's to pick up the horse trailer.

Electra danced on the balls of her feet. "Yeah! We get to go get Trixi tomorrow. Yay!"

Horace chuckled. "You gals have fun. Drive safe now, ya hear?"

***

The next morning, Sam loaded Jace's wheelchair in the back of the pickup and helped her into the passenger side. Electra slid to the middle, and they took off for Billings. She and Jace chattered about horses and life on the ranch versus the anthill hustle in the city.

Sam drove without a word, not responding to Electra's questions. She tried again. "Will Miss Ellie teach us the commands for Trixi, so I can learn trick riding? …huh, Sam?"

"What? Sorry, didn't hear you."

She repeated her question.

The cowgirl glanced at her. "Yes, I'm sure she will."

Electra squirmed in the seat. "I can't wait! Can't you drive faster?" *Another horse to rescue and work with and love. I really, really can't wait.*

"Not towing that trailer." Jace looked out the side window. "I don't want to be in another wreck."

Oops. "Oh, sorry." *Sore subject. My bad.*

Jace chuckled and cuffed Electra's shoulder. "It's okay. Just joking. Sam's a good driver." She turned up the radio, and they sang along as they covered the last miles to town.

***

A plump, motherly woman met them at the door. "Hi, I'm Doris, Ellie's caregiver. Come on in. She's so excited to see you."

Electra ran into the living room and gave the old woman a hug and a kiss on the cheek. "Hello, dear."

Sam introduced Jace.

"Good to meet you." She beamed at them. "This is a happy day indeed. I'm going to move to the Manor on Monday, and now I know Trixi will have a good home." She scooted forward in her chair and grabbed her walker. "Doris, get the girls some carrots, please. Let's go out to the patio, and you can say hello to her."

Doris helped her up, and Sam pushed Jace's wheelchair outside. Electra immediately hurried to the fence and whistled. Out in the pasture, Trixi's head lifted from grazing, her blonde mane shifting in the breeze. She trotted to Electra's outstretched hand and lipped a carrot from her palm. Sam joined them and caressed the mare's face and scratched behind her ears. Trixi blew softly and leaned into her.

Oh, she's so beautiful. Electra exchanged a glance with her friend. "I can't believe we're getting her."

"I know. Me too. Let's help Miss Ellie get a little closer, and she can show us some of her signals."

The caretaker brought a patio chair out into the yard, and Miss Ellie shuffled out to it. Jace's chair bumped over the grass to join her.

"Okay, the first thing. If you want her to lie down so you can get on, you do this." She made a motion, and the horse got down. She motioned again, and Trixi stood. "Now you try it."

Electra swung her gaze to Sam. Anticipation bubbled like a spring. "Can I?"

"Of course. And when you're on her back you can signal her by touching her, like this." Again Ellie demonstrated.

After murmuring to the mare softly, "Good girl," she mimicked Miss Ellie's hand motion, and Trixi lay down again. Electra climbed on, they rose and walked around the pasture.

"Good job." Ellie beamed her approval.

Jace's eyes were wide. "Wow. That is awesome."

Oh, yes, this is awesome. Electra's breath floated through her smiling lips. *If Mom could see me now.* A few months ago, she was a cynical Goth-girl, didn't know anything about horses, didn't like horses…*and now I'm riding a trick horse.*

Sam nodded. "Isn't it though? I'm so impressed, Miss Ellie. I wish I could've seen some of your exhibitions."

Me too! I want to do that. She pictured herself hanging from the side of the mare, like Miss Ellie in the pictures. *That'd be so cool.*

The woman's white curls bobbed. "Oh, it was a thing of beauty. And most of all, we had such fun together. She's really my favorite of all my trick horses. She understood me almost immediately, like we were one."

Ellie continued with her lessons, first Electra, and then Sam giving the signals. Jace applauded with each successful execution.

At last, Sam circled back to the old woman's side. "Well, I suppose we should get her loaded and get on the road before it gets too late. Let me grab my purse, and I'll write you a check."

"Oh, my dear, I almost forgot." Ellie gave a cackle of delight. "You know that program that delightful young man did—Brad, was it?—it has resulted in several very nice donations. But when I contacted the people to try to return the money, they wouldn't accept it."

Electra furrowed her forehead. *What does this mean? Is Miss Ellie going to keep the horse now?* Her heart was a lead weight.

"You mean you're not…?" Sam's face had turned ghostly.

Ellie peered at the cowgirl. "Goodness gracious, you look like you've been hit with a horseshoe. I'm not reneging on the deal. You still have a horse, a wonderful horse. But…" she smiled, "…I'm not taking your money. I'm set up pretty well now with this windfall, and with the sale of my house, I'll be comfortable in my 'golden years.'"

Sam shook her head, her face still scrunched in disbelief. "What did you say?"

Ellie laughed. "I'm giving you my horse, dear. You don't owe me a dime. Just take good care of my baby."

Relief flooded Electra like a warm summer shower. "Yippee!"

"Oh." Sam's shoulders lowered. "Oh, my goodness. Are you sure? I mean…"

"Of course, silly girl. But I'm going to be coming out to visit…often." Ellie stood. "Before you take off, please come in and have some coffee and cookies. Doris baked them in your honor."

Sam giggled and nudged Electra's arm. "We'd love some. C'mon, girls."

"Yeah!" Electra skipped ahead to the house, sing-songing, "We're getting Trixi, we're getting Trixi."

***

Electra kept swiveling her head and craning her neck to stare back at the horse trailer. "I just can't believe this. Can you believe it, Sam? Can you, Jace? We got Trixi, and Miss Ellie *gave* her to us. I can't believe it!" Delight jingle-jangled through her body. She squealed.

Sam exchanged a grin with Jace. "I know. Isn't that the best thing ever?"

"I can't wait to get home. I want to try all those things I learned. I want to be a trick rider like Miss Ellie. Do you think I can?" Electra spoke to Jace.

Jace nodded. "Yes, I do. You are an incredibly determined young woman, and I know you can do whatever you set your heart on."

"I agree," Sam said, "absolutely."

They're talking to me? She blinked. "Aww, thanks." A

tender spot opened in her chest. No one had ever said anything like that to her. For once, she couldn't say a word, simply sat, basking in the afterglow of the compliments and the headiness of the day.

When they got home, Sam unloaded the wheelchair and helped Jace into it so she could watch the unloading procedure. She backed the trailer up to the chute, getting it aligned after a couple of false starts.

Electra was out of the truck, climbed over the fence, and was trying to open the doors by the time her friend came around. "Hey, Trixi, you're home now, hey, girl," she crooned.

"Take it slow now. We don't want to scare her." Sam unlatched the fasteners and talked softly to the mare as she moved close to her head to untie the halter rope. Trixi blew, and as if on cue, backed out of the trailer. "Good girl. Easy as pie. You're so well-trained." The cowgirl led her into the corral. "Such a good horse." She patted her neck.

"Can I ride her now?" Electra's body reverberated. "I just can't wait, I'm so excited!"

"Let's let her roam the corral for a while and get used to her new surroundings, meet the other horses over the fence. Later I'll take her into the barn and feed her. She's really a good horse, but we need to let her be for a bit." Sam pushed Jace up the incline. "Let's go in and fix supper. It's been a long day."

"Okay. But tomorrow… Tomorrow I want to ride her." *A new horse to ride, a trick one. Oh, I can't wait.* She hopped and skipped beside the other two like a six-year-old with a new toy.

As they entered the kitchen, Sam's head automatically shifted toward the answer phone. The blinking light beckoned.

Electra held her breath. *Oh! Good. Maybe…*

Her friend clicked the play button. "Hey, Sam, it's Brad." The baritone voice came over the speaker. Sam had a hopeful, raised-brow look on her face.

"Sorry, I didn't get your message until today. I've been working out of state, out of cell range. Uh…anyway, I'd like to talk. I left a message on your cell too. Give me a call."

"I didn't get any message." Sam fished her phone out of her pocket. "Oh, I forgot to charge it last night." She explained to Jace, "With no cell service here at the ranch, it's hard to remember sometimes."

Electra arched her forehead. "Are you going to call him?" His message sounded promising. *He wants to talk to her.* She crossed her fingers.

Sam's head jittered in small movements up and down. "I think so." She sat abruptly. "Oh my. I don't know. Maybe we should…" she peered at her friends, "…should eat first."

"No!" Electra nearly shouted, but then flashed her a pleading look.

Jace laughed. "Call him now. We'll go in the living room and give you some privacy." She wheeled her chair around and beckoned Electra with her head.

When Sam came into the room, she was chewing her lip. "He wants to talk. He's coming out tomorrow afternoon."

"That's great." Jace raised her fingers in a V sign.

"Yippee!" Electra bounced on the sofa. "About time." Happiness for her friend welled up inside like bubbles.

***

The next morning, Electra could barely take two bites of oatmeal before she fixed her focus on Sam. "Can we go out and work with Trixi now?"

The corners of Sam's mouth twitched. "Well, I don't see why not. But," she quickly added as Electra picked up her still-full bowl and pushed back her chair, "you need to finish breakfast first."

"Aww." Electra slumped back into her chair, but then straightened her shoulders. "Okay. We need nourishment to work, right?"

"You're absolutely right." Electra saw Jace's grin even though she quickly put her napkin over her mouth. "I think I'll have another piece of toast. Watching you guys is going to take a lot of fuel."

Sam chuckled and passed her the plate of buttered toast and the strawberry jam.

Soon the three were on their way to the corral, Electra leading the way. She inhaled deeply the familiar perfume of the dried grass, musty corrals, and horses. The sun hung bright in the clear blue sky.

Trixi hung her head over the fence where Apache and Sugar stood on the other side, like gossipy old ladies. Electra climbed into the corral and approached Trixi with a cake pellet. She scratched the mare's neck, then leaned through the fence to give Apache and Sugar treats. She spoke to Sam who wheeled Jace through the gate. "I probably should brush Apache first. I don't want him to be jealous."

Sam nodded. "Good idea. Let's give our babies some attention before we start working with Trixi." She let the two horses into an adjoining pen.

Electra hugged Apache and gazed lovingly into his dark, expressive eyes. "You're my boy. I'm not abandoning you. We'll go for a ride a little later, okay?" The gelding nuzzled her neck, and happiness unfolded like a flower.

After she and Sam spent a half hour grooming the two horses, Trixi whinnied from the other side. Electra laughed. "Okay, girl, it's your turn now."

She offered Jace a brush. "Want to help?"

The young woman's face lit up. "Sure." She wheeled closer. While Electra and Sam worked on Trixi's withers and back, Jace brushed the horse's shoulder and caressed her legs. Trixi stood patiently, contentment on her face. "Such a pretty girl," Jace murmured, "such a good girl. I wish I could ride you."

Sam and Electra stopped mid-brush and exchanged a glance. "Why couldn't she?" Electra asked.

Sam hesitated a moment. "Oh. Well. I don't know. Maybe it's not…"

Electra squatted beside Jace's chair. "Why not? Trixi is trained to lie down. We can help you get on, and we'll be right here beside you. Do you want to?"

The young woman's eyes widened. "I would." Then to Sam. "Can I? Please?"

At the cowgirl's continued hesitation, Electra pleaded, "Sam. Trixi is meant for this. Don't you see? We were meant to get her because of Jace. C'mon. Let's do it."

Sam let out a fluttery breath. "Well, okay. Go get your saddle and bridle." She reached out and touched Jace's shoulder. "You sure you want to?"

"Absolutely." Jace nodded. "Nothing ventured, nothing gained, right?"

Electra raced to the barn and back, saddled the horse, and gave Trixi the signal. With a nod, the mare bent one knee, then the other, and came to a rest on the ground with all fours under her. Jace wheeled up closer to her side, scooted her body to the edge of her chair, and with her arms, lifted her right leg onto the saddle. Sam stepped forward to help her, but she shook her head. "Let me try. If I start to fall, catch me." She grinned, grabbed the horn with one hand and the cantle with the other. With a grunt, she heaved herself up and inched her way to a sitting position on the saddle.

"Woohoo!" Electra high-fived her. "You did it."

Sam clapped. "Good job. That's great."

Electra gave the signal, and Trixi stood. Sam and Electra put Jace's feet into the stirrups, which were the perfect length. Jace gave the reins a bit of slack and clucked, and she rode around the corral, first at a walk, then a trot, reining like a pro.

"Ohmygosh, ohmygosh!" Electra's body vibrated with excitement. "She's riding. Do you see that? She's riding."

Sam broke into a grin and whooped. "Yes! She's riding. Jace, you're riding!"

Jace cantered up to them and reined the horse in. Her face glowed. "This…this is amazing. Thank you." Tears glistened in her eyes. "Thank you so much."

They took a break for lunch, and after a short nap for Jace, she wheeled back out to the porch where Sam paced, and Electra sat. "Could we go for a real ride, the three of us?" she asked.

Electra jumped up from the swing. "Yeah. Let's."

Sam peeked at her watch.

Jace gave her a sly smile. "It'll keep your mind off Brad…"

Sam shook her head and laughed. "You're right. Okay. We have time for a short ride."

Once again, Trixi got down into a sitting position, and Jace pulled herself onto the saddle. She wiped the sweat from her forehead. "Hard work." She gave the signal, and Trixi stood.

Electra led Apache and Sugar into the corral, already saddled, and she and Sam mounted. The horses ambled calmly through the pasture toward the small, nearly dry reservoir nearby. A gentle breeze cooled the hot August sun, insects whirred and clicked as hooves disturbed their resting places, and meadowlarks trilled to each other from their perches on fence posts.

She led the procession with a feeling of weightlessness. *I'm riding my Apache, I'm with my Sam and my new friends Jace and*

Trixi. This is the best day ever. Who needs Goth-girls when I have all this? She shook her head. They would *never* in a million years get it.

Sam rode beside her old friend, keeping a close eye on her balance. Jace sat strong in the saddle, with no problems.

"What a beautiful day. I love this place." The young woman beamed. "I feel whole. For the first time in years, I'm not handicapped. I feel normal."

Electra's eyes stung. She tried to speak but the words stuck in her throat. A sensation like warm light flowed through her body. *This was meant to be.*

Sam took Jace's hand and gave it a squeeze. Lifting her head skyward, she whispered, "Thank you."

Electra's heart swelled with pride. *Yes, thank you!*

***

As they rode up a small rise back toward the corral, Electra saw the white pickup parked by the barn. "Brad's here," she shouted and urged Apache into a trot.

When he saw them, he smiled and touched a finger to his hat.

She immediately went to work unsaddling Apache and talking at Brad a mile a minute. "Do you see this? Jace is riding and Trixi is perfect for her. She gets down and lets her get on. Oh, it's so cool. Just watch." She pointed at the pair as Trixi lowered herself to the ground.

Brad stepped forward, his hand out, but Electra stopped him. "It's okay."

Jace slipped out of the saddle and maneuvered herself back into her chair, with Sam's help.

Brad gave an appreciative whistle and flashed a thumbs-up as Sam and her friend approached him. "Awesome, ladies." He switched his penetrating gaze to the cowgirl. "Hello, Sam." His voice was even, friendly.

Sam's neck and face reddened. "H-hi, Brad. How ya

doing?" She handed Electra Sugar's reins. "Would you go ahead and unsaddle all the horses, and maybe you and Jace could brush them? Thanks."

"Let's take a walk." Brad touched her arm to guide her, and they headed out into the pasture, dried grass crunching under their boots.

"I'd sure like to be a mouse in her pocket." Jace tittered. "They like each other…a lot, but I don't know if they know that yet."

Electra gave a tiny squeal. "Yeah, they do. And no, they don't know it, at least Sam doesn't." She giggled.

About a half hour later, the couple sprinted toward the barn, holding hands, and laughing.

Electra exchanged a glance with Jace as they waited expectantly by the corral gate.

"Well?" She peered into Brad's face and then Sam's. *It must have been okay.*

"Brad just gave me the most wonderful news."

"Yeah? What?" Electra held her breath.

Sam held up a piece of paper that read *Bank Statement.* "We…have…money." Her voice choked, and she stopped, brushing her cheek with the back of her hand.

"Money?" *Ohmygosh, how did that happen? What's going on?*

Brad stepped in. "As a result of my program about Miss Ellie and Sam's rescue horses, the donations have been pouring in. I set up a bank account"—he faced the cowgirl—"and now you can take care of the three horses you own without worrying about whether you can feed yourself too."

Sam sniffled, giving him a—what? adoring—look.

Ohmygosh! Her dreams are coming true. Electra whooped and leaped in the air, her fist shooting toward the clouds.

Brad stood off to the side, grinning broadly.

Jace applauded and wheeled closer to him. "You're our hero."

"Naw. I'm just the messenger." He stared down at the ground, a flush rising to his cheeks.

Sam touched his arm. "Yes, you are a hero. Without your pictures, I probably wouldn't have gotten Apache back, and without your feature story, I wouldn't have this." She waved the paper. "I have steaks in the freezer. Let's go up to the house and celebrate. I'll call Teresa and have her come over too."

She set up a table on the front porch, and Brad barbecued the steaks. Teresa arrived with a bottle of wine, sparkling juice, and corn on the cob. Soon they were laughing and eating, toasting Brad who kept denying his hero status.

Electra couldn't help giggling at his discomfort. *He's not so bad after all.*

"So, what are you going to do with the money?" Teresa pushed her plate back and leaned toward her. "Invest it, buy the ranch, more horses?"

"More horses. Yes!" Electra grinned.

Sam shook her head. "I don't know. I haven't had much time to think about it." She chuckled. "I could afford the breeding fee for Sugar now, and maybe I could start my Thoroughbred herd."

Brad cocked his head to the side. "Thoroughbreds, huh?"

"Like racehorses? Like Sugar?" Electra widened her eyes. *That'd be cool.*

"Yeah, it's been a dream of mine for a long time." Sam gazed out over the maize-colored prairie. "But I have to be practical too. It wouldn't take long to burn through the money if I just go chasing dreams. I have a lot of thinking to do."

"Well, now you can follow your dream, wherever it takes you." Jace gave her friend a happy smile.

The group sat visiting by lantern light as the moon rose and stars dotted the darkened sky. Finally, Brad stood. "I'd better let you ladies get your beauty rest.”

“Yeah, we have to work tomorrow. Another group of dudes coming in this week.” Sam nudged her. “And your mom will be here Friday.”

She nodded, suddenly unable to speak. Her eyes welled up and threatened to spill. Sam put an arm around her shoulder.

“I don’t want to go.” She sniffed. “I mean, I’m really happy to be seeing Mom, but…” Her voice broke, and she buried her face in Sam’s shoulder. “I’ll miss you,” her words muffled.

The cowgirl rocked her in a hug as she sobbed out her already-growing loneliness.

CHAPTER EIGHTEEN

Friday lunch at Clyde's was a hubbub of conversation and laughter as the three visiting families rehashed their week. "Such fun!" "Never thought I'd enjoy being out in the middle of nowhere, but I want to come back." "When does hunting season start?" "Can we go for one last ride this afternoon?"

As Electra swallowed the last bite of her sandwich, a white car drove into the parking area. A dark-haired woman got out and stretched.

"Mom!" Electra shrieked and ran toward her, and they enveloped each other with a long hug and tears. Then she broke the embrace and pulled her mother by the hand toward the picnic area. "Come and meet our clients and there's Sam and oh, Mom, you gotta come to our place and meet Apache and Trixi and just wait till you see what we've been doing."

Sam snickered as she stood and greeted her mom with a hug. "Welcome back."

"Oh, it's so good to be here. I've been looking forward to this ever since I left." She gave her a huge smile, hugging Electra close with one arm. "This one has grown a couple inches, I think."

"Mom, Sam and I are going to take the kids out for a short ride now. Do you want to come along?"

"I sure do. Let me go get my boots out of the car."

"Your mom would probably like some lunch before we go." Sam addressed her mother. "Have you eaten?"

"No. A sandwich would be great."

After Mom had eaten and Sam rounded up the kids, they took off for their ride over the sun-kissed prairie, trotting through low coulees and over rolling hills.

Electra rode ahead but close enough she could hear her mother say, "I can't believe the change in her. It is absolutely night and day. I really felt bad leaving her with you last spring, with her attitude the way it was. She's a different person."

My attitude? She snorted. *Yeah, I guess I was kind of a beast.* But she had to admit she *had* changed. *Things are so different here. I like it better.* She couldn't explain it, but she felt at home, at peace.

Sam replied, "It was Apache, our rescue. Those two bonded immediately. She helped save his life."

"And he saved hers."

"Yes, he did."

Sunshine flooded her soul. *Yeah, I'm so glad we got him back. He's my best bud. And Mom noticed.* She nudged her horse into a trot and bounced over the golden prairie.

When the group returned to the corrals, a familiar dark-haired figure leaned against the poles near a white truck. Electra threw up a hand to greet Brad.

"Hey, Brad." Sam waved as she trotted by him and stopped by the barn to unsaddle and supervise the kids as they untacked.

Electra bounded over to him, her mother in tow. "This is my mom. Mom, this is Brad." She emphasized his name.

"Alberta." She put out a hand to shake.

Sam came beside them. "Thanks for introducing your mom, Electra. Let's go see what Clyde needs us to do to get everyone ready for the hayride and barbecue."

"Sure. You're coming too, aren't you, Brad?"

He nodded. "Wouldn't miss it."

She caught his grin as he asked the cowgirl, "Good week?"

"Pretty good. This bunch hasn't been as…challenging as some." Sam sighed. "But I'm still glad the week is over."

He touched her arm. "I missed you."

Electricity skittered through Electra's chest. *Oooh. All lovey-dovey again.*

"Yeah. Me too." Sam swiveled her head toward the group. "Um… I'd better go up and help."

"Sure. I'll tag along, if you don't mind." He fell in step beside her.

Electra giggled as she dashed toward the house.

For the next hour, they all bustled around, helping Irene load food into the old-fashioned, canvas-domed chuck wagon while Clyde and Brad hefted hay bales onto the other flatbed wagon and hitched up the team.

"Okay, everybody," Clyde announced. "Time to load up."

The kids ran to the hay wagon, jostling each other to be the first and get the best seat in front. The adults followed somewhat more sedately but climbed aboard with enthusiastic shouts and laughter.

After helping Jace onto the seat beside Irene, Sam and Electra jumped onto the hay wagon as well, and the procession took off toward the rocky outcrops in the pasture, where Clyde had prepared a fire ring. The early evening sun hung low on the horizon and painted a golden promise of a spectacular sunset. The breeze cooled the day's heat, and crickets chirped a symphony in the sage.

At the site, everyone piled out. Irene opened the back of

the chuck wagon, and Electra hung back with her mom, clutching her hand as they watched Sam help the ranch woman open the steaming pot of barbecued beans, bowls of potato salad, baskets of home-made rolls, and all the fixin's. Clyde dug into the fire pit and brought out foil-wrapped packages of beef. The aroma made Electra's mouth water and her stomach rumble. *I'm going to miss stuff like this.*

The families and their kids fell in line to dish up, exclaiming over every platter and bowl. Carrying heaping plates, they settled on logs around the campfire, and dug in with enthusiasm.

Brad approached Sam and Jace, Electra and her mom with a loaded plate. "May I join you ladies?"

Before Sam could respond, Electra jumped in. "Sure, Brad." Between bites and "mmm's" of ecstasy over the melt-in-the-mouth beef, she smirked to see Sam stealing glances at Brad, him doing the same. She averted her gaze to hide her smile to catch Mom covering hers with a napkin.

"So, have you thought any more about what to do with your money?" he ventured after half his plate was emptied.

"Oh. Yeah. Had an interesting conversation with Clyde. He suggested starting a non-profit to continue my work with kids and horses." She related her boss's proposal to partner in the endeavor and idea to meet with his accountant. "I hadn't really thought of that angle, but it is something that intrigues me."

"But of course." Brad set his plate on the ground. "It's a natural. *You're* a natural. And you have a great start already."

Electra jiggled on the log beside them. "Well, *yeah!* It's a no-brainer. Right, Mom?"

Her mother stroked her chin thoughtfully. "I agree. You already have clientele. Why not create a business out of it?"

Sam shrugged. "I don't know if I could pull it off as a going concern. This is such an out-of-the way area. Where would I find clients? What about wintertime?"

Brad's chocolate eyes gazed into Sam's. "You can do it. I have confidence in you. With Clyde's help—he already has his dude ranch clientele—and I'll help in any way I can, you can do it."

"And Mom's an accountant. I'll bet she can give you some good advice." Electra nodded like a woodpecker, punctuating the air with her fork.

"I would certainly be honored." Mom squeezed the cowgirl's shoulder. "You've done such good work with this one here, and I know you have great potential in working with other kids that need healing, and you and your horses are such a big part of that."

Sam's neck turned rosy. "You guys really think I can do this?"

"Absolutely!" Brad bumped his fist on his thigh. "It's settled then. You've got a plan."

"Yeah! Go for it." Electra high-fived her friend. "And I wanna come back and help, okay, Mom?" She focused her best beseeching look on her mother.

Her mom chuckled. "Okay. Next summer. You got a deal."

***

That evening, the women gathered in Sam's kitchen over lemonade, all chattering about the highlights of the day and her plans for the future.

"You know what?" Jace gazed up at her friend from her wheelchair. "Ever since we went for that ride, and I realized how 'normal' it made me feel, I've been thinking. You have a golden opportunity here. You can use Trixi to work with disabled people."

"Yeah!" Electra bounced in her chair. "Isn't that what I said about getting her?"

Sam appeared to be thinking. Then, "You're right. That

opens up new possibilities."

"I think you should take Clyde up on his offer to work with him on the dude ranch, at least until you can build up your facilities here," Mom suggested. "That way, you could build up your clientele and save some money at the same time."

Gee, Mom sure is smart. That's a great idea.

"Oh wow. So much to think about. So many plans to make." Sam's eyes shone bright.

Ohmygosh! This is huge. Then a dark cloud hovered momentarily. *I want to be a part of this…so bad!*

Sam pushed back her chair with a loud scrape. With a big grin, she walked to the high cupboard and took out the vodka bottle.

Electra's mouth fell open. She stood, ready to—what? Stop her?

"Uh… Sam…" Jace stammered.

The cowgirl pivoted to the sink and upended the bottle, spilling the remainder of the liquor down the drain. Then she lifted the empty bottle toward the women. "I no longer need this. Here's to a bright future. A new beginning. For all of us. We have so much to be thankful for, to look forward to. To my friends." She raised the bottle high, then dropped it in the garbage.

Electra wilted into her chair. Jace began a slow, rhythmic clap. Mom joined in, and after several beats, so did she. "Woohoo!" she yelped. "Here's to you, Sam, rescuer 'extraordinaire' as Brad calls you."

They all raised their lemonade glasses in a toast. "To the future!"

CHAPTER NINETEEN

An empty ache tugged at Electra as she and her mom left Sam and walked to the boarding gate. She peeked over her shoulder at her friend who swiped at her cheek with the back of her hand. Tears prickled in her own eyes, and she touched her cowgirl hat with two fingers, like Horace and Clyde and Brad would do.

She slumped into the plane seat, buckled her belt, and peered out the window, hoping to catch a glimpse of Sam at the terminal windows. The sun shone white-hot through the clear turquoise Montana sky.

Mom leaned over her to peer out the window too. "Well, back to the smog and rat race of the city, huh?"

"Meh," Electra grumped. "I wish I could stay here."

Patting her knee, her mother sighed. "Me too, honey. This is such a beautiful state, so pristine, so unhurried…so unspoiled. I like it here too."

"Why don't we move here?" The idea perked her dejected attitude.

"Oh, gosh, wouldn't that be nice. I'd love to get out of the city rat race. But…my work is in New York. I can't see a lot of need for a corporate accountant in Ingomar, Montana."

Electra frowned. "Don't ranchers need accountants too? Didn't Sam say she was going to talk to one about her idea of working with clients and horses?"

"Well, yes, they do, but that would be on such a small scale, compared to what I do. I don't know that I could make a living for us here. You know, keep us in the manner to which we've become accustomed." She winked.

"Hmmph." Electra leaned back in the seat and closed her eyes as the plane taxied for takeoff. The summer played across her mind like a video—finding and rescuing Apache and helping him heal, losing him and then getting him back, only to have to go home now. *He's* my *horse*. She didn't understand how that happened. She'd never had a desire to ride, to be around horses before, even though she and Mom had done some riding. It wasn't something you thought about in the city.

But that first meeting with the broken-spirited, emaciated, nearly-dead animal, and how he peered into her very soul with his huge, liquid brown eyes… An immediate sense of kinship had darted into her heart. She couldn't have escaped it if she'd wanted to. And she didn't want to. It wasn't something she could explain to her mom. Nobody else would understand…except Sam. And maybe Sapphire and Wendy. *How am I going to relate to my friends back home now that I've had this?*

***

The first day back to school, Electra dressed in jeans, a western shirt, and her boots, trying to hold on to her strong connection to the west. She knew she'd be inviting comments. She shrugged. *I don't care. I'm a cowgirl now.*

But she wasn't prepared.

Her little group of Goth-girls passed by her in the hall without acknowledgment, all still dressed in their various black costumes, pale makeup, and black-rimmed eyes. Then

Ashley stopped in mid-stride, swiveled on a chunky black heel, and faced her, mouth open wide. "Electra? Is that *you?*"

The other girls switched direction as well, staring at her as if she were an alien from Mars.

"*What* are you wearing?" Josclyn screeched.

"You look like a hayseed from an old western movie." Ashley's black-lipsticked mouth curled in a sneer. The others tittered.

The words deflated her confidence like a pinprick to a balloon. She tried to explain. "Well, I did spend the summer on a ranch in Montana."

Snorts. "Lame." "Outta place." They turned as a choreographed unit and slouched down the hall, giggling and making rude, gagging noises. "Not Goth." "Definitely not Goth."

Behind their backs, she made a face and stuck out her tongue at them. But it didn't help. Pain hit her like a horse kick in the stomach. She'd wondered how her change would affect her friendships. *This was a mistake. Now I don't fit in anywhere. Dumb, dumb, dumb!* Tears stung her eyelids. She bit the inside of her cheek until she tasted the coppery acid of blood. *Nope. Not gonna cry. Not gonna let this get to me.* She marched to her class, head high, shoulders back. But when she slid into her desk, the titters of the Goth-girls wafted her way. She dug her fingernails into her upper arms through the shirt sleeves as hard as she could.

At home, she roamed the hallway, once again tapping on Jimmy's bedroom door as she passed. She couldn't go inside. Pain grew like a carnivorous plant in a sci-fi horror movie. It hovered; it stole into the crevasses of her mind.

After two days of being shunned by her only friends at school, she dug out her old black pants and long-sleeved, baggy shirts.

"Hey, Electra," Ashley greeted. "Now that's more like it.

You look like yourself again. Except no makeup?" She shrugged. "Oh well. Tomorrow, huh? C'mon, let's go get lunch." The other girls followed suit, welcoming her back, putting an arm around her shoulders, whispering conspiratorially.

But the old persona was not comfortable anymore. It was a skin she had shed during the summer in Montana, when she learned there were more important things than "fitting in" or being part of a rebel group. No other groups in school accepted her, they ignored her as a cowgirl, and simply looked at the Goth group with disdain as they passed in the hallways. So she dutifully put on the clothes and the makeup like a Halloween costume, so she could still be a part of something familiar. *This is where I live and go to school. If I can't be with Apache and Sam, I have to do this.*

One evening, as she sat in front of some mindless TV show with her mom, Electra sat up straight. "Is it okay if I call Sam?"

Mom flicked her attention from the screen. "Oh. Sure. Go ahead. You must be missing her."

"Yeah. I just want to see how Apache and Trixi and Sugar are doing."

"Of course. Tell her hi."

When her friend's voice came over the line, she nearly burst into tears. "Hey, Sam."

"Hey, Electra. Good to hear from you. How are things?"

"Oh, Sam, I… I don't like it here." Her voice quavered. "I want to come back to you…and Apache."

"What's wrong, honey? Why?"

"School sucks." She emitted a long, drawn-out sigh. "My friends—they don't understand. They're still, like, stuck. They're still into Goth, kinda like I was when you first met me." She sniffed loudly. "They make fun of me, call me names, call me hayseed and cowherder."

"I'm so sorry. But you know how much better you feel. You've simply grown past that stage. You're much more mature than they are. I'm sure they can see that, and they're probably jealous."

"Yeah." Defeat colored her voice with a muddy hue. Being more mature didn't bring much comfort in her dark loneliness.

"Have you been able to ride since you've been home?"

"Mom's taken me to the riding stables a couple of times." Her words came out in a small, hushed voice. "But it's not the same. It's really lame, like equestrian style—so *prim and proper*—not like riding with you. Not Apache." She choked out a sob. "I miss Apache." Loneliness curled next to her heart and grew tendrils.

Sam sighed. "I know you do, my dear. I wish I could help you somehow. All I can say is, hang in there. It *will* get better. And before you know, it'll be summer, and I think your mom is willing to have you come out here again and help me."

Electra knew her friend was trying to sound upbeat and make her feel better, but it wasn't working. "Yeah, but that's…like…for*ever* away!"

"No, no. It'll go quickly, I promise. Keep working hard at your schoolwork, and don't let your friends get you down. Do you think they'd go riding with you sometime? Maybe they'd like it."

She snorted. "I doubt it." She let silence build. "Anyway, gotta go."

"Wait. Let me talk to your mom."

"Okay. Here she is. 'Bye, Sam." She gave the phone to her mom and stood just around the corner, listening to the one-sided conversation.

"Sam? How are you? What's going on?"

"…I know. I'm not sure what to do either. She doesn't like the riding stables, she's not into school, and she's started to wear black again. This isn't good for her. I'm concerned."

Electra winced. Mom hadn't said anything to her about any of this, but she'd sensed her disapproval. *Well, sheesh, she doesn't have to try to fit in where she works. She already has her group.* The disapproval of her friends was much harder to deal with.

"…Yeah. I'm afraid her friends are trying to drag her back into that Goth thing again."

Why not? What else is there…here? She dug her nails into the soft flesh of her upper arms. Sam's faint voice whispered in her mind, *You're not that girl anymore.* But she couldn't believe it, not right now.

A moment of silence. "Christmas? Well…I'd have to think about that, financially and all. But…" Mom paused again. "You know, it might give her something to plan for."

Electra dropped her hands. *What did she just say?*

"All right. I'll see what I can work out. Thank you, Sam, that's a good idea." Mom disconnected the call.

"What, Mom? Are we going to Sam's for Christmas?" She bounced on the balls of her feet. "Can we, huh, please, please, please?"

Her mother put an arm around her shoulder. "I'm going to check into the cost of airline tickets, and I'll see if I can get time off from work. But yes, I think that might be just what the doctor ordered—for both of us."

"Yippee! Yay! Oh, Mom, you're awesome. This is the best day ever. I get to see Apache again…and Sam…and everybody!" She skipped around the room like a first grader. "Christmas! C'mon, Christmas!"

Nothing mattered anymore—not school, not her so-called friends, not the Goth-look. She still dressed like they did and ate with them and sat in class with them, but she had her big wall calendar at home, and it was rapidly filling with big red X's.

CHAPTER TWENTY

Electra pressed her nose against the window, scanning the snow-dusted tarmac as the plane taxied to the terminal. "Where is she? Did she forget we were coming?"

"Of course not, honey. She has to wait inside, for us to get off the plane."

She giggled. "Oh, I know. I just can't wait to see her, Mom!" Happiness bubbled up like spring water.

Her mother nudged her arm with an elbow and grinned. "Me too."

As soon as they came to a stop and the seatbelt lights went off, Electra jumped out of her seat and grabbed her bag from the overhead bin. She surged into the crowded aisle, inching toward the door. In the terminal, she craned her head around taller people in front of her. *She's not here. She didn't come.*

Then she saw her. Her worry changed to glee. "Sam! Sam! Sam! We're here!" She dropped her carry-on and rushed through the crowd to latch onto her friend with a crushing hug. "Oh, Sam, I'm so glad to see you, so glad to be here. Ohmygosh it's just been terrible, how's Apache, is he okay, how are you, are you okay? Ohmygosh, I'm so glad to see you."

Sam hugged her back. "Well, I'm glad to see you too. Apache is fine and so am I, now that you're here." She released her and held her arms out as Mom came up, pulling both cases.

"She's been insufferable the last few days, heck, the last few weeks," her mother whispered as they hugged, but Electra heard her and snickered. Mom glanced at her and wrinkled her nose. "Gee, it's good to be here," she added. "All right, Electra, let's go get our suitcases."

Electra grabbed Sam's arm and dragged her toward baggage claim. "Oh, Sam, I can't wait to get to your place and see Apache and ride and play in the snow and..." She couldn't help keeping up a nonstop chatter as they waited. "I'm just *so* excited to be here."

"I'm excited too." Her friend crooked Electra's arm in hers.

Baggage claimed and loaded into the back of the truck, the women piled in. "Anything you need here in Billings before we head out? Last-minute Christmas shopping?"

"No, I think we're good. We'd better get down that road to see Apache before this girl detonates."

"Mo-o-m." She bounced in the middle of the bench seat. "I can't help it, I've just missed Apache—and you too, Sam—so much, there's nothing in New York like this, and riding there is lame, and I don't have any friends, and..." Her voice trailed off, and she nibbled at her chipped black nail polish.

Sam patted her knee. "I've missed you too, and I'm so glad you're here now."

On the drive to the ranch, she could barely contain herself. Thoughts dove into her mind and skittered out through her mouth. "Oh, I just can't wait to see Apache and Sugar and Trixi and pet them and feed them and brush them. New York horses are so different, aren't they, Mom? I think they're *city* horses, ohmygosh they wouldn't even know what to do if we brought them out here." She stopped long enough to take a breath. "Ohmygosh I'm so excited to be here, I love the snow and I want to build a snowman and take a ride in it and oh I wish you had a sleigh! Wouldn't that be so cool?"

Mom sighed. "Electra, could you chill for a minute? You're not giving Sam a chance to talk."

Her friend laughed. "That's okay, Alberta. I've missed this. It's good to see you both."

As they approached the ranch, Electra leaned forward, searching for a glimpse of the horses. "Where are they? Will Apache remember me, do you think? I can't wait to see him, I can't wait to ride him. I. Just. Can't. Wait!"

"Well, I guess we'd better find out first thing." Sam drove directly to the barn, where her little herd waited in the adjoining pasture, all four heads hanging over the fence.

"Oh, there he is! Oh, Sam, there's Trixi too, and there's Sugar, and oh yeah, your new horse. What's his name?"

"That's Toby. I've been working with him, because he had a traumatic experience in a vehicle accident and is still a little shy and skittish. But maybe you can help me with him, like you did with Apache."

Electra widened her eyes hopefully. "Yeah. I could do that." She pushed on her mother's arm. "Mom, let me out. I gotta go see Apache."

"Okay, okay. But take it slow. It's been a while, and you don't want to scare him." Her mom opened the door, slid from the seat, and let her out.

Taking a couple of running steps, she stopped in mid-stride when Sam called out, "Wait!"

Sam scooped from a bucket in the back of the truck. "Here's a handful of cake pellets."

She took them and stood in place for a moment,

quivering. Then she walked slowly toward the horses, holding out her hand, her boots crunching through the snow. "Apache. Hi, boy. It's me. Do you remember me?"

All the horses, except Toby, crowded the fence in anticipation of a treat. Sam and Mom also grabbed pellets and approached.

Apache tossed his head and whinnied. He pressed his chest against the wire. His greeting rumbled as she held out the treat. He sniffed her hand, took the pellets, and then nuzzled her arm as he chewed. "Oh, Apache. You do remember me, don't you? I'm so glad to see you." She laid her cheek against his and stood like that for several long moments, drinking in his horsey aroma and the smooth texture of his hair. Peace flowed from him into her heart, erasing the past months of pain and rejection. "Mmmm," she murmured. *This is home.*

Behind her, Mom spoke softly to Sam. "She needed this." An audible deep breath. "And so did I."

While Sam opened the gate for Apache to come into the corral, Electra went to the barn and came back with a comb and brush. She stood by the horse, gently rubbing and brushing his neck and mane, moving to his withers and back. "Oh, Apache, you're looking so good. You're such a handsome fellow. You're so much better now."

Mom and Sam gave the other horses their treats and petted them for a few minutes —even Toby had come forward to claim his.

Finally, the cowgirl suggested, "Well, what d'you say we drive on up to the house and get you settled? We can have some lunch and catch up."

"That would be great," Mom said. "I've been waiting to kick back for quite some time."

At the house, Sam led the way as they carried the luggage upstairs to the two tiny bedrooms. "I know this is cramped, but I hope it'll be okay for a few days anyway."

Mom scanned the room. "It's perfect. Thank you."

"Yeah, it's fine." Electra shrugged. "Besides, I'm gonna be out with Apache as much as I can."

"When you're ready, come downstairs, and I'll fix you a cup of coffee and some lunch if you're hungry."

Electra's stomach rumbled. "Yeah, I'm starved. And after, could I—we—maybe go for a short ride?"

"Yes, of course we can. But you better get fueled up. It's chilly out."

Over coffee and sandwiches, the women chatted to catch up. "How is your friend Brad doing?"

Sam told them about how he had volunteered to bring her latest rescue horse from Arizona, had been caught in a snowstorm, and ran off the road, wrecking his truck. She related the latest, about him being in a coma, having pneumonia, and her fears that he wouldn't wake up. "I'm really scared, Alberta, but there's nothing I can do. I feel completely helpless."

Electra's heart thumped in shock. "Oh no. Brad? Ohmygosh, I hope he's going to be okay."

"Oh, my dear, I'm so very sorry. I know this is the hardest thing in the world to endure." Mom's eyes took on a distant focus as she gazed out the kitchen window. "My son was in a coma for several weeks before he…" Her mouth worked as she swallowed hard. "But that was a different story. I knew from the beginning, there was no coming back." She patted Sam's hand. "But I do know what you're going through. And if I can help in any way, I'm here."

Memories of the days following Jimmy's accident swelled into the old ache. Electra held her hands over her heart. *Ohmygosh, Brad can't die too. Sam doesn't deserve this! Just when they were getting along again.*

Sam blinked. "Thank you. I appreciate it. You're a

wonderful friend." She clasped Mom's hand and changed the subject. "But what about you, Electra—black again? Are you okay?"

Mom sighed and put an arm around her. "She's been going through a tough time. Her friends made fun of her when she got back to school and had no interest in going riding with her. So, she's gradually gone back to the dark Goth look and attitude, just to fit in again."

"Yeah…well…if that's the only way they'll talk to me." She flashed what she hoped was a bright smile. "But I'm better now that I'm back here. This is where I belong, Mom. I *need* to be here!" She gathered empty plates and took them to the sink. "I'm going back out to the corral and get ready for our ride."

As she slipped out the door, she overheard Sam say in a low voice, "Oh dear. Back to Goth. That's what I was afraid of when I saw her. But at least her face is fresh-scrubbed, not the white and black makeup."

"Yeah. That was just for you." Mom's voice, also nearly a whisper. "I don't know what we're going to do. I don't think going back to that school and those kids is a good idea."

She closed the door quietly, hope rising in her chest. *Maybe Mom will let me stay.*

***

She stood with her face pressed against the gelding's neck, once again taking in the peace of being with her horse. The old pain and need for new pain to deaden her loss faded into the background as she breathed in his unique scent.

"Gee, I think if he was a cat he'd be purring." Sam's voice startled her.

She swished her face to the side. "Yeah, he would. Can we go for a ride?"

"Sure. I'm glad the snow has melted enough we can go. I'll get Trixi." The cowgirl got a bridle, went to the pasture, and whistled. The other horses grazed on dry tufts of grass a short distance away. Trixi raised her head and came trotting.

"Expecting another treat, huh? Golly, are you spoiled!" Sam rubbed the mare's face, gave her a cake pellet, and slipped on the bridle. Then she led her through the gate into the corral by the barn.

"They're all spoiled, aren't they?" Electra couldn't keep the grin off her face. "But they deserve it. They're our friends. Oh, Trixi is so pretty."

"Yes, she is, and I'm looking forward to working more with her."

They went into the barn, retrieved saddles, and tacked up their horses. Within minutes, the horses' hooves crunched in the snow and dried grass through the pasture, toward the large, flat-topped butte in the distance. At first, Electra was content with Apache walking, but finally, she nudged him into a trot, and then a canter. She squinted at Sam. "Race ya!"

"You're on!" Sam pressed her heels to Trixi's flanks, and the mare willingly joined the race.

The cold December air bit at Electra's face and ears, but she pulled up her neck scarf and leaned forward, caught up in the exhilaration of the run. She reined in at the base of the hill, laughing. "*That* was fun! Ohmygosh, I missed this *so* much."

"Me too." Sam shivered and pulled her coat collar up farther. "I haven't been out as much as I should be, with the snow and cold and with Brad in the hospital..." She swallowed hard and gave her what seemed like a forced smile. "But now that you're here, I hope we can do this a lot more before you go back home."

Home. Electra's euphoria evaporated, and she stared down at the frozen ground. For just a moment she was tempted to dig her nails into her arms to dull the ache of the misfit so alone. *I can't go back there.*

Sam studied her for a moment. "Electra?"

She avoided her friend's gaze.

"Are you okay? What's going on?"

Instead of answering, she nudged Apache and took off up the side of the butte. Sam followed. At the top, they stopped and slipped out of their saddles. Below them, the red and white Herefords gathered around the reservoir.

"I…love this place." She sank onto a boulder and wrapped her arms around her middle. "I love Apache, and I love those cows… and I love you." Her eyes watered.

Sam sat on the rock, put her arm around her shoulders, and drew her close. "I love you too They sat in silence a few moments. "What's going on? Is it more than your Goth friends? Did something happen back home?"

"No. Not really." She squirmed a bit on the rock. "But…it's a big city. There's too many people and not enough horses."

Sam chuckled. "I can understand that. I don't think I'd want to live there."

"My friends… I guess I changed last summer. But they didn't." She swiped at her cheeks with her gloves. "They didn't like me anymore. They didn't understand me…and they didn't want to go riding. They made fun of me."

"So, you went back to being Goth, so your friends would like you again?"

"I didn't really want to." She picked at a clump of grass and stared out at the horizon. "B-but what else could I do? They weren't going to change. I don't have any other friends."

Tears trickled again. "I went to the stables a few times, but it…it wasn't the same. No galloping allowed. Sit up straight and hold the reins in two hands and be all prim and proper." Her voice rose in a mimicking tone. "The girls at the riding academy were all too snooty—they didn't want to be friends. And the horses… I couldn't relate to any of them." She blinked at Sam. "They weren't Apache."

"I understand." Sam chewed her lower lip. "I'm sorry about all that. I wish I had a magic wand and could make everything better." Then she grinned. "But, you know what? We will just enjoy the heck out of the horses and riding and having the time of our lives while you're here. And then it'll soon be summer, and you'll be back again." The cowgirl gave her shoulder a squeeze. "Sound like a plan?"

Electra wiped her cheeks again. "Yeah. You make everything better." She stood. "Let's go back. It is kind of cold up here."

The horses loped at an easy stride in and out of the low coulees, through the spicy sage, and back to the barn. Another brushing for Apache and Trixi, and then Sam and Electra ambled back up to the house, arm in arm.

***

That evening, after supper, Sam brought a fir tree she'd picked up in Billings from the barn and set it up in front of the big window in the living room. Electra squealed as she opened the boxes of ornaments. "Oooh, come look, Mom! This is so cool." She held up a horse figurine and then a cowboy hat and a pair of boots. "Where did you get all these?"

"Oh, here and there." Sam hung the boot ornament on the tree, front and center. "A few have been gifts from friends who know I love horses, and some I've found in little gift shops." She added a hat ornament and a gold garland.

Mom brought in cups of hot chocolate with marshmallows and a plate of cookies. "Here's something to sustain us during our hard work."

"Thanks." Sam took a cookie. "You appear a little more rested this evening."

"Yeah. I feel much better. That nap helped. And this fresh

air and the peace and quiet here are just what I needed." She picked up an angel ornament and added it to the growing bling on the tree. "I see you have 'theme' areas all over—cowgirl stuff here and angels there. It's lovely."

Electra exclaimed over every piece and asked the history of each—Sam explained some were from her Grandma Anna who had come from Germany, some were from her great-grandma Nettie, and others depicted milestone years of her childhood. When the tree was finished, Sam plugged in the glowing, multi-colored lights.

This is so cool. We don't have anything like that at home. Just a lot of lights and bling. Big fancy parties. Affection for her cowgirl friend washed through her like the glow of the lights.

"This is such fun. I'm so glad you're here to celebrate Christmas with me. It's my favorite holiday and if you hadn't come, I might not even have put up a tree this year." Sam shook her shoulders and sipped her steaming chocolate.

"We're happy to celebrate it with you too." Mom came up behind the cowgirl and wrapped her in a hug.

Electra threw her arms around them both. "Me too!" *I never want to leave this place.*

CHAPTER TWENTY-ONE

Snowflakes drifted lazily from a pewter sky as Electra helped Sam finish chores the afternoon of December 24. The horses had been ridden, groomed, and fed, and the door to the barn left open if they needed shelter.

"This is perfect—snow on Christmas." Sam held the door open to the kitchen where cinnamon and yeast aromas greeted them.

Mom straightened from the oven where she took out a tray of cinnamon rolls. "Yes, it does seem more like Christmas."

"Mmm. Yum." Electra reached for a roll.

Her mother swatted at her with a spatula. "No, these are for tomorrow morning. We have other goodies for today."

"O-kaay." She giggled. "Sam, why is Christmas Eve at four o'clock such an important thing?"

"Well, it's a family tradition. That's when Grandma Anna and Grandpa Neil were married in 1948." She retrieved a china coffee pot from a glass-fronted cabinet, measured coffee grounds into it, and then poured boiling water over them to steep like tea.

"That's a weird way to make coffee." Electra cocked her head. "Why don't you just use the coffee maker like you usually do?"

"This is another family tradition." Sam smiled. "My grandparents made their afternoon coffee this way, and it's delicious."

She made a face. "If you like coffee."

"For you, we have cocoa. Do you want to get out all the cookies we made and put an assortment on this plate?" Sam handed her a gold-rimmed china plate.

"Sure." Electra took out containers from cupboards and the refrigerator. "Mmm, we finally get to try them all." She arranged fudge bars, lemon bars, multi-layered bars, date-filled spice cookies, and the sugar cookies they'd decorated the night before. "Hey, why did your grandparents get married on Christmas Eve?"

Sam set her grandmother's dainty china cups on the table and poured the coffee and cocoa as Electra and her mom sat. "They met in Germany after the war. He was in the Army, and she was a nurse. When he went to visit a friend in the hospital, they met and became friends. Then a couple months later, Grandpa was shipped back to the States, and by the time he got home, he realized he'd fallen in love with this girl. So, he wrote her a letter and asked her if she'd come to the U.S. and marry him. And she said yes."

"Ooooh!" Electra took a bite of cookie, her forehead high. "Cool." *This is a true love story, like in novels or on TV.*

"But it took her two years to get all the paperwork and visas approved before she could come. And Grandpa wasn't able to go back to visit her. But they wrote a lot of letters."

Mom grimaced. "That must have been so hard."

"I think it would have been." Sam nodded. "I've always thought it took a lot of courage to come to a new country where she didn't speak the language, to a different culture, out here in the middle of nowhere with the cows and horses and cowboys. And this country had just fought a war with Germany, so people still saw her as the 'enemy.'"

Electra gasped. "Oh no. That's awful!" *And I thought the Goth-girls were mean.* Her heart ached for Sam's grandmother.

"Yeah, I think she fought prejudice all her life." Sam sipped her coffee. "Anyway, she arrived here in November, and then in early December she got a letter that had been lost or rerouted in the mail for weeks, telling her that she still didn't have all the documentation she needed, her visa would run out on December 31, and she'd have to go home."

Electra paused in mid-bite. "What? Ohmygosh! How could they do that?"

"Well, you know, the government… So, they decided to get married before that deadline, and the pastor only had December 24 available because he was going on vacation the next day. It had to be at four o'clock since the kids' Christmas program was later that evening."

"Wow. Mom, isn't that the most romantic story? Married on Christmas Eve, so she wouldn't have to go back to Germany?"

"Yes, it is." Her mom blinked several times. "Your grandmother must have loved your grandpa very much to move out here." She stared out the window at the snow drifting down on wide-open spaces. "I can see why you keep up this family tradition and why you want this ranch. You have a special history here."

After a light supper, Sam gathered her friends around the tree. "Another family tradition is to open gifts on Christmas Eve. When I was growing up, we opened the Moser family gifts that night, and then on Christmas morning, we had Santa's presents."

"The best of both worlds." Mom smiled.

"Yeah! I love that idea." Electra's body jittered with

excitement to see the brightly-wrapped boxes. "We should do that, Mom."

Her mother laughed. "Yeah, right, now that you're too old for Santa."

"But not too old for more presents!" She burst into giggles, and Mom and Sam joined her.

They took pictures of each other by the tree "Another tradition," Sam explained. "We used to spend hours opening presents, carefully cutting the tape so we could save the paper for another year. And then at the very end, Grandma would pull out the box her family had sent from Germany, and oh my, the treasures we found there—like special German chocolate, *Lebkuchen* cookies, and hand-crocheted items."

"Thank you for sharing these wonderful traditions with us." Mom hugged Sam.

Electra squealed. "Can we open them now? Can we?"

"Of course. Let's do it." Sam gave her the first box.

She started to rip the paper and then stopped and looked at Sam. "Do you want me to save this?"

Sam burst into laughter. "No, that's okay. I'm frugal, but I don't save paper like we used to. Well, maybe some of the pretty stuff. But you're a kid, you go ahead and rip."

"Oooh." Electra held up the light blue western shirt with dark piping and silver sequins. "Wow. I love this. This is so cool. Thank you!" *If the girls could see me now—from black to bling.* She giggled.

When Mom opened her gift, she wore a broad grin, and Electra squealed again. "Oh, Mom, we got matching shirts. Ohmygosh! That is so awesome. I can't wait for us to wear them. Can we wear them tomorrow to the Bruckners'?"

"That sounds like a great plan. Thank you, Sam. This is perfect." Mom hugged her again.

They opened one gift at a time, oohed and aahed over

each one, savoring the moment. "Now, your turn." Electra handed her friend a box.

Sam caught an audible breath as she opened it—a soft, turquoise, tooled leather handbag with a silver cross on one side and her initials on the other. "This is beautiful. It must have been expensive. You shouldn't have."

Mom beamed a soft, tender smile. "Nothing is too good for such a wonderful friend. We appreciate everything you've done for us."

"Yeah." Electra's eyes blurred. "What she said." *I think Sam is my best friend. Maybe she's my only friend, besides Apache…*

***

A light cover of snow greeted them Christmas morning, and after feeding and chores, the three drove to the Bruckners' for dinner. Sam brought a fruit salad, along with a rum-soaked fruit cake she said she'd been basting for a month.

Horace joined the party, bringing a mincemeat pie he'd made. Sam gave him a hug. "My, I didn't know you were a pie-maker."

"I have a coupla kitchen skills." He winked. "But mostly I keep 'em secret."

An inner smile grew. *I love these old guys too. They pretty cool.*

The group lingered at the table laden with turkey, all the trimmings, salads, sweet potatoes, and then pies and cakes and cookies. Soft music and scented candles, laughter, and friendship bathed Electra from head to toe in the warmth and spirit of Christmas. She'd never experienced anything quite like this, and the more she learned about life on a ranch, the more she wanted it…*needed* it.

As Sam drove them home later that evening, Mom marveled over the day, the food, and the gifts they'd exchanged.

"This is the *best* Christmas I've *ever* had!" Electra declared.

Contentment spread warmth through her whole body.

Her mom's face was bathed in a happy expression. "I think I have to agree."

They went inside, shedding their winter gear. Sam gestured toward the fridge. "Anybody ready for supper?"

Mom groaned.

"No way!" Electra draped herself over the couch.

"I don't think I'll have to eat for a week." Mom lifted Electra's feet and sat at the end of the sofa.

"Me too." Sam headed for her rocker and then stopped. "Oh yeah, Brad's sister Melissa was supposed to call yesterday to let me know about Brad." She went back into the kitchen to make the call.

A couple minutes later, Sam trudged into the living room, her face ashen, lips quivering.

Oh no! It can't be… Electra bounded over to hug her, Mom following close behind. They held her for several minutes until she stopped shaking.

"Not good news?" Mom peered into her face.

A huge boulder sat in the pit of Electra's stomach. "What's wrong with Brad? He's not…?"

The cowgirl shook her head. "Melissa said they tried to take him off the ventilator for about five minutes yesterday and today, but it's not going very well." Her voice broke.

"Come sit. Electra, would you make us some hot chocolate?" Mom led Sam to the rocker. "Now, of course, I'm not a nurse, but I know these things take a while. Sometimes it doesn't work at first. He simply needs more time to heal."

Heart hurting for her friend, she heated the milk, listening to her mom trying to inject a note of optimism into the situation.

She brought the cocoa in and handed Sam a cup. "I put marshmallows on top."

"Thank you, dear." Sam took a sip. "Mmm, good. This helps." She rewarded her with a tiny smile.

Mom took her chocolate, sat on the couch, and leaned forward. "Next time they try, it will work. I know it will."

Closing her eyes, the cowgirl sat for a moment. Then she opened them. "Yes. I have to believe that. Thank you for being here with me."

"Why don't we go to the hospital tomorrow?" Mom suggested. "It might help ease your mind to be with his family."

Sam nodded. "That's a good idea. Let's do that."

***

After they left the hospital the next day, Sam settled behind the wheel of her pickup and exhaled a whoosh of air. "Melissa said they tried him off the ventilator again this morning, and he went for the full five minutes."

Electra leaned closer and put her head on Sam's shoulder. "That's good, isn't it?" Was this a sign Brad would get better? *Please, God, don't let him die…like Jimmy.*

Mom's eyes glistened. "Oh, Sam." She blinked hard.

"Yes. This is a good sign." Sam's voice came out raspy, and she cleared her throat.

They sat in silence for long minutes, Electra wondering what her friend was thinking. Brad's accident and coma had to be really tough on her. *I think I kinda know how she might feel…a little. I'll bet she's scared.* She patted the cowgirl's knee, trying to convey peace and love through her jeans.

Sam smiled at her as she guided the truck down the road. When her cell rang, she said, "Would you put it on speaker for me?"

Mom answered, identified herself, and clicked the speaker button.

"Hello, Sam, it's Nick Seward, from the community college."

"Oh. Yes. Hello, Nick."

"I know it's still Christmas vacation and this is short notice, but I wondered if you might be able to bring your trick horse in to Miles City, maybe tomorrow or the next day. Some of my board members would like to see what you do with the veterans and your horse. It'll be a good time, with no students on campus, and Del and Garrett want to try riding again."

Sam stared straight ahead, her mouth open. Several seconds ticked by.

"Sam? Are you still there?" Nick's voice came over the speaker.

"Uh, yeah. Yes, I'm still here. I'm quite surprised, is all. I wasn't expecting…"

"Well, like I said, it is short notice, so if you can't, I understand."

Veterans? Trixi? What? Electra bobbed her head up and down. "Yes, yes, do it," she mouthed.

Sam blinked. "I think I can swing that. How about day after tomorrow?"

"Sounds great. We'll see you then. Looking forward to it." Nick clicked off.

Mom's face held a quizzical expression. "That sounds intriguing. Working with veterans? What is that all about? I want to see this too. Is it okay if we come along?"

"Of course." Sam told them about the two veterans who had come to her, asking to help them overcome PTSD by working with horses. "Electra, you can help me demonstrate."

"Can I? Yeah! I can do that! Yesss!" Excited tremors raced through her body. "Oh, Mom, this is going to be so much fun." She high-fived her mother.

***

At the ag center the next day, Electra helped Sam unload

the mare, and they led her into the indoor arena, where a group of men and women waited.

A man with no legs rolled his wheelchair up. "Hi, Miss Sam. Thanks for doing this. We're so excited."

"Hi, Del. Good to see you again." The cowgirl shook his hand.

Ohmygosh. He lost his legs. Shock and sadness rested heavy on her heart. *But maybe we can help him with Trixi.*

"Ladies and gentlemen," Nick boomed, "I'd like to introduce you to Samantha Moser, her famous trick horse Trixi, and her friends Alberta and Electra." Polite applause, and he continued. "Sam will be demonstrating the kind of work she and Trixi can do to help disabled veterans. I hope to bring her on as a certified trainer, which I've already explained to all of you."

He gestured to Sam with a flourish. "Take it away, ma'am."

She nodded to Electra and gave Trixi the signal. The horse kneeled and came to rest in a sitting position. Electra slipped into the saddle, gave another signal, and Trixi rose.

An audible "Ahhh" came from the group.

She rode the mare around the arena a couple of times, changing gaits, and came back to where Sam stood, feeling like she could conquer the world. Another signal, the horse kneeled, and Electra dismounted. She hugged Trixi's neck.

"That's amazing." Nick applauded. "Something like this will be a great tool in assisting with the mounting process. Good job, ladies. Thank you." He turned to the vets. "One of you want to give it a try?"

The man in the wheelchair propelled forward, but another guy limped in front. "I'll go."

"Great! You've made such good progress." Sam gestured. "Electra, meet Garrett."

"Hi, Garrett, you're gonna love this." She took his hand. *It's shaking. He must be scared.* "It's okay. She's very gentle."

Sam led him to the mare who knelt again on cue. "Okay, Garrett. Go ahead and get on."

The group remained silent as if collectively holding a breath.

He stopped, leaned down to rub Trixi's neck for a moment, and then lifted his leg over the saddle.

Electra stifled a gasp. *He only has one foot!*

Sam helped him place his prosthetic foot into the stirrup and grabbed him firmly by the belt. "Okay, clamp your knees against the saddle, put your weight on the stirrups and hold on to the horn."

He took a shuddering breath and finally nodded.

Sam met Electra's gaze and nodded.

She motioned to Trixi, and the horse rose to her feet. *C'mon, Garrett, you can do this.*

The young man stayed centered in the saddle. He flashed her a momentary grin. "Better?"

"Superb." She and Electra led them around the arena, Electra silently rooting him on. When they returned, they were met with applause.

Dismounting from the kneeling mare without mishap, Garrett stood in front of the group. "I've only been to Sam's a few times, but I can tell you that she is a very patient teacher." He cleared his throat. "She never pushed me to do anything I didn't want to. She started me—and then Del—out with simply getting to know the horse, feeding her treats, and gradually beginning the grooming process."

Several people nodded, intently listening. "When I'm with a horse, it's…" his voice faltered, "…it's like a calm comes over me. I forget everything else… what happened…" he glanced down at his prosthesis, "and all the demons I fight daily in the regular world."

Wow. Electra stared at him in awe. *Kinda like what Jace said when she rode.*

Garrett continued. "With winter arriving, I've missed being able to do this on a regular basis. A program here at the center would be a godsend."

Yes, these men need our help. Electra blinked against the sting in her eyes. What would it be like, not to have a foot or even legs, or be paralyzed like Jace? It was obvious they all could be helped by Trixi. *Horses can heal hearts.* Apache had given her the gift of peace, deep in her soul.

Sam smiled at the veteran. "Thank you, Garrett. That means the world to me."

Del volunteered to ride next. Slow and painstaking, he maneuvered himself from the wheelchair into the saddle—Sam hovering behind—and centered smoothly as Trixi stood. He flourished a bow from her back. The group whistled and clapped.

Electra cheered too. "Yay, Del. That was awesome." She couldn't help herself.

After his ride, he repeated Garrett's sentiments and ended with a plea. "We need Miss Sam here to help us vets heal."

Electra felt like her heart would burst with pride for her friend. *Yes, they do need her! And oh, how I would love to help.*

***

"That went very well." Mom leaned across Electra in the pickup.

"Yeah, that was so cool." Electra chortled. "I love showing people what Trixi can do. And that was so awesome to see Garrett and Del ride and what they said. Wow, Sam."

"Yes, I'm so thankful it was successful. I'm still blown away by Garrett. I didn't think he'd ever come back, that he'd probably be even more afraid of horses after he fell off and injured himself."

"That was amazing. You could have a future with this."

Mom's voice held a note of awe.

"Yeah, you do." Electra beamed at her friend. "See, I *knew* there was a reason for you to get Trixi."

"Yes. Well, it all depends on the board and if they approve Nick's proposal."

"They will. I *know* they will." Electra bounced in the seat. "And I want to help you. I want to work with the horses and the vets too! Can I, Mom? Can I? Please?"

Her mother grimaced. "I don't know, honey. How would it all work? This is so remote—where would you live? Where would you go to school? My job is in New York."

Sam glanced at Electra's mother. "Would you ever consider moving to Montana?"

Mom whooshed a long sigh. "Believe me, I've thought about it. But I don't know how on earth that could happen." She gestured toward the window. "This is a wonderful, peaceful place, and I can see why you love it, but it's so far from…everything. What's the nearest town—Forsyth?— and that's how far?"

"Forty-some miles. Almost an hour from the ranch." Sam nodded. "I know. That would be the closest for school and maybe a job."

"Well, can't think about that right now. I'm just going to enjoy the time I have here and worry about the future later."

"Sounds like a good idea."

Aww, Mom. Electra's heart sank. "Mom. I could live with Sam, right, Sam? And I can… uh… I could home-school."

"Good grief, girl." Her mother gave her a stern look. "That is so rude. You haven't even asked Samantha about this…or me. You can't be making assumptions about these things. There's so much more to it…" She trailed off, shaking her head. "You can come back next summer, but right now you're coming home with me, and that's final."

Electra lowered her head and pressed her lips tight. Tears trickled down her cheeks. How would she get through the next five months without her Apache and Trixi and Sam? *I'm gonna die without them!* She crossed her arms over her chest and dug her fingernails as hard as she could through her sweatshirt to her flesh.

CHAPTER TWENTY-TWO

The day after New Years, Electra sat in silence as Sam drove them to the Billings airport. Her chest hollowed, already feeling the void. Her body slumped under a weight as if a cow sat on her. *My life is over. Summer is forever away—it'll never get here.* Sam kept making attempts to cheer her up with remarks like "It's going to go by so fast. You'll be back before you know it."

She merely grunted.

Mom got into the act as well. "You can call every week and keep up with Sam's progress with the horses and the kids and the veterans. And I'll take you riding at the stables more often too, if you want."

She snorted. Yeah, like that was gonna cheer her up. Lame-O horses. Lame-O girls and their fancy clothes and prissy manners. *Nope. The horses are not Apache, and the girls aren't Sam.*

At the terminal, Sam hugged her long and hard. She stood stiffly, refusing to reciprocate. Stepping away, she dragged her carry-on down the ramp, swiping at the mascara tears bleeding onto her cheeks. On the plane, she turned her face to the window and showed her mother her shoulder. She chewed the inside of her cheek until it stung. *I'll make it*

so miserable for her she'll send me back to get rid of me!
***

The days at school stretched like the longest, empty road in the world, one without an end in sight. She slogged through the halls from one class to the other, barely listening to the teachers, not caring if she understood the lessons or did her homework. *If I flunk, maybe Mom will listen to me. If she even cares.* Her mother was always busy. When she wasn't at work, she was on the phone to clients or coworkers. *I wonder if she'd even notice if I was gone.*

Despite her dark clothing and stark makeup, she no longer fit in with the Goth-girls. They began to keep their distance from her too, just like the cheerleader types, the jock types, the brainiac types. *What else is left? There are no cowgirls in New York City.*

She sat alone at lunch, picking the olives out of the tuna surprise and arranging them in various shapes on her plate. Her stomach was a hard mass. Nothing tasted good.

"What's up with you?" Ashley's voice startled her from her dismal musings.

"Huh?" She peered into the girl's black-rimmed eyes. "What do you mean?"

"I *mean* you are the world's most pathetic little nobody. You ignore your friends. You don't talk. You don't do anything. You just sit here like a schmoe. What's wrong with you?"

She wrinkled her nose. "Nothing."

"Ever since you got back from Podunk, Montana, you've been off in some other world. Are you missing your *horses* and your *hayseed friends* back there? Why didn't you just *stay* there?" Ashley's mouth twisted into a sneer. "We thought you were *our* friend, but who needs friends like you anyway? You don't belong with us anymore, so you might as well take off your Goth clothes and put your cowboy hat back on."

She stood, knocking Electra's glass over. "Bye, *cow*-girl." She flounced away.

Red Kool-Aid ran across the table. Electra stared at it. She made no move to sop it up, merely watched each drop dribble onto her lap. *Like a river of blood.* She jammed her fork into her palm, an exquisite pain radiating into her fingers. Turning her hand over, she let her own blood drip into the stream of Kool-Aid.

At home after school, she wandered the apartment. Mom wasn't home from work yet. She ran a glass of water in the bathroom and carried it with her into the hallway, taking small sips. Pausing at Jimmy's door, she leaned her forehead against it. Fear, grief, and hate wrapped her lungs in a tight cocoon. She could barely breathe. Finally, she put a hand on the knob and rotated it in slow motion. She hadn't been inside since...

The room was just as Jimmy had left it—down to the unmade bed. Mom hadn't been in here either. His rock star posters adorned the walls, sports memorabilia on his dresser. The toe of one tennis shoe peeked from under the drooping bedspread.

It was as if he hadn't left. But he had. He'd never be back. She'd never see him again. She took a drink of water and set the glass on the side table. The room swirled around her, and she collapsed on the bed with a strangled scream of anguish. Cries rose from her depths, like tormented souls in hell. She buried her face in the pillow and screamed until she couldn't utter another sound.

She lay panting into the bedding, her throat raw with pain.

Finally, she sat on the side of the bed, her eyes dry and swollen. She took another drink of water. Then she hurled the glass at the wall. In slow motion, it shattered and dribbled down the plaster. For what seemed like hours, she stared at the wet puddle on the carpet, the shards glistening. They lay there, mocking her. *Jimmy's gone. You don't have any friends. You don't belong here.* Ashley's words echoed in her mind. *You're a nobody.*

Zombie-like, she slid to the floor and crawled to the glass. *You're a nobody. You're a nobody.* She reached a finger to one of the pieces, touching it tentatively, caressing the polished surface. Then she traced the edges. So smooth, yet so sharp.

She picked it up. Pushing back the cuff of her sweatshirt, she touched the pointed end to her skin on the inside of her forearm. She held it there for long moments. Then she pressed it a little harder, making a dent on her skin.

With a swift motion, she sliced. An angry red line appeared. Beads of blood pooled and ran in tiny rivulets down her arm. The sting bit at her, the pain a welcome relief from her howls of anguish minutes before. She leaned her head back against the bed and savored the feeling.

After that, every afternoon when she came home from school, she padded into Jimmy's room where the glass lay. The release of pain became her guilty secret. Almost like a blood pact with her brother. *I won't forget you, Jimmy.*

***

As the weeks crept by, Electra came to the realization she couldn't keep on the way she was. She knew what she was doing was wrong. That it wasn't going to get her back to Montana and Apache any sooner.

One evening, when Mom was in the living room on her phone, she sneaked into the kitchen where her mother's purse sat on the counter. Keeping an ear open for "goodbye" sounds, she opened the wallet and selected one of the credit cards—one she didn't think Mom used very often. As an afterthought, she grabbed a couple of twenties, put them all in her pocket, and headed for her room. She threw her jeans and western shirts into her small carryon suitcase and shoved it under the bed.

The next morning, Mom bustled around the kitchen, buttering a slice of toast with one hand and grabbing a travel mug for coffee with the other. "Okay, honey. I'm off. I may be a little late tonight. We have a big meeting at the end of the day." She reached into her wallet and pulled out a ten. "Here's lunch money. Have a good day, sweetheart."

Way to shove me out the door. "Okay, thanks. You too, Mom. 'Bye." *She really doesn't care.*

When her mother was gone, she called the airport and booked the next flight. Then she dressed in her cowgirl clothes and boots, pulled her suitcase into the elevator, and headed for the bus stop.

At the airport, she held her breath, waiting for someone to question her traveling alone, but no one did. She secured her ticket and boarding pass, and soon she was on the plane.

Only then did she relax and allow a smile. *I'm going home.*

***

She slept most of the trip, waking for the complimentary bag of pretzels and a Coke when the flight attendant came by. *Sam's going to be so surprised. I can't wait to see her.* A delightful shiver of anticipation coursed through her.

When the wheels touched down at Billings Logan Field, she gathered her things and followed the other passengers into the terminal. Perusing the terminal for a pay phone, for the first time the thought crossed her mind that maybe she should have called Sam before she came. *If I had, she would've been here to meet me, I know she would.* Dark wings fluttered in her tummy. What if she wasn't at home? But no, if she'd called ahead, her friend probably would've alerted her mom. She hadn't wanted anyone to stop her from coming. *She'll be home. Where else would she be?*

At the ticket counter, she asked where she could make a call, and the woman directed her to a courtesy phone. With trembling fingers, she punched in Sam's number. The recorded message came on. "Hi, this is Sam. Please leave a message."

Her heart thudded to the pit of her stomach. *Oh no. Now what do I do?* She didn't know Sam's cell number. Tears stung her eyes, and her throat closed off. "Um…um…" A sob choked her words. "Hi… Sam… It's Electra. I'm at the airport…in Billings…" She hiccupped. "I don't know what to do. Can you come get me?"

She wandered around the terminal, staring out the window at another plane arriving, watching passengers come and go. The wing-like fear flapped, and she shivered. *Oh man, I really messed up. What am I going to do tonight if she doesn't get my message?* She thought of calling Miss Robin but didn't know her number or the name of the group home. Her shoulders drooped. She slumped into one of the hard, plastic chairs in the waiting room, chewing at her chipped black nail polish. The urge to force her nails into her flesh was overwhelming, but she thought of Sam and what she would say when she found her.

After sitting another half an hour, she went to the courtesy phone and tried Sam's home number again. "Sam, are you there? Pleeease pick up! I can't stay…h-here. The airport closes at…ten." Her voice wound down to a choked wail.

Her body slid down the wall to crumple on the floor. Tears flowed freely now. *Ohmygosh, ohmygosh, what am I going to do?*

When she was able to control her sobs, she sat upright. *Okay, Electra, think now.* She had Mom's credit card. She could call a taxi and go to a motel. She inhaled deeply. *Okay. If Sam hasn't called in another half hour, that's what I'll do.*

Then she heard the loudspeaker: "Paging Miss Electra Lucci. Miss Electra Lucci. Come to the security desk please."

She leaped to her feet and ran to the counter. "I'm Electra Lucci."

The man behind the desk gave her a kindly smile. "Oh good. You have a phone call from a Samantha Moser."

"Oh." She squeaked out a syllable.

He handed her the phone.

"Sam? Is it you? Sam, are you there?" Her voice came out high-pitched, little girl-like.

"Yes, it's me. What on earth are you doing in Billings?"

She broke into sobs.

"Electra. Electra. Listen to me. Calm down now. You're okay. I'm going to come and get you, all right?" Sam's voice was calm, soothing.

"All…all…right."

"Take a couple of deep breaths and let them out slowly."

Electra complied, her chest heaving. "Okay, Sam. I'm okay."

"I'm going to leave now. It's going to take me a couple of hours or maybe a little longer, depending on the roads, so I should be there around 8 or 8:30."

"O-okay."

"Have you called your mom? I had a message from her, and she's really worried about you."

"N-no." A sniffle. "She'll be…so…mad."

"Well, I suppose so. This was a pretty bone-headed stunt. I'm going to call her now and let her know I've talked to you. But you should call her too."

"Yeah…prob'ly should." More sniffles. *No, that's the last thing I want to do.*

"I'll be there as soon as I can. Do you have any money to get something to eat in the café there?"

"Yeah."

"All right, you do that. I'm coming to get you."

"Okay. See you soon." She swallowed more tears, of relief

now, and handed the phone back to the man. "Thanks."

He looked at her with concern. "Are you okay? Can I help you?"

"Got a hold of my ride now. I'm fine, thanks." She headed to the Gateway Restaurant, where she ordered a BLT, fries, and a Coke. Food hadn't tasted so good in weeks. Then she went back to the waiting area and found a seat where she could observe the main entrance. Her hunger satisfied, she dozed off and on for the next hour.

Stiff from the hard chair, she stood to stretch. In the light outside the glass doors, someone approached with a familiar stride. *Sam!* She sprinted to meet her friend, nearly bowling her over. "Sam! Sam! You're here. I'm so glad you're here. Ohmygosh, ohmygosh, ohmygosh," she wailed and buried her head in Sam's neck.

The cowgirl wrapped her arms around her and rubbed her back, murmuring and rocking side to side.

"Oh Sam, Sam, Sam, I'm so sorry. I couldn't stand it anymore, I had to come see you, and I was so scared when you didn't answer. Please don't be mad at me!" She hiccupped and fell into inconsolable sobbing.

When the torrent finally subsided, Sam put gentle hands on her shoulders. "You're okay now. Let's go wash your face." She led her to the restrooms, pulling the suitcase behind.

Electra splashed cold water on her face and took long, deep breaths. When she was more composed, they headed outside to the pickup. Sam loaded the suitcase, got in, and drove down the hill to the highway toward home.

"Did you call your mom?"

Electra fidgeted. "No." The small voice again. "I couldn't. I know I made a mistake. I shouldn't have done this. She's gonna hate me."

Sam fluttered her lips. "No, she's not going to hate you. Yes, she is upset and angry. But she loves you, and she was scared when she found you missing." She reached for her cell. "I want you to call her right now."

"Do I *have* to?"

"Yes. Do it right now," Sam repeated in a firm tone.

As Electra made the call, snowflakes hit the windshield. *Oh-oh.*

Whiteness swirled in the headlights. Sam flipped on the wipers and the defroster fan.

Oh man. That's all we need, a snowstorm. I've caused so much trouble.

When her mother answered, Electra gulped. "Hi, Mom. I'm okay. I'm with Sam."

"You! I. Am. So. Upset. With *you*. You stole my credit card and took off on this wild trip all by yourself. What on God's green earth were you *thinking?*" Mom's voice rose to shrillness. "That's just it. You weren't thinking."

"But Mo-om," her little girl voice whined. "I said I'm sorry—"

"This is simply not acceptable! I have half a mind to tell Sam to put you on the next plane back here."

"I know, Mom. I just couldn't..." Electra held the phone away from her ear while her mother ranted. Peering through the whirl of snow, she blinked to keep from being hypnotized.

Sam slowed the truck's speed.

"Well, you're coming home, whether it's tonight or tomorrow or... Let me talk to Sam."

"I can't, Mom. I can't go back there. Please..." She held the phone out. "Mom wants to talk to you."

"Not right now. I'll call her when we get home." Her friend hunched forward over the wheel.

"We're in a snowstorm, Mom. She'll call you later."

"Oh dear. Now she has to drive you through a snowstorm?" Her mother whooshed out an exasperated-sounding breath. "All right, I will be talking to you later."

"Okay, Mom, 'bye."

Wind gusts whipped the snow into a frenzy. Electra sat quietly, staring out the windshield at the falling snow. *Oh man. How can she see where we're going?* Guilt shot through her like an arrow. After a while, she moaned. "Geez, this is bad, Sam. I'm so sorry."

Sam's jaw tightened. "Maybe time to say a prayer." She smacked the steering wheel.

Electra bowed her head, her heart pounding. *Hi, God. It's me, Electra. I'm really sorry I've caused so much trouble for my friend. Please help her drive and keep us safe.* She opened her eyes and peered up into the dense sky. *And please don't let Mom take me back to New York. Um…thanks. 'Bye.*

Finally, visibility cleared a bit, and Sam's shoulders seemed to relax from their hunched position. Then the bright lights of a semi beamed through the darkness toward them. Sam clamped her hands around the steering wheel as the wind blast from the big truck rocked the pickup and blew snow across the windshield. The vehicle slid sideways.

Electra shrieked.

Eternal seconds stretched as the old pickup continued in its long swerve. *Oh, oh, oh, no, no, no.*

Sam hugged the steering wheel and pushed the brakes slowly, intermittently. Then as suddenly as it began, the vehicle straightened itself, and they drifted to a stop on the side of the road.

Electra panted. *Ohmygosh, ohmygosh, ohmygosh!*

Sam closed her eyes and lowered her forehead to the wheel. After a long minute, she sat upright. "You okay?"

"Yeah." The word came out in a tiny squeak.

"Good." Sam huffed a semi-laugh. "We dodged a bullet,

that's for sure."

"Ohmygosh, ohmygosh, ohmygosh!" Electra felt like all the blood had drained from her face. "I… I was so…scared. Ohmygosh."

"Well, we're all right. And it's only another forty-five minutes or so home. We're going to make it." Sam shifted into gear and eased the pickup back onto the road. The snow drifted now rather than swirling.

With no further incidents, Sam pulled into the ranch yard at nearly midnight. They sat in silence for a minute, simply breathing.

"Th-thank…you…Sam." Electra's voice still quavered. "I've caused you so… much trouble. I-I'm s-sorry."

"Hey. We made it. We're okay." Sam squeezed her arm. "Let's go inside and make some hot chocolate."

Electra pulled out her suitcase, and they went in. The phone message light blinked. Horace's voice held concern. "Sure hope you decided to stay in Billings tonight, little gal. Give me a call when you get this, no matter what time it is."

Mom's message was equally tense. "Oh my, I hope you guys are all right. I didn't want to call your cell again if you were driving in a storm. Oh, I hope…" Her voice trailed off. "Call me when you get home. I don't care what time."

Sam took milk out of the fridge and the box of cocoa from the cupboard. "Go ahead and fix it. I'll make the calls." She punched in Horace's number first. When his sleepy voice wafted from the speaker, she said, "We're home safe and sound. Thank you for checking on us. Sorry I didn't call you, but I was a little busy with the roads."

"Yeah. When it started to snow, I kept picturing you in the ditch somewheres. You shoulda stayed in town. But I'm glad you're home."

"I know. I should have stayed. Didn't think it was gonna storm. Kinda sneaked up on us. Oh well. Go back to sleep. Sorry we worried you."

Mom was apparently still awake, despite it being 2 a.m. in New York. "Yes?" Her tone high-pitched, expectant.

"It's Sam. We're home, and we're fine."

A long, low sound almost like a moan soughed over the speaker. "Oh good. When Electra said you couldn't talk because you were in a snowstorm…" Another puff. "Golly, talk about feeling helpless."

"Yeah, it was a little hairy for a bit, but it's okay. We're going to have some cocoa, chill out a bit, and hit the hay. Can we talk more in the morning?"

"Absolutely. I'm going to have to figure out what to do with that girl. But you both get some rest now."

That girl. That meant she was *really* angry. Electra's stomach did flip-flops. *Ohmygosh, what have I done? Mom and Sam are both mad at me. I'm going back to New York for sure and will probably be grounded for the rest of my life. I might never get to come back here.*

She poured two cups of steaming chocolate and sprinkled marshmallows on top. "Sam… please don't be too mad at me. I'll make it up to you…somehow… I promise." Her eyes filled with hot tears.

Sam spoke in a stern tone. "We'll see what your mom has to say tomorrow."

"Do you think she'll let me stay?"

"I don't know. You'll just have to wait and see."

CHAPTER TWENTY-THREE

A hard rapping startled Electra awake.

"Time to rise and shine!"

Her eyes felt like sandpaper. It was still dark. She closed them again.

Another knock, a little harder. "Electra! Time to get up." She moaned.

"Are you awake?"

"Yeah." Her voice was raspy. "Okay, I'm up." She slid to the edge of the bed and went to open the door. She blinked against the light in the hallway. "What time is it?"

"Time to get the chores done. If you're going to prove what you promised, you're going to have to work hard. Harder than you've ever worked before." Her friend headed back downstairs. "Get dressed. I'll have breakfast ready in a few minutes."

The clock on the nightstand read 6 a.m. *Ugh.* She sighed. *Well, I asked for it! Might as well take my punishment.* Yet, even though she was still exhausted from the stress of her trip, a quickening stirred inside. The thought of seeing Apache and Trixi again gave her a rush and prodded her awake.

When she came downstairs, Sam gave her a cup of cocoa and set a steaming bowl of oatmeal in front of them both.

She took a sip of the hot chocolate. "It's not even light out yet. How do we see to do chores?" She'd forgotten how much darker it was out here in the winter.

"It's getting light. We'll be fine." Sam gestured to the center of the table. "There's brown sugar and raisins if you want them on your oatmeal."

"Okay." As Electra reached for the dish of raisins, her sweater sleeve rode up.

Sam stared at the angry red marks on her forearm. "What happened to your arm?"

Electra snatched her hand back and pulled down the sleeve. "Nothin'."

"Did somebody…?" Her friend's face crinkled with concern.

She shook her head and stared into her oatmeal.

"Did the girls at school do this?"

She shrugged. "No."

"Did you…cut yourself?" Sam persisted though a note of shock in her voice.

Electra bent closer to the bowl. A tear dripped into the oatmeal. *Will Sam think less of me now?*

Standing, her friend came around the table and put an arm around her. "Oh, honey." She compressed her shaking shoulders. "What can I do? Do you want to tell me about this?"

Electra stood abruptly. "I'm going to the barn."

Sam pushed out a breath and backed away. "Okay. You can chop the ice in the tank and feed the horses some of their pellets. I'm going to call your mom, and then I'll be out to throw down some hay. Horace is coming over in a while to help with the feeding."

Electra slipped into the coveralls Sam had set out, and left, head bowed, legs dragging. *I've been caught. Mom'll never let me stay now.* Dark dread spiraled from her stomach to her chest.

Inside the barn, she stopped to inhale the sweet aroma of hay and horse. Then she headed straight for Apache's stall. When he saw her, he hung his head over the gate and gave a low, rumbling whicker.

"Hello, boy. I'm so glad to see you." She caressed his face and then buried her head in his mane. "I've missed you so much." He arched his head and neck around her. Sobs erupted, and she could only lean into the strength and love he radiated while she cried herself dry.

Then she felt him move his head and rumble a greeting to someone behind her. She jerked back. "Oh. Hi, Sam. I didn't hear you." She swiped a mitten across her cheek. "Sorry, I didn't get anything done yet. I only wanted to…to…see Apache." The last words came out in hiccupped sobs.

Sam stepped into the stall and wrapped her arms around her. "I know. That's exactly what you needed. And he knows that." They stood, entwined and rocking, for several long moments.

Then Electra eased back. "I'm okay. Let's get to work." She sniffled, reached into her pocket for a tissue, and blew loudly.

"All right then. If you want to give the horses some pellets, you know where the bin is. I'll go up in the loft and toss down a bale."

"What did Mom say?" She peered at her friend. *What if I can't stay here? What can I do to convince her?*

"She's going to give us a few days to work things out. She'll call you tonight."

An exhale lowered her shoulders. "Okay." *Maybe there's hope.*

When the horses were fed, she and Sam each grabbed an ax and chopped the four-inch-thick ice from the tank, throwing the chunks into a growing pile to the side. Electra hacked at the ice with more strength than she realized she had, as if beating down her demons.

As Sam lifted the last chunk of ice from the tank, Horace's truck roared up the driveway. Electra waved both arms. When he eased himself from the vehicle, she ran to give him a bear hug. "Ohmygosh, I'm so glad to see you, Horace. I missed you *so* much."

"I missed you too." He hugged her back.

"Well, I'm here to work… hard…" She moved back and spoke with a serious expression. "I want to prove to Mom and you guys I can do it." Her eyes welled with tears. "I want to stay here…so bad."

"All right then." Horace swept an arm out. "Let's get to work. There's cows to feed. You can help me stack the truck."

Sam threw down the hay, and Horace showed Electra how to arrange the bales. He grabbed one end of the bale with a hook, and she took the other, puffing and grunting as they maneuvered it in place. When the pickup was loaded, they all piled in, and Horace drove to the pasture, where the cows awaited with eager white faces looking in the direction of breakfast.

"Okay, you come up top and help me distribute the hay while Horace drives." Sam cut the twine and tossed down a flake.

Electra threw herself into the job with gusto, dropping hay as fast as she could.

"Whoa. Slow down. A little at a time, like this." Sam showed her.

She relaxed into the task. *This is actually kind of fun.* It felt good to work hard physically. "Look at those cows." She laughed, pointing. "They take one bite and then run behind us to get the next one. It's like they're racing each other."

"Yup. Cows are greedy…just like people sometimes."

When the truck bed was emptied, Horace drove to the reservoir. Sam handed Electra an ax. "More ice to chop."

She gulped, but again, she attacked the chore with all her might.

When the ice was cleared from holes so the cattle could drink, they all got back into the truck. Electra rubbed her hands together. "That's the only part of me that's cold." Her arms quivered, and her whole body shook with tiny tremors. "This is really hard work. You do it every day?"

"Twice a day, during the cold, snowy months." Sam grinned at her shock. "About every other day when the snow's not too deep and the cows can get to some grass. Now, we go home for lunch, and then do the same thing at Horace's."

The girl's eyes widened. "Can I drive the truck at your place?"

Horace guffawed. "I see right through ya, young lady. Nope, not this time."

***

When they got home that evening, Sam went into the kitchen to fix supper. Electra collapsed on a chair. "I can't raise my arms."

"You're probably going to be pretty sore tomorrow. You worked very hard today. I'm proud of you." Sam flashed her a thumbs-up. "We'll get a day to rest though. I want to go to Billings to see Brad. I hope he'll be able to stay awake soon."

"Oh. Yeah. I hope so too. I miss his teasing."

"Me too." Sam flipped burgers in one frying pan and stirred sliced potatoes and onions in another. Then she set ketchup, mustard, and pickles on the table. "Hungry?"

"Am I ever!" Electra scooted the chair up to the table and stuck out a hand to grab a napkin, slowing in mid-reach and wincing. "I'm sorry I didn't help with supper. I actually *can't* move my arms."

"You'll get used to it." Sam sat and dished up the food. When they finished, she made hot chocolate and brought out oatmeal raisin cookies.

Electra took a bite and closed her eyes. "Mmm, so good."

Her friend cleared her throat. "I know you've been going through some hard times lately."

The cookie turned to a sour taste in her mouth. *Oh-oh. Here it comes...*

"I don't know what it's like to lose a brother and then having your dad leave." Sam peered at her with an earnest expression. "But I do know how painful it was for me when my grandparents died. Grandma Anna and Grandpa Neil were so important to me while I was growing up. I really felt empty when they were gone."

Electra stared at the cookie in her hand.

"And now my whole family is far away, living off the grid in Alaska, and I hardly ever hear from them. Haven't seen them in about three years." Sam sighed. "And my best friend, Jace, got into drugs and alcohol. You know what happened—you met her. She's paralyzed for life." She closed her eyes a moment. "I always blamed myself for not being able to stop her."

Electra nodded but continued to stare at the cookie.

"It's not the same as what you've gone through, but..." Sam put a hand on her arm, "I want you to know you can talk to me about anything."

Electra nodded again, her cheeks wet with tears. *Maybe...*

Sam stood, came around the table, and wrapped her in a long, warm hug.

***

After the supper dishes were done, Electra punched in her mother's number with icy fingers, dread churning the food in her stomach.

"Hi, Mom."

"I'm glad to hear from you."

"Me too. Please don't be mad at me. I couldn't stay there anymore."

"I know. How are you feeling?"

Oh boy. That was a switcheroo. Did Sam tell her about my arm? She worried her bottom lip with her teeth. "I'm fine, Mom. I worked *really* hard today, Sam can tell you… So can I stay?"

"Well…we'll have to see. I talked to your teachers and the school counselor today, and I'm going back in a couple of days. They're checking into setting up some kind of study program so you can keep up with your class for a while…whether it's for a couple of weeks or the rest of the school year. That is yet to be determined."

Relief flooded her core. "Okay. Thank you, Mom. I'm going to work really hard on studies and helping on the ranch and everything and you'll see I can do it and please let me stay and thank you, Mom, I love you."

Her mother chuckled. "Let me talk to Sam."

When Sam hung up, she smiled and winked. "Well, it sounds like she's going to give you a chance to prove yourself…at least for a little while. But you're going to have to work extra hard—at your schoolwork, as well as here and at Clyde's."

"Oh, I will, I truly will! Thank you, Sam." Suddenly feeling light as a feather, she floated into the living room. *Mom's giving me a chance, and so is Sam.* She peered out the window into the night sky. *Oh, thank you, Lord.*

CHAPTER TWENTY-FOUR

"How are you feeling today?" Sam asked when Electra came downstairs the next morning.

"Oh man. I could barely lift my arms to get my sweater on." She giggled. "I might not be able to help you chop ice today. I'm sorry."

Sam took a couple of waffles from the toaster and spread them with peanut butter for a quick breakfast. "That's okay. Eat and then come down to the barn and feed the horses. I'll go ahead and open up the water on the tank." She shot her a grin. "But tomorrow, you're back on the job."

She spoke solemnly. "All right. I'll do it." *Anything, Sam, anything to stay here.*

As quickly as possible, they finished the chores, and headed for Billings.

"Did you talk to Brad's sister last night? Is he okay?"

Sam told her the doctor was planning to take him off all sedation this morning and would see about moving him out of ICU if he responded well.

"Awesome! Can I come and see him too?"

"I'm sorry, honey, but he's still in ICU, and they won't let anyone but family in. Melissa had to fib a little and tell the nurse I'm his fiancée so I could see him."

Electra widened her eyes. "Really? Do you think you and—?"

"No! It's way too soon for that. All I want right now is for him to wake up and have no brain damage." The cowgirl leaned against the backrest. "So, while I'm at the hospital, do you want to visit Miss Robin?"

"Will Sapphire and the girls be there?"

"Probably not. It's a school day. But you and Miss Robin could talk…"

"Meh." She made a noncommittal sound. "I dunno." She swiveled to look out the window, sitting in silence for a while. *Do I really want to see a counselor—even if it is Miss Robin? What would she say that Sam hasn't already?* Finally, she asked, "So what about that program in Miles City with the vets? Are you going to do that?"

"I think so. I haven't talked to Nick for a few days, just waiting to hear if the board is all right with me starting before I'm certified."

"Well, if you do, can I help, like I did when I was here for Christmas? That was so fun."

"I think so. We'd probably have to get permission for that too. But… I'm a little concerned about using Trixi too much. She's about twenty years old, still in good shape, but I don't know if all the up and down will eventually be harmful to her."

"Oh. Yeah, I hadn't thought about that." Electra shook her head. "That wouldn't be good." She sat silent for a couple of minutes when an idea came to her. "Hey. I wonder if I could teach Apache to kneel?"

"Hmm. That's a good idea. Do you know how you would go about doing that?"

"Not for sure… But Miss Ellie still lives in Billings, doesn't she?" She focused a huge, hopeful smile on her friend. "Could I go visit her today? I could ask her how she trained Trixi."

"Sure. I'll bet she would love to see you." Sam pointed at her cell phone on the seat between them. "Go into my contacts list and call her."

Miss Ellie was more than excited to have company, so Sam drove by the assisted living facility to drop Electra off. She came inside to say hi and double-check that leaving her was okay.

"Oh, yes indeed!" the tiny white-haired lady chortled. "This is going to be so much fun. Come here, dear, and let me give you a hug."

***

The mid-afternoon sun slanted toward the horizon when Sam came to pick her up.

"We baked cookies." She held out a plate of oatmeal raisin delights.

Sam bit into one. "Mmm. Tastes wonderful."

She hopped from one foot to the other. "Miss Ellie and I had so much fun today."

The old woman grinned from her recliner. "Oh, we sure did. Help yourself to some coffee and come sit."

Sam poured a cup for Ellie and herself and eased onto the sofa.

Electra bounced beside her. "Miss Ellie gave me a lot of ideas for training Apache to kneel. She thinks I can do it. I'm so excited, I can't wait to get home and get started! Oh, it's going to be *so* much fun."

"Okay. That's great." Sam patted her arm. "It'll be a big project though."

The former trick rider's white curls haloed her beaming face "Yes, but if anyone can, Electra can. With your help, of course."

"Oh yes, Sam. It's going to be awesome and Apache is such a good horse and I think he's going to learn really quick!" She couldn't help but chatter away about the signals and everything Miss Ellie had taught her. *I can't wait! Mom is going to be proud of me. I can do this. She'll see...*

Her friend chuckled. "Well, it sounds like fun. Miss Ellie, when the weather clears up a little more, I'd love to bring you out for a visit. I bet Trixi would be happy to see you."

The woman's eyes grew bigger. "That would be wonderful. I would enjoy that so much."

***

Electra woke just before dawn the next morning. She slipped on warm clothes and hurried out to the corral before Sam was up. Giving Toby and Sugar a couple of pellets and a pat on the nose, she led Apache into the round corral. "Good morning, boy, how are you today? Guess what? We're going to have some fun, and I'm going to teach you how to kneel. Would you like that?" She brushed his black mane and hugged him.

Then she saddled him and put a halter and lead rope on his head. She spoke softly as she stood in front of him, putting pressure on the rope. "Okay, we're going to back up now." The gelding tucked his head toward his chest and took a step backward. "Good boy." Electra kept talking to him and backing him. Then she brought the rope along her side and around to the saddle horn. She stood next to the stirrup and pulled back on the lead. Apache kept his head tucked and after a moment's hesitation, backed again easily. She released the pressure and repeated the exercise several times, each time rewarding him with praise and a treat. "You're doin' great, boy."

Finally, she noticed Sam resting a foot on the bottom rail, her arm slung over Toby's neck. "G'morning, Sam. Apache is doing *really* great already."

"Well done. You are so patient and good with him. I'm sure he'll catch on quickly."

She led the bay to the fence, where Sam handed her a breakfast bar and gave Apache and Toby a handful of pellets.

"I 'spose we have to get the chores and feeding done now?" Electra caressed her horse's neck and gave her a wistful sidelong glance.

"Yes, ma'am. That's our number one priority." The cowgirl spoke firmly. "I see you chopped ice in the tank already. Thank you. So if you want to unsaddle him, we can feed them all some hay. Horace should be along any time, and we'll head out to the pasture."

"Okay. We'll do this some more later, Apache. Good boy!" She planted a kiss on his nose and led him to the barn.

Horace arrived in his usual fashion, cheerful and rarin' to go. "Mornin', ladies. It's a beautiful day in the neighborhood."

"Yes, it is," Sam greeted him.

Electra squinted into the clear blue sky, the sun's golden beams reflecting from the snow. *Yes, it is beautiful. And I get to be out here, working with my horse.*

"Horace! Guess what. I'm starting to train Apache to kneel, Miss Ellie told me all about how to do it, and she's going to come out and visit and help me some more when the weather is better, and now we'll have two horses to help with the vets in Miles City. Isn't that exciting?"

The old man raised his bushy gray eyebrows. "Well, yes, I'd say it is. Very good, Miss Electra." He grinned at Sam. "Let's get the truck loaded."

After feeding the hay to the cows in the pasture, Horace unloaded the axes. "How's the muscles today, little gal?"

She giggled. "Oh, I'm sore, but not as bad as yesterday and the day before. At least I can lift my arms again." She hoisted her ax high in the air to demonstrate.

Sam and Horace laughed. "We'll get you in cowgirl shape yet," he said.

***

The following morning dawned as another cold, but sun-sparkling day. Again, Electra rose early to work with Apache. The crisp morning was silent except for the crunch of horses' hooves on snow. She breathed in the peacefulness of the ranch. First, she buried her face in the gelding's neck, gathering the strength she needed to get through the day. All her tension from New York had drained away in the last few days, leaving a feeling of almost weightlessness. She realized she hadn't even thought of the glass…the pain…since she'd been back. "Oh, Apache," she murmured. "You're my life saver."

With loose limbs, she calmly tacked him up and began the backing process again. "Good boy. You remembered what we did yesterday. Okay, let's do it again."

"You need to eat a proper breakfast before you come out here." Sam's voice startled her from her concentration.

She frowned and turned her mouth down at the corners. *Killjoy.*

Sam handed her a protein bar, and then smiled at her and the gelding. "He's making good progress."

"Yeah, he's so easy to work with." Pride welled up, and Electra flashed a hopeful grin. "So far, anyway. I guess I'll keep doing the backing training for a couple more days. Miss Ellie told me about putting a hobble on his legs to start the lying-down process." She grimaced. "That's a little scary. I wouldn't want him to fall."

"I can see that it would be, but I'll help you if I can. And maybe if you can wait until Ellie comes out here, she'd probably have some more good tips for you."

"Okay. Good idea." Electra gestured toward the water tank. "I chopped the ice first and gave everybody some pellets but haven't fed the hay yet. Are we feeding the cows again today?"

Sam studied the hills, still covered by a coating of snow with maize-colored wisps of grass poking through. "I think they can get enough grass for today, but you and I can drive out and open up the water and give them some cake."

"Can I work with Apache again and maybe Toby this afternoon?" Electra flashed her a hopeful look.

"We'll see. I want to drive in to Ingomar and get the mail. Your mom said she'd mailed your books, so they might be here by now."

"Aww." *Schoolwork*. Her hopeful attitude collapsed, and she lowered her head. Then she gave a resigned sigh. "Okay. I s'pose I better be doing that, or Mom won't let me stay."

"Yup. Hard work, keep up with your studies, and maybe you'll win her over."

In town, Sam retrieved her laptop from the truck, downloaded the therapy course materials Nick had sent her for the veterans' program, and printed out a number of pages on Billy's office printer at the Jersey Lilly, just in case the slow dial-up at home wouldn't handle it. Then she and Electra walked over to the post office. Sure enough, there was a big box with Electra's name on it. Sam smirked. "Well, now we both have homework."

Electra made a face but then grinned. "Okay. As long as we do it together."

That afternoon, she went back out to work with Apache. The gelding was so patient, backing and backing and backing again for his girl. "Good boy. You're my boy."

She glanced over at Sam. "Can I put a hobble on him, just to get him used to it?"

"Sure. I'll get one for you." Her friend went into the barn and came back with a braided heavy cotton rope. Ellie had told Electra to use it to lift one foot, altering Apache's balance to try and get him to kneel.

"Miss Ellie said I need to help him get used to feeling the rope. But I might need your help."

"Okay. First, let's see if he'll let you lift his leg."

Electra rubbed Apache's leg and murmured to him. Then she reached down and tugged at his foot. He willingly allowed her to pick it up and cradle it in her arm. She grinned.

"He's pretty used to having his feet worked on, so that's a good first step." Sam stood close by, also talking to the horse, and caressing his neck. "Now, just put the rope under his foot to cradle it."

Electra followed her instructions, and the gelding stood calmly, although watching them out of the corner of his eye. "Good boy, Apache. Good boy."

She released his foot, repeated the exercise several times on that side, and then the other.

"I think maybe that's enough for the first time." Sam smiled at them.

Electra's body thrummed with the energy of a successful exercise. "He's such a dream to work with."

"I'm so proud of you and what you've accomplished already. You're both doing very well." Sam hugged her. "Well, I hate to be the bad guy, but now we need to go inside and do our homework."

"Aww." She made a pouty face. "I know." With one last pat to her horse, she let him loose in the pasture. "Be good, boy. I'll see you tomorrow."

An hour later, across the kitchen table, she snapped her Algebra book shut with a groan. "This is too hard. I'll never get this stuff and I don't know how Mom and Mrs. Nelson thought I could do it all without classes and teachers and..." She huffed and stood.

Sam raised her focus from her work and reached out a hand. "I know it's hard, really hard, and I'm not sure how much help I can be. I didn't do all that well in Algebra myself."

She scrunched her face in a scowl. "Yeah. What was Mom thinking? She needs to be here to help me." She strode to the wall phone and punched in the number. After a few seconds, her mother's voice answered. "Mom? I can't do this! I'm stuck on Algebra and I need help and you need to come here and help me and…" Her voice broke with a sob.

"I know it's hard, honey, but you made the choice to go to Montana, and you're going to have to prove that you will keep up with your studies."

"Mo-om!" Electra's voice rose. "I *do* want to keep up with school, but—"

"Otherwise, you're going to come home and go back to school here." Her mother's voice was stern.

"I don't want to come home! Please, Mom!"

"All right then. You'll have to do the work. Let me talk to Sam."

Tears trickled pathways down her cheeks. "She wants to talk to you."

Sam stood.

"Please don't let her make me go back. Please." Her face was hot, and her lips trembled. "I'll do whatever it takes. I'll study more. I'll get this stuff. I promise."

Putting her arm around her shoulders, Sam drew her closer. "Let me talk to her. We'll see if we can work something out." She peered into her eyes. "Okay? Deep breath now."

Electra hiccupped another sob. "Okay. Please…" She stopped on the other side of the doorframe, listening.

Sam picked up the phone. "Hi, Alberta. We seem to be having a little trouble with math here at this end."

Electra's chest filled with a hundred dreadful flapping crows' wings. *Can Sam talk her into letting me stay?*

Sam leaned against the kitchen counter. "I'd like to give it a try. And if I can't, maybe the tutor-thing could work from this end. Mrs. Bruckner does some of the bookwork for their dude ranch. Maybe she could help or maybe she or Teresa would know of someone nearby."

Oh, a tutor. Yes, maybe Mrs. Bruckner will help me. She's nice. She could barely breathe.

"Let's see how it goes here for a while longer. She's been doing so well with the ranch work and training Apache. I think Electra and I can do this together." Sam had a confident note in her voice and motioned for her.

She took the receiver. "Mom? I'm sorry." She sniffed.

"All right, sweetheart. Sam has some ideas to help you. You do what she tells you, okay?"

The flapping in her chest quieted. "Okay, Mom. I'll work hard with Sam, I promise. Love you. 'Bye."

CHAPTER TWENTY-FIVE

Phone calls to Irene Bruckner and Teresa brought the same answers: "I took Algebra in high school, but I'd have to have a refresher to remember any of it now." Teresa suggested someone from the school, but that was in Forsyth, forty-five minutes away.

Sam shook her head as she related the news. "No way can we make that drive every day or even a couple times a week."

Her heart sank. "Mom's not going to let me stay."

"Oh yes, she *will*. We'll figure this out." Sam tried to encourage and joke with her.

While her friend prepared supper, Electra slouched on the sofa staring at her textbooks, discouraged. *It might as well be Greek!*

The phone rang after they'd eaten. "It's your mom."

Again? What now?

Her mother didn't waste time on pleasantries. "I'm taking a few days off work and coming out there. I need to see what's going on."

Electra gulped. *Oh-oh. She's coming to get me.* Her heart shriveled like a raisin in the sun. *I can't go back there, I just can't!* Tears streamed down her face as she hung up. "She's not going to let me stay. I know it. She's not." A wail burst from her lips. "If I have to go back there, I'll… I'll…just die!"

***

As Friday and Mom's arrival approached, Electra's concentration on her studies wavered. She slammed her books shut. She paced. She ran her fingers viciously through her hair, spiking it in all directions. She was impatient with Apache, and the horse refused to even back up for her.

"Oh, man, what's wrong with you? You were just doing this!" Her voice rose to a crescendo. Tears prickled her eyelids, and storm clouds hung heavy on her shoulders. *It's no use. I can't do this. I'm a failure, and Mom will make me go home with her.*

Thursday late afternoon, her face held tight, Sam gathered their tack. "Let's go for a ride."

Electra nodded, eyes downcast. She saddled her horse, swung up, and took off at a gallop.

"Stop! Let him warm up," Sam yelled behind them.

Ignoring the warning, Electra urged the gelding faster. "Go, Apache, go!" The cold breeze whipped knifelike into her face, and she leaned forward in the saddle, screaming as if she could leave all her demons behind. She wanted to keep on going, over the miles and hills, until she came to the end of the earth where no one could find her.

Finally, guilt overtook her, and at the top of a rise overlooking the reservoir and its few winter-bared cottonwood trees, she reined Apache to a stop. She rested her cheek on his neck, tears flowing. "I'm sorry, boy." She hiccupped. "I shouldn't have run you so hard." He blew and stomped as she slid off and slumped onto a boulder nearby.

Sam rode up but stayed in the saddle for a few minutes before dismounting, her disapproval like the presence of a grim specter.

Electra sneaked a glance from the corner of her eye. *Oh*

man. She's really gonna let me have it now. And then she'll probably agree with Mom and make me go home. I blew it.

Then her friend sat next to her on the rock. "Okay. Tell me what's up."

She turned her wind-stung face toward her. "Mom's not going to let me stay."

"You don't know that."

"Yes, I do. She's not happy with me being here without her and not doing good in my schoolwork." Her chin drifted to her chest. "And I've disappointed you too."

"Hey. No, you haven't." Sam put an arm around her. "You and I have been working very hard on your Algebra, and I think we're doing much better. We'll get 'er done."

Her shoulders edged toward her ears. "I dunno about that. What if I can't? What if she insists I go home?"

"Listen. Your mom misses you. And she's concerned about you. She just wants to come visit and see for herself how things are going. I get that. We have a lot of progress to show her—with Apache's training and that you *are* trying hard with your studies."

"B-but Apache won't… He quit…" A sob broke through her throat. *I was mean to him and now he won't like me anymore.*

Sam gave her a squeeze. "Apache is sensitive to your moods. He knows something is wrong. He wants to work with you, but you've been, maybe, a *little* impatient with him lately?"

"Yeah. I know." Electra buried her face in her hands and sobbed harder. The cowgirl gathered her into her arms and patted her back, murmuring, "It's okay, honey. It'll be okay."

Finally, her wrenching cries stopped, and she pulled back. "I'm sorry, Sam." Lip quivering, she stood and walked to her horse standing patiently, watching her. "I'm so sorry, Apache." She rubbed his face and head and then leaned into his neck. "Please forgive me. I didn't mean to treat you bad." A hiccup. "I love you, Apache. I'm sorry."

The gelding encircled her with his head in a horsey hug. All was forgiven.

***

At the airport the next day, Electra's body tensed when she spotted Mom, clad in a dark blue puffy winter coat, at the baggage carousel.

"Hey there," Sam called out. "Welcome back to Montana."

Mom's face lit up, and she held her arms open. Sam gave her a quick hug, and then both faced Electra who hung back, her head down. Her stomach roiled, and she only wanted to run out of the terminal. *I'm doomed!*

"Sweetheart, come here," her mother coaxed in a soft voice, continuing to hold her arms out.

Electra swallowed, lifted her face, and then ran into her mother's arms, sobbing. "Mom…Mom… I'm so glad to see you. I-I…m-missed you."

Her mom hugged her tight. "I missed you too, honey."

At last, the tears and hiccups subsided. *I have to be brave. I have to show her everything I've done already.*

Grabbing her suitcase, Mom linked her arm with Electra's. "Okay, ladies, I'm ready to head to the ranch. I need some peace and quiet."

Sam tittered. "Well… I hope you can find some."

Electra let out a long, slow breath. *Maybe she really does need a rest. Maybe she won't force me to go back.* She sat in silence for several miles, trying to figure out how she could convince her mom. Then the excitement of what she'd been doing bubbled up. "Oh, Mom, I gotta show you what I'm doing with Apache, he's backing up, and I have him getting used to hobbles, and pretty soon I'm going to teach him to kneel down, and then we'll have another horse to work with when we go help the veterans learn to ride. I'm *so* excited, I can't wait to show you!" She gasped for air.

Her mom widened her eyes and spoke into the pause. "Wow, that sounds great. I can't wait to see."

"And Sam's been studying with me and helping me with my math and schoolwork and I think I'm doing okay now and I'm going to keep it up and I just… Mom…" She cocked her head in what she hoped was a pleading, puppy-dog look. "I just love it here and I love working with Sam and the horses, and I don't want to go back to New York…oh, Mom."

Her mother put an arm around her. "Let's not worry about that right now. I'm glad you're doing well." She peered at Sam. "I'll still be here Monday, so I'd love to come in with you and see how it goes with the veterans."

"Yay, Mom! That's awesome. How long do you get to stay?" Electra bounced on the truck seat.

"Gotta go back Wednesday. But we're going to enjoy every minute while I'm here." Alberta grinned. "I'm not even going to *think* about taxes for the next five days."

They chatted about Brad and ranch chores and neighbors for the rest of the trip, and Electra couldn't help but add her excitement and enthusiasm—jumping into the middle of their sentences. Soon, they were all laughing to the point where Sam had to take a breath. "I'm going to run off the road if I don't settle down here. Hey, let's stop and get a bite at the Jersey Lilly."

As they entered the café, Horace waved from a table in the back. "Hey there, ladies, come join me." After hugs all around, the women sat.

"Good to see ya, Miz Alberta. What brings you back to these here parts so soon?"

She picked up a menu. "Well, I was just missing my girl too much, so I decided to come for a short visit."

"I kin understand that. Good to see ya again." He took a sip of coffee as Billy brought his meal and took the women's orders. "So, Electra, how's the horse training goin'?"

"Oh, it's so fun, I love it, and Apache is the most wonderful horse in the world, he's so patient and he's learning everything so fast." She beamed at him as she recounted, once again, everything she and Apache were doing.

Horace burst into laughter. "That's great, little gal. I'm proud of ya. And how's the schoolwork coming along?"

His question dampened her joy, and she shot a quick glance at her mother. "Well, I was having some trouble with Algebra, and Mom came to check on me. But Sam's been helping me, and I think I'm…well yes, I *am* doing okay. I *am* going to get it." She sat up straight in her chair. "I don't want to go back to New York."

Mom's face hardened into stern lines. "Yes, Electra needs to keep up with her studies and get good grades to be able to stay here."

Sam told her neighbor about her search for a tutor, with no luck, and that she'd been boning up on the subject, studying along with Electra.

Billy brought their meals. They all began to eat with gusto. After a few minutes, Horace leaned back in his chair. "W-e-l-l… You probably don't know this, but I went to college for a while when I was just a pup, and…I was a math major." His mouth quirked up at one corner. "It was about a hundred years ago, but I'll bet I remember enough to be able to tutor you, young lady. Algebra was kinda my *thing*."

What? Electra's jaw dropped the same time she saw Sam's mouth open in a huge O, and her mom's eyebrows rose toward her hairline. They all stared, speechless, at the old man.

Electra recovered first. She squealed, scraped her chair

back, dashed to Horace's side, and threw her arms around his neck. "Ohmygosh, thank you, thank you, thank you! You are my angel, you're my lifesaver. Thank you, thank you, thank you!"

Horace gave them a lop-sided, aw-shucks grin.

Electra disengaged and widened her eyes at her mother. "Did you hear that, Mom? Did you? Horace can help me, and Sam's already helping me, and I'm going to keep up with my studies, Mom, did you hear that?"

Her mother sat silent for another moment. Then peals of laughter erupted. She stood and grabbed her daughter in a bear hug. "Yes, honey, I heard that. It's wonderful. Thank you, kind sir."

He shrugged and scrubbed his fingers over his salty-gray crewcut. "W-e-l-l, let's see how much I actually remember." He guffawed, and Sam, Electra, and her mom couldn't help but join in. Their laughter ricocheted around the room, infecting the other patrons and Billy behind the bar too.

***

When they arrived home, Electra leaped out of the truck. "Mom! You've gotta come see. I *need* to show you what me and Apache are doing."

Her mother rolled her eyes but left her suitcase in the pickup and followed her to the corral. Sam came along, chuckling.

"Okay, sweet boy. Let's show Mom what we can do. Please work with me. I'm sorry I was impatient with you before. You can do this." Electra attached a lead rope to the gelding's halter and put him through his paces, backing with his chin tucked toward his chest. Then she tapped his front shoulder and reached down to pick up his foot. Before she took hold, however, he lifted it on his own. Her heart leaped. *Oh! Wow.*

She heard Sam gasp and a "hmm" from her mother.

"Good boy." Electra supported the foot with the lead and ran the rope around the saddle horn. Apache stood patiently and quietly for several seconds, head down, leaning back slightly. She released the foot, patted his neck, and caressed his face. Giving him a cake pellet from her pocket, she again murmured, "Good boy, Apache, good boy." Then she turned toward her mother and Sam, a glow warming her face.

"Wow." Mom released a breath. "Oh, my goodness, honey. I'm impressed."

"I'm so proud of you." Sam stepped forward. "When did you do this last bit? I had no idea."

Electra shrugged, her face aglow. "I dunno. Little by little. We still have a ways to go before I teach him to kneel though."

Her mom and Sam engulfed her in a group hug.

"You're doing great, daughter. I'm so, so very proud of you and what you've accomplished with this horse." A tear trickled from the corner of Mom's eye.

She's proud of me. She suddenly felt taller, bigger, and stronger.

"She is gifted, a natural." Sam gave Electra another squeeze. "Now, let's do chores and head on up to the house. You can show your mom what you've accomplished with your schoolwork."

Electra scrunched her face in a mock scowl, but then she couldn't prevent her grin from returning. "Okay!" She bounded off to the loft to throw down flakes of hay for the horses. One hurdle down, one more to go. Confidence rose once again inside. *Maybe…just maybe, I can pull this off.*

A pleasant afternoon included a ride for the three women and more horse demonstrations, including a gentling session with Toby who was still afraid to enter the barn after the vehicle accident with Brad.

After supper, Electra cracked open her books and showed Mom where she was working and having trouble. Her tense body relaxed as her mom patiently explained the problems and methods of getting the answers.

"Okay. I understand that one now." A hope-filled glow suffused her chest. "Mom. Thank you for not yelling at me when I don't get it."

"Oh, sweetheart, I never want to yell at you." Mom's eyes softened. "That's not the way to help you learn. You just need to understand the basics, and then you'll be able to figure the rest out."

"Yeah. I hope so."

"Well, I *know* so, and with Horace's help, you're going to do just fine." Her mother rose from the table, came around and gave her a hug. "I am very proud of you, young lady."

Aww. "Thanks, Mom." She blinked back tears. *Ohmygosh, I never thought she would be saying* that *when she came.*

"What you've shown me today is leaps and bounds of progress." Her mother sat again, leaned forward, and took her hands. "I need to apologize to you for not paying more attention to how you were feeling back home. I got so caught up in my own whirlwind life, I didn't see how much you were hurting."

Electra's heart filled with a new sense of connection. "You were too, I know. Losing Jimmy—" Her voice broke.

A tear slipped down her mom's cheek. "That is said to be the worst loss a person can go through—the loss of a child. And then your dad too… The way I coped was by working longer and harder. But I wasn't thinking how deeply that affected you too." She sighed. "I guess I figured you're young and resilient, and kids bounce back quicker than adults."

Electra snorted. "Nah."

Mom caressed her arm. "And then Sam told me…" She pushed back Electra's sleeve to peer at the now-healing scratches.

Her muscles contracted. It was all she could do not to snatch her arm back and cover it again. *That was really stupid to do it where it could be seen.* She bit her cheek. *It was stupid to do it. Period.*

Mom spoke hesitantly. "I don't want to drag up a sore subject, but…how are you feeling? I mean, really? Are you still wanting to do this?" Her eyes flicked to the scars.

She shook her head, just a little. "I'm doing a lot better, Mom, honest. I've been in to talk to Miss Robin a couple times when Sam visited Brad, and that has helped me a lot. She's very understanding, and she explains things really good. And Sam is so nice to me too. She's my best friend." She turned an earnest face toward her mother. "And Apache… He's really my bestest friend, and when I'm with him, I don't feel the pain anymore."

Her mother wrapped her hands around hers tightly.

She took a shaky breath. "He needed me. Somebody, something needed *me*. That's why I ran away—I needed him too. I'm sorry, Mom. I know it was wrong, and I should've talked to you."

"Oh, sweetheart." Tears flowed down her mother's face. "Thank you for talking to me now. Yes, it is important, and we need to be better about that—talk things out, share our feelings, and come up with solutions together."

"Okay. It's a deal. I love you, Mom." She drank in the moment, to remember this feeling forever.

CHAPTER TWENTY-SIX

Saturday evening, Electra and her mom joined Sam for supper at the Bruckners'. Irene met them at the door with giant hugs and a smile to match. "Come in, come in. We're so happy to see you."

Clyde shook hands, his weathered face beaming. "Sure hope you've come to stay."

Mom paused. "Well, I've thought about it, and that would be lovely. Not quite yet, but after April 15… It's a possibility. I'm thinking on it."

"Well, if you'd like a job here with me, we sure could use a good accountant." The rancher leaned forward. "And I know all the ranchers around here would use you for their taxes. And you could live here, in one of our cabins."

Electra stood beside her mom, nodding like a woodpecker on fast-forward. *Ohmygosh. She said it's possible.* This was the first time her mother had hinted that it might happen. And Clyde would give her a job? Is this real?

Mom's face registered open-mouthed surprise. "Thank you. That's a very generous offer, and it means a lot to me. I love Montana and its slower pace. I'm going to do some soul-searching and see what happens." Then Mom put a hand on her arm. "But, young lady, we'll have to see how your math tutoring goes first, along with everything else. The decision hinges on you."

Electra's body vibrated, but she remained calm and quiet. "Okay, Mom."

It was taking everything she had in her not to erupt. Sam patted her shoulder. Electra beamed and mouthed *We can do this.*

The rest of the evening, she settled into the easy rhythm of friendship offered so freely by these wonderful people. She'd never known anyone in New York like them. They were not only friends—among Sam, the Bruckners, and Horace, she'd found a second family.

***

Monday morning, Sam loaded Trixi into the trailer for their trip to Miles City.

"Could we bring Apache too? I can show Nick and Del and Garrett and everybody how well he's doing." Electra sent Sam a pleading look. "And maybe do some more training at the same time?"

Sam scrunched her mouth to one side as she considered the request. "Hmm. I dunno. Do you think he'll cooperate, with a group watching? I wonder if he'd be too distracting to the lesson and work I'll be doing with the vets."

"Please." She couldn't help her little-girl voice. "He loves to show off, and I think they would like to see how he's doing and that they're going to have another horse to ride."

"Well…okay. We can try and see how he reacts. Maybe it would be good to get him used to being around more people while you're doing your thing."

"Yesss!" Electra fist-pumped the air, pivoted, and ran toward the barn to get Apache.

She heard her mother chortle. "You're such a pushover."

"Yeah, I am." Sam giggled. "But this just might be good for both of them."

Electra giggled too. *We'll show them all!*

After the hour and a half drive, they pulled up to the chutes at the ag college, where Nick Seward met them. "I've got six vets here today, very interested in what you are doing."

"Six?" Sam's face had the deer-in-the-headlights expression. She gave him what appeared to be a forced smile. "That's great, Nick."

"You'll do fine, Sam." Electra rubbed her friend's arm. "And I'm here to help you."

"Thanks. I'm glad you are."

They unloaded the horses and brought them into the arena, where about a dozen people stood watching. Even more of an audience. *Wow. I hope Sam isn't too nervous.*

Sam swallowed visibly and straightened her posture.

You can do it. Electra sent her telepathic encouragement.

Nick introduced her friend, then Electra, and Trixi.

Sam cleared her throat. "Good morning, ladies and gentlemen." Electra heard a quaver in her voice. "First, I'm going to demonstrate with Electra and Trixi what we can do for those of you who are unable to mount easily. After that, I'll let you meet the horses and get used to being around them. Then, if anyone would like to try to mount and ride, you are welcome to. But please don't feel pressured. If you are more comfortable just watching this time, that's fine."

The cowgirl turned to her. "Are you ready?"

She gave Trixi the signal. The mare bent her legs and knelt on the ground.

The audience gave a collective gasp.

She slipped onto the saddle, put her feet into the stirrups, and gave another signal. Trixi rose, and they trotted around the arena.

The audience clapped.

When she returned and dismounted, Garrett and Del

came forward. Garrett told the group how much the lessons and riding had helped him with his fears and doubts. Then he nodded at Sam who signaled Trixi. When the horse kneeled, he swung his good leg over the saddle and eased his prosthetic foot into the stirrup. Sam made sure he was secure in the saddle and then led them around the arena.

After Garrett's successful ride and applause, Del showed how well he could maneuver onto Trixi's back, even without legs. The audience again responded with enthusiasm.

Electra demonstrated how she was training Apache, with backing, lifting his leg, and leaning him slightly back. The gelding reacted as docile as a lamb and gave a perfect exhibition.

"The next step is to train him to kneel, like Trixi, so we'll have two horses to work with here," Sam explained. "Now, I'd like to simply let you get acquainted with the horses. Do whatever you're comfortable with—petting them, feeding them, or just watching."

Two of the veterans came forward eagerly. A couple hesitated when they came close to the large animals as the horses blew and snorted and watched these new humans approach. A woman stopped several paces away, watching the horses warily.

"It's okay if you don't want to get close today." Sam offered each person pellets and spoke softly, trying to encourage them to go ahead and touch, talk to, and interact with the horses. The woman stayed back.

"Hi." Sam introduced herself and held out a hand to shake.

"Sondra." The petite veteran shook her head, a long brown braid flapping. "I faced the demons from hell back in the sandbox, but…" her eyes widened, "horses are so *big!*"

Sam ruffled Trixi's bangs. "Yes, they are. But they are also very gentle, loving animals and quite intuitive. Mine always seem to know what my mood is."

"Yeah. Apache sure does mine too." Electra demonstrated how to brush Apache.

"Hmm." Sondra paid close attention, from a distance.

"Here's a treat." Sam handed her some pellets. "When you're ready, just hold them out in your palm, like this, and the horse will take it without biting you."

The woman hesitated a few more seconds, and then stepped forward, holding out her hand to Trixi. The mare sniffed and gently lipped the treats from Sondra's palm. She drew in a sharp inhale. "Her mouth is so soft."

Trixi nuzzled the veteran's hand, and Sondra slowly stroked the velvety nose. "Wow." She continued to caress the mare's face. Trixi's ears rotated forward and after a moment, she rubbed her head against Sondra's arm. "Oh…" She breathed the word, almost a sigh, as she leaned into the horse, cheek to cheek.

Electra exchanged a glance with Sam.

Sam closed her eyes for a moment, nodding.

That's a good thing that just happened. Horses can heal grown-ups too. Electra allowed a satisfied grin.

***

"You two girls are awesome." Mom leaned forward in the truck as Sam shifted gears to go up a hill. "You never cease to amaze me when you work with horses. You are so calm and patient, and you both have this instinct, or some kind of ability, to communicate with them." She put an arm around Electra.

"Thanks, Mom." She snuggled against her mother. "I love them…and I love you."

Sam smiled back. "Thanks, Alberta. This girl is learning twice as fast as I ever have. She's a great help already with the program."

"Does this mean I can stay, Mom?" Electra bit her lower

lip, nerves tingling her arms, and cast her eyes sideways toward her mother.

"For now. I'm very pleased with your schoolwork as well, and now that you have Horace to help you with math, I think we can make it through this year."

A feeling of weightlessness lifted her spirit. "Seriously? Yay!" She bounced in the truck seat and threw both arms wide to hug her mom, nearly hitting Sam in the process.

"Hey, careful there." Her friend hooted. "We don't want to run off the road."

"Sorry, Sam, but I'm so excited. Thank you, Mom, thank you, thank you, thank you! I can't wait to get home and work with Apache some more and Trixi too and maybe I'll learn more about her tricks, and when are you moving here, are you coming after tax season?"

"Take a breath, honey." Mom cast a bemused look at her. "One step at a time, okay? You just keep up the good work with the horses and schoolwork. I'll also work very hard at how to get here as soon as I can after I finish with my clients. But there's a lot involved with moving." Her face settled into a serious expression. "New York and Montana are two very different places, and I'll be taking a big cut in pay. Got to figure that out."

"I know that's a concern." Sam spoke up. "However, Montana is a lot cheaper to live in than New York, and you'll have free board and room if you accept Clyde's offer. I have this gut feeling it is going to work out just fine."

Mom nodded. "You're probably right, and with possible extra income doing other ranchers' taxes, I think it will."

***

The atmosphere was somber as Sam drove Mom to the airport on Wednesday. Electra sat quietly, hugging her mother's arm and leaning her head on her shoulder.

"Well, at least the sun is shining. No more snowstorms." Sam tried to lighten the mood. "You should have good weather for the trip."

Mom gave her a half-hearted smile. "Yes, it is. I'm glad of that."

They drove on in silence, the miles stretching like a rubber band.

Electra sniffed. "Mom?" She peered into her mother's face. "You *are* coming back here to live, aren't you?"

"That's the hope." Mom smoothed a wisp of Electra's hair from her face. "Just a few more months. I'm going to try my hardest to make it sooner, rather than later."

"Time will go by super fast. You'll see," Sam said. "Spring will be here, with all the wildflowers blooming, green grass, and new calves being born."

Electra brightened. "That'll be cool. Can't wait!" Then she snuggled back against her mother. "But hurry. I'm going to miss you."

On the way home, she could barely contain herself. "This is just so cool! Mom's coming to live here and we have three horses to work with and I get to be with Apache—and you—forever!"

Sam chuckled and gave her a thumbs-up. "Yes, it is. And I'm very happy you're staying too.

CHAPTER TWENTY-SEVEN

Apache greeted her at the pasture fence with a low, rumbling nicker. She gave him a treat, giggling at the soft, tickling sensation as he gently lipped it from her palm. Smoothing the velvet skin of his nose, she worked her way up his face, between his eyes and then his ears. "My Apache," she whispered.

Her arms encircled his neck. His hair smelled of musty hay and fresh air, of horse sweat and saddle leather. She breathed in his healing essence.

From the moment she had seen him, so broken and abused, something inside her had given way, had shoved aside her own great pain and loneliness, to make room for this new feeling of love. He had needed her, and she had needed him. Two broken beings that found a safe haven in each other. This *was* an answer to prayer.

And now, thanks to this horse—and Sam—she had a new life, a new beginning, a sense of purpose. She was whole again.

Enjoy this book?
You can make a big difference.

Reviews of my books help bring them to the attention of other readers.

If you've enjoyed this book, I would be very grateful if you could spend just five minutes of your time leaving a review (it can be as short as you like) on the book's Amazon page.

Or let me know through my website:
http://www.heidimthomas.com

Thank you very much!
Heidi

ACKNOWLEDGMENTS
So many have been involved in making my books a reality. I thank God for the gift of the writing gene, my family for their continued support and encouragement, the teachers and editors who believed in me, my fellow Women Writing the West members, my Word Spinners critique group, and my Chino Valley critique group who have given me such valuable feedback: Sally Bates, Leta McCurry, and John J. Rust. Thank you also to Brenda Whiteside, critique partner and editor, for helping make my work better. And, of course, thank you to all my readers for supporting my writing habit.

ABOUT THE AUTHOR

Heidi M. Thomas grew up on a working ranch in eastern Montana, riding and gathering cattle for branding and shipping. Her parents taught her a love of books, and her grandmother rode bucking stock in rodeos. She followed her dream of writing, with a journalism degree from the University of Montana. Heidi is the author of the award-winning "Cowgirl Dreams" novel series and *Cowgirl Up: A History of Rodeo Women.*

Seeking the American Dream and *Finding True Home* are based on her mother who emigrated from Germany after WWII. She makes her home in North-Central Arizona.

Rescuing Samantha, Rescuing Hope, and *Rescue Ranch Rising* continue the fictional Moser family story.

Goth-girl to Cowgirl is the "rescue" story from Electra's point of view.